Dear Reader,

*T*he Biblical story of Esther—whose beauty was matched only by her wisdom—has inspired women for centuries. In THE GILDED CHAMBER, she comes to life through the eyes of a contemporary woman, debut novelist Rebecca Kohn.

The response has been overwhelming; the "word of mouth" is huge. Buyers and booksellers across the country have made a point of letting us know how much they loved the story. Readers called.asking for extra copies for their reading groups, mothers, rabbis. And all this resulted from sending out only 500 copies. So, we reacted to this demand by going back for a sizable second printing—of advance reading copies. This is a first for us here at Rugged Land.

If you haven't already read the book, open it up and see what you think. You may just become part of the word of mouth – before that word of mouth reaches you.

BEST,

CHRIS MIN
EDITOR

THE GILDED CHAMBER

A Novel of Queen Esther

Rebecca Kohn

PUBLISHED BY RUGGED LAND, LLC
276 CANAL STREET · NEW YORK · NY · 10013 · USA

LIBRARY OF CONGRESS CONTROL NUMBER tk

PUBLISHER'S CATALOGING-IN-PUBLICATION DATA tk

ISBN 1-59071-024-X

BOOK DESIGN BY HSU + ASSOCIATES

RUGGED LAND WEBSITE ADDRESS:
WWW.RUGGEDLAND.COM

1 3 5 7 9 10 8 6 4 2
FIRST EDITION

RUGGED LAND | 276 CANAL STREET · NEW YORK · NY 10013 · USA

For Meir

Vast floods cannot quench love,
Nor rivers drown it

[Song of Solomon 8:7]

One

It came to pass in the second year of the reign of Xerxes—who ruled from Hindush to Kusha—that I was orphaned. My father was trampled in the street during the first revolt of Babylon. My mother followed him an hour later, reaching the end of her days in childbirth. I heard her cries grow weak and shallow, after the midwife sent me from the room. When she died, I was not allowed to see her or the stillborn baby. But I saw them in my dreams. The creature had the head of a man and the body of a lion. Its claws tore through my mother's womb and her blood ran like a river.

I was in my tenth year.

My only surviving kin was Mordechai son of Yair, my father's brother. Mordechai lived in the capital city of Susa, on the east bank of the River Sha'ur, a journey of five days from Babylon. He had served as a minor treasury official during the years Xerxes spent as the viceroy of Babylon. When King Darius died and Xerxes inherited the turban of the kingdom, my cousin was among those who followed the new king out of Babylon to Susa. He left his home, seeking to do good for his king and his kin.

Mordechai soon rose to a position of honor in the court of King Xerxes, holding the second place under the minister of the treasury. From dawn to dusk, he sat at the king's gatehouse receiving men from throughout the empire, dignitaries and common people who came to the palace bearing gifts of gold and silver coin for the royal treasury. He also held responsibility for checking the revenues of the tax collectors, to ensure that none stole what belonged to the king.

Mordechai's absence from Babylon saddened his family, but we spoke with pride of his loyalty to the king and his success. The Jews of Babylon knew him to be a good son who honored his parents. He enriched them with gifts of coin and cloth, and after the death of his father provided for his mother's needs.

We held Mordechai in great esteem for his accomplishments and his generosity, but we knew little of his life in Susa. We did not know that he went by the name of Marduka the Babylonian. Or that his fine house in the fortress stood apart from the homes of all the other Jews, who lived in the town below the acropolis. We never imagined that he employed a Babylonian housekeeper who was not a Jew and did not keep the dietary laws.

I am glad that my father never knew how Mordechai hid himself among the Zoroastrians who worship Ahura Mazda and the Babylonians who worship Marduk. He would have grieved as if for a lost son.

Yet Mordechai's efforts to gain advancement were not uncommon. Many Jews of Babylon had chosen to turn away from their heritage, forgetting that King Nebuchadnezzar had exiled their grandparents from Jerusalem. They dwelt in Babylon as if it were their ancestral home and concerned themselves only with building lives of wealth and prosperity. Some of these men even took Babylonian wives, who taught their children to pray to Marduk and Ishtar.

A smaller group, my father among them, lived for the hour they might return to Jerusalem. These Jews prayed three times each day for the rebuilding of the Temple. They observed the laws of Moses with utmost strictness and set themselves apart from their Babylonian neighbors in worship, speech, and dietary habits. They scorned Jews who adopted Babylonian ways, and kept watch on each other like spies. When someone committed a violation, it was reported in the prayer tent. Three judges determined the punishments. A minor infraction, such as missing a prayer service without cause, might require a fine to be paid as charity to the poor. But some infractions were so grievous that the sinner would be banished from the tent forever. These included murder, adultery, one man laying with another, and violation of the laws of Sabbath rest.

My father was revered as a pious scholar among these devout men. His brother Yair was neither as learned nor as observant. But he followed the dietary laws and prayed each morning in the tent of the Jews by the market square. And my father considered Yair's household suitable for his daughter.

I was still an infant when Mordechai came into his full beard. But our parents wanted to preserve and strengthen the family by uniting their children in marriage. Mordechai agreed to the match and so we were betrothed. I, Hadassah daughter of Avihail son of Shemei, was two years old. Mordechai son of Yair son of Shemei, was twenty.

Mordechai left for Susa six years later, promising to return when I came of age. But the subject of our marriage was never far from the lips of my mother and aunt. They sat together in the afternoon, weaving plain towels on their hand looms and imagining the fine cotton robe I would wear to my wedding, embroidered with azure rosettes and silver beads. They argued over whose bridal veil I should use—my mother's, crimson wool fringed with gold coins, or my aunt's, saffron wool with silver coins—until at last they agreed I

7

should have my own. They spoke of the delicacies that would be served at the celebration—almond honey cakes and rosewater syrup—and the music that would herald my arrival to my new home. Sometimes they spent an hour or two imagining all the gifts guests would bring—the hens and the cooking pots, a heavy wool blanket for the cold nights, a fine wooden loom.

And so my young heart learned to look forward to the day of my marriage with joyous anticipation.

Sometimes I wondered why Mordechai, who did not hesitate to put aside the traditions of his upbringing and the heritage of his people, did not take a Persian or Median bride in Susa. I was a child when he left Babylon, with a child's shape and a child's ways. He was already a man, with a man's desires. He could not have known if I would grow up to be beautiful in form or pleasing in disposition. He could not have known if I would be skilled with the loom or capable of managing a house.

After I was taken away from him, I formed in myself a harsh explanation of our betrothal. He had agreed to wait for a girl who was eighteen years his junior because he did not wish to be married. And when at last I came of age, and my tender young breasts ached to suckle his children, he continued to wait because he did not wish to marry. I told myself that the years would have passed and his manhood shriveled, and still I would have remained a virgin in his household.

Later I exchanged this bitter story with one that was truer to my cousin's kind heart: I was promised to him as his wife, but became a daughter to him instead.

When I was orphaned, my father's friends wrote to my cousin in Susa. They did not tell him how I wept all day, or that I woke at night screaming. They said only that my parents had left this world and I was in need of protection. It was his duty to take me, they reminded him, for I was his betrothed and he my only living kin.

Mordechai did not come for me himself. Instead, he sent a purse of gold coins and instructions for my guardians to hire a guide to escort me to Susa. They chose an old Jew and his wife who had made the trip once before across the River Tigris, the vast marshland, and the high hills. They owned two donkeys that we could ride upon.

I remember almost nothing of the journey, except that the donkeys stank and the couple was not kind to me. My heart was consumed with grief and my vision was blurred by the horrors I had witnessed. I ate little and could not sleep. The guide ignored me and spent each evening counting the gold remaining in Mordechai's purse. His wife forced me to obey all the customs of mourning, though I was only ten years old. I was forbidden to wash, wear shoes, or sit on anything but the bare floor. We stayed at homes along the way, but I was not permitted to play with the other children. Had Susa been closer, they would have made me walk.

We arrived on a bright day in early spring and dismounted from the donkeys just outside the settled area. The king's white palace rose above us high on the acropolis and the town of Susa spread before us on the plain. Birds flitted among the reeds on the riverbank where wildflowers bloomed. I stooped to pick a beautiful yellow tulip, its full bud ready to burst. The guide's wife slapped my hand and tried to take the flower from me. But for the first time I

9

stood defiant. "I am giving it to my cousin Mordechai," I said, pressing the stem close to my heart.

We made our way to the Jewish quarter. The huts appeared much like those in Babylon, made of mud and reeds. But the people here supplied many fine crafts and services to the court of King Xerxes, and so they were more prosperous than the Jews of Babylon. They wore dyed wool robes and leather shoes. Their cheeks were full and their mouths curved up in cheerful smiles. The children were bold in their curiosity and several girls my own age waved to me as I walked by one donkey's side. The heavy cloud of sorrow began to lift from me and for the first time in many weeks I tasted hope.

The guide stopped several people to ask for directions to the house of Mordechai the treasury official. But no one had heard of such a person. I grew alarmed, and feared that my cousin, too, had been taken from me. I imagined him dead, his flesh devoured by vultures and his remains deposited in the Valley of the Bones. I could no longer believe, as my father had, that the vision of the Prophet Ezekiel would soon come to pass. I had seen death and I knew it did not rise into life.

Someone suggested that we inquire at the market square on the acropolis. As I climbed the steep road to the fortress—a ragged orphan with swollen bare feet and dirty hands clutching a yellow tulip—no one who saw me could have imagined the heights I would reach before I traveled down that road again.

When we came to the fortress gate, a guard asked my escorts to state their business.

"I am come to deliver this child to Mordechai the treasury official," the guide replied in clear Aramaic.

The guard looked puzzled for a moment, before the light of recognition passed across his face. "Do you mean Marduka, the treasury official?"

The old Jew and his wife looked at each other with confusion.

"Marduka the treasury official has told us to expect his cousin, a young girl of ten years old," the guard continued.

"I am his cousin!" I burst out with excitement. The guide's wife pinched me but I did not care. The journey was over and I would soon see my cousin. As the guard gave directions, my feet grew light with joy.

I approached Mordechai's house, resolving to forget my parents and all I had lost. I would begin this new life by pleasing my cousin with a cheerful disposition. I would make myself useful to him with my busy hands. He would start each day by catching me in his arms and thanking God for such a blessing, as my father had done with my mother. We would be married and I would bear him strong sons. I would be safe in his household and never know danger again.

Such were the foolish hopes of a childish heart. For no one is safe in this world forever.

Two

When we found our way to Mordechai's house, we could not
see what lay beyond the high white limestone walls. The solid
wooden gate revealed nothing, but yielded to the guide's hands. He
closed the gate behind him, leaving me outside with his wife and the
donkeys.

I looked up and down the wide street, marveling at the
fortress city, so different from Babylon. The walls of every house
were scrubbed clean. Not a single beggar accosted us. The streets
were paved with flat stones, and clear of refuse. Babylon had once
gloried in such splendor. But by the time of my birth the pavement
had long lain hidden beneath a rising layer of animal droppings and
garbage. And the population had grown so great that the authorities
no longer removed the homeless and indigent.

Perhaps one day Susa will be the same.

At last the guide returned, his eyes wide from all that he had
seen of my cousin's wealth. "A water well and cooking hut!" He
clicked his tongue, urging us into the courtyard. I advanced with
caution behind his wife and the donkeys, hoping to glimpse my
cousin before he saw me.

The courtyard was more splendid than the guide had
described and large enough to hold a second house. Two cypress
trees rose in the center, each giving shade to a stone bench. In a pen

at a far corner, a goat nibbled its bedding straw. She had her own little hut for shade and I guessed that she provided the household's milk. She was a pretty animal and I longed to pet her.

The door to the kitchen hut opened and a tiny, very old woman shuffled out. She stood no taller than me and her bones protruded from a thin face. Her large eyes sank deep into fleshless sockets and when she drew close I saw that all her eyelashes had fallen out. The front of her robe was sprinkled with flour and she was wringing a towel with fingers as brittle and gnarled as twigs.

"This is the girl?" Her voice was a succession of nervous high trills, like the song of the yellow bee-eater.

"We have another purse coming to us now that she is delivered to you," the guide insisted.

The old woman inspected me from head to foot. Her frown curved low with displeasure. "Whose house is this?" she asked me. I recognized the Aramaic words, which I had learned from our housekeeper Ninsun.

"My cousin Mordechai son of Yair," I replied in a whisper.

"Speak up!"

"My cousin," I repeated a little louder.

"His name is Marduka the Babylonian," she corrected me. "I am Aia his housekeeper and I do all the work. I cook, I clean, I wash. You are a guest in this house. Remember that."

I nodded my head.

Her eyes scanned my body again. "I will not let such a dirty girl into my house."

"She cannot wash until her mourning is over!" the guide protested.

Aia flashed him a look of scorn. "Then she will have to sleep with the goat." The old woman turned away from us, shuffled to the house, and disappeared inside.

I gazed at the goat while the guide and his wife cursed each other. They had believed more payment would be forthcoming.

"We should have sold her to the slave trader," the wife growled. She grabbed at the black wool shawl, which I had draped over my head and around my neck. It was the handiwork of my mother and I had clung to it since the hour she was taken from me.

"Give it to me!" the woman demanded.

I dropped the tulip and fought with both hands to hold on to the shawl. We struggled for a moment but I could not match her strength. The garment slid through my fingers and the woman ran out the gate, clutching it to her chest. Her husband took the donkey leads and followed.

I had promised myself not to cry in my cousin's household. But I had not yet seen Mordechai and my mother's shawl had been taken from me. The housekeeper seemed no kinder than the guide's wife and my stomach ached with hunger. Tears pooled in my eyes and flowed in a river to the dust.

Aia shuffled up behind me. "Where are your companions? Did they leave without this?" She held up a small red purse.

"They are not my companions," I sobbed. "She took my shawl."

I wiped my eyes on my sleeve and saw the wrinkles on the housekeeper's face soften.

"Your cousin can buy you a better shawl."

"It was my mother's," I explained.

The housekeeper shrugged. "She is gone and so is the shawl."

The housekeeper heated a big kettle of water and drew a bath for me in the cooking hut. She placed in my hands a little bowl of washing powder and left a towel and a comb on a stool next to the tub. Ordering me to undress, she moved to the other side of the room where she began kneading dough for bread.

I sank into the tub and felt all my fears wash away with the dirt. I renewed my resolve to look to the future. I would learn to please both Aia and Mordechai, to be the sun of their day and the moon of their night.

When I rose from the tub resolved to forget the guide, his wife, the journey to Susa, and the lost shawl. I remembered only my mother's smile and nothing of her death. I remembered my father's good name but not his end.

I told myself these things as I combed my hair with an ivory comb, more beautiful than any I had ever seen. I told myself these things and willed myself to believe them. I wrapped my memories in a dark shroud that day and hid them deep in my heart. It would be many years before they found me again.

When I was done, I sat on the stool and waited for Aia. She placed the bread in the brick oven and turned to me, eyeing my appearance. "Such a face," she muttered. She shuffled out of the hut and soon returned with a fine wool robe the color of a ripe pomegranate and leather sandals. I thanked her for my beautiful new clothes.

"Save your thanks for your cousin when he comes home," she replied. I did not dare ask her when he would return.

She pointed to a low table and cushions near the tub, indicating that I should sit. She brought me bread, beer, and a wooden bowl of stew. I was so hungry I forgot to say a blessing before I tore into the bread. A mouthful of stew lodged in my throat as I realized my mistake.

"You do not like my goat stew?" Aia asked. "It is good enough for your cousin."

I lowered my eyes. "I forgot the blessing."

Aia laughed. "No blessings are wanted here! Eat up and I will show you the house."

The house, much grander than our mud hut in Babylon, seemed like a palace to me. Light-blue glazed tiles covered the floors and crimson and black wool carpets hung on the walls. A room was set aside for dining, and another for entertaining guests. I had a room of my own, with two yellow silk cushions, a soft wool blanket, and a thick mattress to sleep upon. I spied a white night robe waiting for me on a trunk at the foot of the mattress.

"My cousin is a rich man." I ran my fingers over the shimmering yellow silk.

"Your cousin is a generous man for taking you in."

Before I could respond, we heard him call from the front of the house. His voice was as sweet as honey and as soft as a lowing lamb.

"Stay here until I call for you," Aia instructed.

I hung back in the doorway of my new room, straining to hear every word.

"The girl has arrived," Aia trilled as she made her way down the hallway. "She is here if it would please the master to see her."

"How is she?" my cousin asked.

"She was unwashed and unfed in the care of those Jews, but I have seen to it."

"I thank you," Mordechai replied as he appeared before me.

I had not seen him in two years. He was a tall man, but he did not carry his height with pride. Rather, he stooped, as if all the cares of his position at court sat on his back. He was neither thin nor heavy, but his round cheeks seemed ready to smile. He had a wide brow, an elegant long nose, and a full lower lip. His kind eyes, hidden beneath heavy drooping lids, had not changed.

I smiled at him, concerned about how tired he appeared, until I noticed his beard. He had trimmed it close to his face in the Babylonian fashion, violating the laws of the Jews. I held my breath in surprise. I had never known a Jewish man without a full and flowing beard. But I soon forgot my concern for he opened his arms to catch me, just as I had hoped he would.

"Little cousin," he said, his gentle voice as soothing as my mother's, "do you like your new room?"

"It is the finest room I have ever seen!" I exclaimed, kissing his hands.

Mordechai laughed. "Aia will take good care of you," he promised.

"She should sleep now," Aia interjected.

"Yes," Mordechai agreed. "She must be tired."

"I will see to it and then draw your bath," Aia replied to him. She turned to me, pointing to the linen night robe. "The master works hard from dawn to dusk. We do not disturb him in the evening."

Mordechai bent down and kissed me on each cheek. "Sleep deep and well, little cousin," he whispered.

And for the first time in a month, I did.

Three

I spent my first weeks watching Aia hurry from task to task. The housekeeper's work began as the sun rose and her hands did not stop until long after darkness fell. She shopped in the market, cooked the meals, cleaned inside and out, washed the clothing and the bedding, and wove cloth and rugs. She waited upon my cousin when he rose and when he retired.

Aia appeared to have no friends or family. I never saw her stop in the market square to gossip or seek the companionship of other women, but she seemed content with her life. I was sorry to intrude, and held myself as still and quiet as I could while I followed her through the days.

When at last she took notice of me, she gave me small tasks and supervised my work with a sharp eye. I peeled pomegranates and chopped figs, swept the goat's pen and laid down fresh straw, scrubbed the floor tiles and washed dishes, drew water from the well and beat dust from the cushions and carpets. Satisfied with my progress, she taught me to knead bread, make stew, and milk the goat.

I sought Aia's approval, though she was a hard teacher who seldom offered praise. She demonstrated a task once and expected me to remember; if I made a mistake, the corners of her mouth sank to her chin in displeasure.

Weaving presented my greatest challenge. Aia strung her smallest loom for me, and I struggled with the linen thread for days, unable to keep the edges even. But I was determined, and so I taught my fingers to relax and let each new row be guided by the one before it. I removed what was not perfect and started over a hundred times. I worked in every spare moment.

I presented to Aia the fruit of my labor, a new kitchen towel, with thanks for her kindness to me. I held my breath as she fingered the cloth with a critical eye. She offered a rare smile. "You will be a good wife one day."

My young heart soared with happiness. She never mentioned my betrothal, but I understood by her praise that Mordechai had spoken of it. From that day I held back my tears whenever she scolded me, grateful to her for training me so well.

But I would never be a Jewish wife in custom or practice, like my mother had been before me. God did not dwell in the household of Marduka the Babylonian. We spoke no Hebrew and said no blessings. We did not observe the dietary laws or celebrate the holidays. We worked every day and took no Sabbath rest. I soon grew used to this and forgot that I had ever lived any other way.

My cousin looked with no more favor on any other religious ritual or practice. Sometimes Aia mumbled a prayer to Ishtar or Marduk when she supposed me out of earshot; if she became aware of my presence, she bit her lips, shook her head, and raised a conspiratorial finger to her lips.

One morning Aia seemed nervous as she kneaded the bread. When the sun had risen to its full height in the sky, she shuffled to the gate and unlatched it. She came back to her work, but often looked out the window. I began to wonder if she was expecting someone.

We heard the gate creek open. Aia threw down her chopping knife and hurried to meet her guest; I followed close behind.

The stranger stood much taller than my cousin. He wore a flowing black cloak and a high white turban that suggested he was someone of importance. His face was shaven clean except for a long square tuft at the chin.

He set down all that he carried: a long stick of polished ebony, a small stove, and a large goatskin bag. Aia knelt at his feet and kissed his hand. When she stood again, he removed his black cloak to reveal a white robe embroidered with silver images of Marduk's dragon. I recognized the creatures from the gates of Babylon. They had the head of a viper, a long body covered with scales, the feet of a lion in front, the claws of a bird in back, and the tail of a scorpion.

As I gazed at the glittering dragons and realized the man was a Babylonian priest. When I looked up, our eyes met.

"Your spirit shall be a slave to our mistress Ishtar," he whispered on the wind that rushed through my ears like a raging river torrent. The man's lips did not appear to move but his eyes burned like fire. I felt a hundred hot needles shooting into my shoulder.

I cried out in pain and rubbed my stinging flesh.

Aia patted my head in a gesture of comfort. "The priest offers you a great compliment. Ishtar holds power over the hearts of men and the wombs of women. But say nothing of this visit to your cousin," she added in a whisper, "or I shall be sent to my ruin. He does not understand what a woman can suffer. Now go inside the cooking hut and do not come out."

I ran to the hut. But curiosity overcame me, like an itch that I could not ignore. I climbed up on the kneading table and crouched to one side of the window, where I could peek into the courtyard without being seen.

Aia bent her head low before the priest and removed her head covering.

I had never seen her without the scarf, even when she slept; now I understood why. The old woman had no hair and patches of oozing white and yellow scales covered her scalp.

The priest reached into his bag and brought out a flint box, a skin pouch, and a small vial. He lit the stove and sprinkled it with liquid from the vial. A smoky sweet perfume filled the air.

Aia remained standing with her head bowed while the priest filled his hands with a white powder from the pouch. He sprinkled the powder on the ground in lines from east to west and then crossed them with lines from north to south.

"This is the prison of your body," he announced. Aia stepped into the center of the crossing lines.

The priest chanted in a language I did not understand. His voice was high and sorrowful. He dipped into the pouch again, drawing forth some small objects that looked like seed pods. He tossed these into the fire one at a time, chanting a different incantation as each one burned. He pulled up his sleeve to reveal a thin strip of undyed linen around his wrist. He removed the cloth and kissed it, then tied it on the tip of his ebony stick. He sprinkled the cloth with the remaining contents of the vial and held it to the fire in the stove.

Flames shot up from the tip of the stick. He held the blazing torch high and then waved it over Aia's head. It passed so close to her, I feared she would be scorched. But the fire soon burned out.

Aia covered her head again. Then she reached into her sleeve and removed a purse that she handed to the priest. After he accepted the payment and kissed Aia's hand, he donned his cloak, collected his things, and left. When the gate closed, Aia shuffled her feet over the white powder to erase all trace of the priest's visit. I climbed down from the table and sat in a corner.

The housekeeper returned to her cooking. "Say nothing of the visitor," she warned, "or I will tell your cousin that you have been praying like a Jew and he will send you back to Babylon."

I promised that I would never speak of what I had seen. Aia was good to me and I wished her affliction gone. But I knew that the healing of an idolater would never work.

I had always been a quiet child in my father's house, surrounded by the voices of women. My mother drew others to her like bees to a jasmine vine in full bloom. The herb seller, perfumer, and henna maker who came to our house in the morning before the market opened could complete a day's business in our courtyard, chattering with my mother and the stream of women who visited her. The midwife, the bride-dresser, the wives of the men who prayed with my father—everyone sought the pleasure of my mother's lively company. I, too, preferred sitting with her to playing with the other children.

In my new life, I became even quieter. Aia and I could work for a whole day together exchanging no more than a few words. I grew to enjoy the sounds of scrubbing and chopping. I listened to the birds—magpies, bee-eaters, and delijah falcons—and learned their calls. I knew contentment in the wind whispering through the cypress leaves. But my favorite sound was that of Mordechai's footsteps in the courtyard.

My cousin returned home every day at dusk. He embraced me with great affection and often asked me to sit with him while he ate his evening meal. I plumped up his cushions and seated myself close to his knee. Aia served his food in silence; he thanked her with a nod. I kept a close watch to see if he liked the dishes I had helped prepare. And when he finished eating, Aia allowed me to clear the plates.

Sometimes Mordechai paused between mouthfuls to tell us of strange sights he had seen, such as a black slave from Kusha with huge holes in his ears, or a tamed lion wearing a jeweled collar. Still, he spoke little more than Aia and often seemed distracted. I told myself that he bore a heavy burden in the king's court and could not put aside his cares even for the length of a meal. I told myself that he did not enjoy the chattering ways of women. I told myself that my company gave him comfort whether or not we conversed.

The new moon came and went many times. Spring burned on the altar of summer. I had never known such heat in all my days. But Susa was home now, and I was happy in my new life.

When the air began to grow cooler, I knew that the time for the holiest days was upon us. But we did not fast, we did not atone for our sins, we did not build a booth and eat under the stars. And I no longer feared the wrath of the One God as my father had taught me. I told myself that as long as I did not commit the gravest sin— idolatry—the God of my father would be satisfied. I told myself that

I must not question the man who was to be my lord. And so I cast off all that I knew of my people's ways, much as a girl forsakes her doll when it is time to become a woman.

I was troubled by only one thing: my cousin never mentioned our betrothal. He had not spoken to me of it once in all the days since my arrival in Susa. But I saw his pleasure in my progress under Aia's tutelage. And so I told myself that the day I came of age would be our wedding day. I looked forward to it with eagerness.

Four

Soon after I arrived in Susa, the king gave a drinking feast for all his officials and advisors, for the military officers of the armies of Persia and Media, and the nobles and governors of the provinces. He sent messengers throughout the realm to proclaim the birth of his second son by Queen Vashti, summoning all men of importance to the palace, to celebrate the glory of Ahura Mazda, the god who had made him king and given him another son.

I saw the visitors coming through the town square, men from all nations. I imagined a grand procession inside the palace, each newcomer presenting himself to the king in a flourish of fine language and dignified manners. I supposed King Xerxes to be a ruler worthy of my cousin's devotion, a man sitting in state on his golden throne, receiving his guests with grace. Nor did Mordechai tarnish my childish fancies with the truth.

Many years later I saw the court's debauchery for myself. I heard of the great gathering and its catastrophic conclusion from those who witnessed the events with their own eyes. For the story remained fixed on the tongues of the court gossips long after it had faded from the king's own memory.

The stream of visitors to the king's palace continued for one hundred and eighty days. They brought gifts, man and man, each with tribute from his own land. They offered objects of beauty: glittering jewels, silk from the east, cotton from the west, jars of gold dust, ivory carvings, and glass bowls. They brought delicacies for the palate: white wheat flour, aged wine, salt in silver cellars, honeycombs, and exotic fruit. They brought weapons and equipment for the king's armory: iron shields, silver daggers, swords, long lances, and two-horse chariots. And they brought animals, both practical and rare: camels, horses, bulls, dromedaries, okapi, lions, and twisted-horn antelope.

Yet their offerings were like a single drop of water in the sea of the king's wealth. The vast palace inspired awe in all who passed through the king's gatehouse. The main courtyard alone could hold ten thousand men and the reception hall, with columns the height of twelve men, could hold a thousand. Materials of rare splendor were commonplace: alabaster columns, granite urns, cedar beams, gilded nails, and doors inlaid with ivory, ebony, lapis lazuli, and gold. The show of workmanship dazzled the eyes: the columns crowned with life-sized double-headed bulls, the wall tiles with molded images of griffins and winged bulls glazed in brilliant hues of pure gold, blue, and green, the marbled walkways, woven hangings tied in cords of fine linen and purple wool. The hanging gardens of Babylon, known as a great wonder throughout the world, paled in comparison to the variety and beauty in the gardens of the palace at Susa.

The wine flowed from the royal cellar for half a year without pause. The king took pride in offering the fruit of vineyards throughout his empire and beyond, from the dry reds of Sardis to the sweet whites of Sogdia. The royal stewards filled the golden wine cups according to each man's request and the normal rule of keeping pace with the king was suspended.

The guests were entertained each evening by dancing girls who made their flesh rise with pleasure and musicians who filled their eyes with tears. The palace kitchens prepared delicacies to appease their hunger and concubines from the soldiers' barracks served their desire.

When deep night crept over the palace, the Zoroastrians among the group gathered in the fire temple. There they drank a potion known as haoma—brewed from the red fly agaric mushroom—and sat before the sacred fires, dazzled by strange and wondrous visions. The Magi threw the pur to foretell the future, but none saw the disaster that was about to befall the king.

When the final week of the banquet began, every adult who lived on the acropolis was invited to attend. The men joined the raucous group in the reception hall and Queen Vashti entertained the women in her private quarters.

Mordechai left his post at the palace gate to join in the celebration and we did not see him for two days. But word of the queen's downfall came to us long before he returned; it swirled through the marketplace like a cloud of red wine in clear water.

The heart of the king was soaked with wine and his spirit was light with laughter. The men in the audience hall could hear the king's merriment above that of the seven princes of Persia and Media, who sat with him behind the royal screen. A brawl broke out between a Syrian and a Lydian. Each was locked in the other's arms, they tumbled and rolled until the screen fell and the king's handsome face and broad chest were revealed.

A gasp of fear rippled through the room until the king saluted the crowd. Amidst thunderous applause, he rose from his cushions to survey the multitude of his guests.

He looked down upon the two men who yet lay on the floor with their hands at each other's throat, too terrified to move. Then he laughed again and called out: "Do none here know better pleasures than embracing their fellow men as the Greeks do?"

"Persian women are far superior in looks and scent to your fellow man," one of the king's advisors added.

"Median women are more beautiful!" someone called out from the crowd.

"Assyrian women!" another shouted.

"Bring on the dancing girls!" exclaimed a third. This suggestion was met with another round of applause and enthusiastic shouts.

The king climbed upon a table, bracing himself on a Lydian who jumped up to attend him faster than his own chamberlains. He motioned for a fresh cup, which an eager courtier filled and handed up to him. The room grew hushed and all drinking ceased. Three hundred pairs of eyes turned to the king and three hundred hearts beat in eager anticipation.

"I am Xerxes!" the king proclaimed. Wine sloshed over the rim of the cup as he hoisted it above his head. "Grandson of Cyrus! Son of Darius! By Ahura Mazda I rule from India to Ethiopia! A hundred and twenty-seven provinces are subject to my will! I alone am possessor of the finest vessel to be had—but for Ishtar herself—and that is my queen, granddaughter of King Nebuchadnezzar whom Cyrus defeated." He paused a moment to take a sip of wine and smack his lips. "I alone am possessor of the finest vessel to be had!" he repeated, "and she is a Chaldean!"

The men cheered. Then the king lifted his finger for the eunuchs and youths who served as his chamberlains.

"Bring me Queen Vashti! Let her leave the women and come to me with the turban of the kingdom upon her head, that all the company might behold her wondrous beauty."

From the time of my arrival in Susa I had heard talk of queen Vashti, reputed to be beautiful and cruel, good to the eye and savage in disposition. The women in the marketplace spoke of how she forced her Jewish servants to work unclothed on the Sabbath. It was said that she set her hand against her attendants and caused those who displeased her to be mutilated and murdered. Other than her beauty, no good was said of her. But the heart of the king was soft toward his queen and he did nothing to check her.

The eunuchs and youths returned empty-handed. Trembling in terror, they conveyed the angry refusal she had spat at them: "Am I to display myself like a concubine?"

The king's fury burned within him until his face was afire. The crowd hissed and several men dared to mock the queen's message in a drunken falsetto. The king turned to his advisors.

"What shall be done to a woman who dares disobey the command of the king?" he roared.

His closest advisor, Memuchan, rose to speak. "It is not the king alone who has been wronged by Vashti the queen," he announced to the assembly with gravity, "but all the princes and all the people in all the provinces of King Xerxes. Shall we permit wives to despise their husbands, as has Queen Vashti, who was commanded to show herself before the king and did not obey? If it please Your Majesty, let a royal edict be issued, that Vashti shall come no more before King Xerxes. And let Your Majesty bestow her royal estate upon one better than she."

"By Ahura Mazda the man is right!" the king proclaimed, lifting his cup yet again and scanning the crowd as if seeking its approval. Someone proposed a toast to the king's authority and three hundred cups rose high. The king drained his own cup, threw it down, and drew a jeweled dagger from his belt. "Let the disobedient queen be banished from my presence forever!" he proclaimed, brandishing the silver blade. "Let her know by this that I am her king!" The men cheered and stamped their feet. They toasted the king's health. They called for the dancing girls.

And so that very night Vashti was banished from the palace and told never to return.

The day after the unexpected conclusion of the feast, Aia sent me to the market for rosewater. Though I had strict instructions to speak with no one, I could not help overhearing the perfumer and the almond roaster speculate on the queen's fate.

"Where will she go?"

"He is a fearsome king. She will pay for her disobedience with her life."

"The mother of his sons will not perish in that way."

"Perhaps she shall live out her days in a corner of the harem. Unwanted, unattended, and unadorned."

I paid for the rosewater and turned for home. But the darkness in the perfumer's voice had lodged deep in my heart, reminding me of how Aia cursed those who crossed her, wishing them into Kurnugi, the land of no return.

And so long before my feet ever passed through the palace gate, I came to imagine the harem of Xerxes as a place of living death.

Five

After the queen's exile, King Xerxes waged war against the Greeks. He marched overland with his soldiers and crossed the seas with his fleet. He laid waste to the enemy and enriched his coffers with spoil, all in the name of the mighty god Ahura Mazda. But the war did not end well. Xerxes returned from the campaign defeated, having lost much of his fleet under the deceitful hand of Themistocles the Athenian.

And so the court at Susa became a solemn and sorrowful place. Musicians put aside their instruments and dancing girls sat idle in the harem. The reception hall remained empty and the wine cellar full. The king passed his days deploring the defeat at Salamis. At night he pined for his beautiful queen. He recalled the last time he had seen her—more than three years earlier—the day she had been banished to Chaldea with her infant son. Her beauty haunted him and he mourned the loss of her council regarding matters at court, upon which he had often relied.

For many months the king's heart hung like a heavy weight in his chest. He continued to rule, hearing the wisdom of his advisors and issuing decrees. He spent hours each day practicing with the sword and challenging the officers of his army to wrestling matches, which he always won. But he found no delight in old pleasures and no distraction in the company of his cup.

The youths who attended the king in his chamber spoke among themselves of His Majesty's melancholy. They sought to

33

devise a plan that would lift the spirits of the great king and return him to his former glory.

And so they became the authors of my misfortune.

They entered the royal bathhouse one warm spring night when the king was bathing. His Majesty sat in the sunken blue tile tub and the eunuch Hathach stood in a far corner, ready to procure whatever the king might request and desire.

The youths came into the king's presence, kneeling on the slick blue tiles. The custom of kings dictated that these youths alone, and a few trusted eunuchs, were permitted to behold Xerxes in his nakedness. His body matched his stature as ruler in size, strength, and beauty. A full black beard adorned his face and thick black hair flowed to his shoulders. No one who ever beheld him, clothed or unclothed, doubted that this was a man favored by the gods and born to the throne.

The king greeted his youths with a nod, granting them permission to speak.

"We suggest a search," the youth began, laying out the strange and terrible plan with care. "We propose that the king in his glory should acquire for his use the most beautiful virgin vessels of his empire."

The king did not reply.

"Let young women be sought for Your Majesty from every province of the realm," a second youth urged, his voice as smooth as oil gliding over sleek flesh. "Virgins with breasts as round and firm as pomegranates, and waists as slender as a reed, and buttocks as full and white as the moon."

"Let the young women be assembled in the palace at Susa," the third one continued. "Let them enter the king's harem under the supervision of the eunuch Hegai, the keeper of the women, who knows best what stirs Your Majesty's passion. Let them be provided with unguents, and cosmetics, and let them have attendants to oversee their beauty treatments, so they shall come to Your Majesty as soft and fragrant as Ishtar herself."

"Let Your Majesty find their loins either supple or unyielding," the fourth one concluded, "whatever his desire shall dictate. May Your Majesty gladden his heart with his fill of these delights. And if it please Your Majesty, choose whichever of these women satisfies him above all others to be first among the women instead of Vashti."

The king continued to sit in silence, his muscular arms braced against the wall of the tub. He closed his eyes and sunk lower into the water, leaning his head back upon the golden head rest. The youths waited in fear that the king would not find the proposal to his liking. But a smile soon rose on the king's full lips. The youths saw that their words alone roused the king's flesh, and knew the plan would be approved.

"Send for a concubine," the king commanded.

The eunuch Hathach sought to clarify the king's desire before sending word to Hegai, the keeper of the women. "Does His Majesty wish for one in particular?"

"One from my harem is the same as another," the king snapped. "Send for any vessel I might use tonight, and let the search to replenish the supply begin tomorrow."

And so the king came to issue his shocking edict: that the fairest young virgins of the realm be taken from their homes and brought to the palace at Susa.

Those who lived in more distant cities and provinces received word of the edict days and weeks before the king's men arrived. Fathers took heed and hurried to save their daughters from abduction. The virgins of Babylon, Ecbatana, and Persepolis, Sardis, Nineveh, and Memphis were soon married or made hideous to the eye. And thus many were saved from serving the king's pleasure.

But my cousin's house was in the royal fortress on the acropolis of Susa. And so I was among the first to be seized.

I often see that evil hour in my memory.

I sat in the shade of the cypress tree in the courtyard of my cousin's house, with the loom upon my lap and scarlet wool in a basket by my side. My days were occupied with work and my heart was filled with love. I was a virgin of fourteen years, a woman, but still Mordechai remained silent on the subject of our marriage.

I reminded myself that Mordechai was a man of honor and would not forget his promise to my father. I assured myself that he returned my affection in all his smiles and sweet words. I told myself to be patient. But I knew of no other girl my age who remained unmarried. I was weaving a wedding belt for my beloved, hoping that this would hasten our wedding day.

I heard the clatter of their leather shoes and iron spears upon the stone street before I saw them, four of the king's ten thousand best, the Immortals. They wore pleated tunics of fine linen, and tall head gear of silver and bronze. Their beards were curled in tight swirls as if they were nobles. Their legs were shaved after the Athenian fashion, and their oiled arms and necks glistened in the sunlight.

They seemed such vain and pampered men, but they were four strong soldiers and I was just one girl. I opened my mouth to scream, but no sound came. They grabbed my wrists, and pulled me to my feet. They laughed at my weakness and trampled my loom in the dust, smashing it into many pieces.

Aia shuffled from the cooking hut, swooping down on the soldiers like a balaban falcon whose nest was under attack. "Leave her alone!" the old woman shrieked, beating her fists on the arms of a soldier. He swatted her with the back of his hand as if she was a fly. She fell to the ground, calling curses upon them in Babylonian.

My heart exploded with fury to see Aia's fragile body crumpled in the dust. "Let me go!" I demanded.

"We will let you go to the king's harem," one laughed, putting his hand on my thigh. "Should we take a taste of her first?" he asked his companions.

"It is virgins the king wants," another replied, touching my hair, which hung loose to my waist.

"Take her and she will be ours to keep," the first one observed. He pulled off my robe.

My bones collapsed, and the light left my eyes. I walked in the valley of the shadows of death and my heart grew cold.

I awoke on the ground with my head cradled in Mordechai's arms. His tear-filled gaze revealed a tender love that must have long hidden in his heart. I imagined that I was rescued. He had received word of this terrible mistake and run from the king's gate in just enough time to save me—his beloved—from harm. We would be married and I would stay with him all the rest of my days.

But the glint of a spear caught my eye and I saw the four soldiers surrounding us. Mordechai had saved me from them so that my treasure might be given to the king. We would be permitted only the briefest farewell.

"Do not reveal your people or your kindred," Mordechai whispered into my ear as he handed me to the king's men. And I knew he feared his position at court would be compromised if he was exposed as a Jew. "Let yourself be known only as Esther, foster daughter of Marduka the Babylonian."

And so ended the days of Hadassah daughter of Avihail.

Six

I told myself that Mordechai did not fight because he did not have a soldier's strength and had no chance of succeeding against them. He did not argue because the king's edict was issued with no provision for exceptions. He did not bribe the soldiers by mention of his wealth or influential position in the king's court because he knew the disobedient would be subject to cruel punishment.

As we said farewell, his resolute silence showed that resistance would not gain my release. And so I submitted to my captors.

I walked with the soldiers across the east side of the acropolis to the market square. I dared not look back to see if my cousin followed. Nor have I ever asked. It is my wish and my desire to imagine that his eyes remained on me until I was swallowed by the harem gate.

The king's gate house loomed large over the market square. A long double stairway—wide enough on each side for four horses to pass abreast—stretched up to its entrance. Mordechai set foot upon these stairs every day. It was his habit to count them as he climbed, and so I knew they numbered one hundred and eleven. I began to count them myself, to ease my fear and sorrow.

I looked down at each stair, and tried to picture Mordechai's kind face. I wanted to see him, to hold him in my heart. But the grip of the soldiers on my arms distracted me. I stumbled and lost count.

I continued up the stairway, as if in a dream, and recalled the hour that I was taken from my father's house. So real was my memory, that it seemed as if the past four years never happened.

The hut was dark. I had been sitting in the alcove of the chamber pot behind a heavy curtain for many hours. My father's body lay trampled in the street beyond our gate. My mother's blood-soaked body lay on the floor in the middle of our hut. Ninsun, our Babylonian house servant, had gone to find someone who could take care of me. My parents had reached the end of their days and I was alone.

I had stayed with my mother through most of her labor. But when wild-eyed death had possessed her face, the midwife sent me to the alcove. She warned me to stay there until someone told me I could come out. Though I could not see my mother in the end, I heard her cries through the curtain. She did not depart from me like a lamb led to the slaughter.

After the midwife had gone, Ninsun told me to remain hidden. "I must get help," she said, her voice worn with weeping for my mother and her dead infant. "Stay there and do not move or Lamashtu will take you." Ninsun lived in fear of Lamashtu, She who Erases. Father was always scolding her for talking about the Babylonian gods and demons. "We are Jews in this household," he would remind her whenever she let something slip. "We worship the One God." But Ninsun would no more give up her gods than Father would accept them.

I do not know how long I sat in the dark alcove in the dark hut, separated from my mother's corpse by a curtain, while the revolt of Babylon raged in the streets around me. I was too afraid to give way to my grief. My blood ran cold and hunger began to eat at my flesh, but still no one came for me.

At last I heard Ninsun's familiar footsteps, and someone with her. Lamp light crept across the space between the curtain and the floor.

The visitor paused in the middle of the hut. "Cover her with something clean," he ordered Ninsun, his old voice filled with disdain. "The women will not be here to wash her until daylight. Where is the girl?"

"There," Ninsun replied.

He pushed the curtain aside and found me crouching beside the chamber pot. I could not move.

"Come," the old man said. He had a long white beard and thick white eyebrows that met above his nose, and he covered his head with a tall black turban. His eyes held sorrow but no kindness. I knew him as the father of Ezra the scholar.

"You will stay with my wife for now," he said.

But still I could not move.

"She is cold," Ninsun observed, her voice filled with pity. She took my mother's best shawl from a peg and wrapped it around me as she helped me to my feet.

"Come," the man said, holding out his hand to me. I gazed past him to the shrouded figure on the floor. The toes of one foot were showing. My father had often admired her beautiful small feet.

And then the light left my eyes. It seemed as if God had reversed his creation and all that had been separated—light from dark and ocean from firmament—was joined into a great nothingness.

The old man touched me. "Come now, child."

"No!" I cried out, my heart exploding into the emptiness of the world. I held fast to Ninsun's robe with both hands, my tears flowing over the birth stains of my mother's stillborn infant.

"I cannot keep you!" Ninsun whispered. "I have children of my own to feed."

"Come," the old man insisted, taking me by a hand.

The soldiers took me through the colossal doorway into the gatehouse, as tall as twelve men. The central passageway was wide enough to hold hundreds of people, and twenty smaller rooms flanked either side. Many men served the king here, Mordechai among them, recording the taxes and tributes delivered each day from the vast provinces of the empire. As a child, I had been told that none of the king's courtiers could be more trustworthy or loyal than Mordechai, who served the king's interest from dawn to dusk. When I came to Susa, I saw for myself how hard he worked and how many people relied upon him. He was a good man and I could have hoped to wed no better.

But I had lost him, as my mother and father had been lost to me.

I stumbled again as we emerged from the gatehouse into the daylight.

"Drinking the king's wine even before she got here," one of the soldiers laughed.

"Let us pray that the king does not like her," another added.

The others agreed and though the wish was not intended to be kind, it filled my heart with hope as a parched Indian dog fills his belly with water after the hunt. The king might not want me, I told myself, and then I could go home to Mordechai.

We descended the stairs into a court large enough to hold ten thousand men. Guards were posted at even intervals, near doorways and colonnade entrances. Each stood at full attention, one foot placed in front of the other. Each held a towering spear with a silver blade and a gold pomegranate-shaped butt. Strange companions stood near many guards: white stone statues of men undraped, in full display of their manhood. I had never seen figures sculpted without clothing.

"The spoils of Athens and the Parthenon!" one of my captors declared, following my gaze to the figures. I shrunk inside myself with shame.

"Victorious strength!" his companions replied in one voice.

"We worship Ahura Mazda, who gave us victory over Pallas Athena!" the first one added.

"Victorious strength!" the chorus repeated, this time shaking their fists in the air. And they said no more. Later I learned that this was the cry of brotherhood among the men who had lain siege to Athens and vanquished the Greek goddess of wisdom and war in her own temple. The heroes who carried off these statues never spoke of the subsequent defeat at Salamis. They remained—among each other—forever victorious.

Three of my escort turned away, leaving me in the charge of a single soldier. He had no reason to fear my escape now; I could go nowhere without being seized.

We passed an open reception hall, with six rows of towering columns, each topped by a stone bull's head. I fixed my attention upon these creatures for only a moment before the sun pierced my eyes. The soldiers had praised Ahura Mazda, the god of Xerxes and the Persian people. And so I resolved to appeal to the God of my own people for help.

But I could not remember the old prayers from Babylon, and none were ever spoken in Mordechai's house. I was mute and the One God did not hear my distress. He did not protect me from the king's own god who appeared above, watching over the courtyard from a cornice.

Ahura Mazda sat inside a winged disc, his head and shoulders twisted in profile away from his wings, spread to their full span. He wore the tall turban of a king and a full beard. His upper body was clothed in a robe; bird's feet and tail feathers floated out from under the disc. His left hand grasped a ring and his right was raised, as if in greeting or blessing.

But he offered no such kindness to me, an intruder from the Jews who could not summon her own God. "I am the keeper of the valley of dried bones," he whispered, his voice like cypress branches creaking in the wind. "The spirit rushes and sits near the skull. The spirit tastes as much suffering as the whole of the living world can taste!"

His whispering enveloped me and I felt the skin and sinew on my bones peel away and evaporate, like a drop of water on the ground in deep summer. And though my obedient legs carried on and the soldier held my arms, I was no more than a shadow in his grip.

Seven

Many young women were taken by force from our families, who received not even a few coins of compensation for a bride price. When I came to know the king, I understood that he never imagined the grief of a father for his daughter, a brother for his sister, or a man for his betrothed. He was the king and what he wanted was his.

The harem was a maze of rooms at the southern tip of the palace, across from the king's gate house. Four soldiers armed with daggers stood before the enormous iron gate that secured the entrance. No man, except those who had lost their manhood to the knife, could gain permission to pass into the harem. No women, except those too old to serve the king's desire, could leave.

My captor saluted the four guards of the harem gate and released me. Two of the men lifted a heavy latch opened the gate, another pushed me through.

I watched the gate close, separating me forever from my life with Mordechai and Aia. I stared with lifeless eyes through the iron bars from Kurnugi, the land of no return. A sudden chill wrapped me in a rigid embrace, though it was a warm spring day and the sun stood at its zenith.

I tried to rally my heart and imagined what Aia might be doing: kneading dough, sweeping the goat's pen, scrubbing the floors of the house, beating dust from a rug. But as I pictured her gnarled hands and thin wrists, my bones began to shake with sobbing. For while I had blossomed into womanhood, the housekeeper had grown frail with illness and age. When she felt well, we worked side by side. When she was too weak to leave her bed, I brought her soup and attended to the housework according to her detailed instructions. She had given my life peace and purpose; I had promised myself to care for her until the end of her days. But now I was gone. And she was alone.

Someone prodded me from behind. I cried out, turning and shrinking back. I fell against the gate and the guards laughed.

"His manhood was cut out before your mother was born," a soldier said through the iron bars.

I looked up to see an old, stooped eunuch. He wore a robe of fine emerald green linen and a tall white turban. Chains of gold and silver glittered around his neck and sandals of soft yellow leather shrouded his feet, twisted and crippled with age. His wrinkled cheek and pointed chin were beardless.

"Illness?" he asked, hovering over me.

I shook my head.

"Pregnancy?"

The guards laughed again. In desperation, I wondered if a lie would release me. But the eunuch seemed to understood all that I contemplated.

"We will know soon enough." He lifted a bony finger to indicate that I should follow him to a colonnade at the other side of the court. I raised myself from the dust. My knees were so weak that I could stand no straighter than the ancient servant. My feet fought for every step forward as if the hands of the demon Druj Nasu held my ankles. "Come where you are coming," the eunuch snapped with impatience, poking me again.

My stomach churned as if I might vomit. I sought relief in tears, but the well of my eyes was dry. Again I tried to summon a picture of Mordechai from my memory, to steady my steps, but he was gone. And so I knew the dread demon Lamashtu had taken possession of me, erasing from my heart all that had ever mattered.

We reached the steps of the colonnade and climbed from sunlight into darkness. The stone floor was polished to the high sheen of a mirror, smooth and slippery. I looked down and saw my face in the shadows. All of my features had been erased.

The eunuch stopped before the door to the harem court. On the door jambs before me, a molded relief of the king fought a rearing lion monster with no more than a dagger in his bare hands. A powerful odor assaulted my nostrils, the rich fragrances of roses, cloves, and mimosa mixed with essence of musk, sandalwood, myrrh, and balsam. And so I came to smell the women of the king's harem before I saw them.

"You are a pretty bit of flesh," the eunuch rasped. "Mind your keepers and serve the king's bed well! You will live here in great comfort until your breasts sag and your sweet honeycomb shrivels. Be warned—the ones for whom we have no use go straight to the soldiers in the barracks."

I looked at the eunuch, my eyes wide with terror. His words rang in my ears and my head spun. The lion monster on the door jamb lunged for me. I fled from the creature's wide mouth and sharp claws into the harem court.

The court was divided into two levels. A cedar wood railing ringed the upper level, on which I stood. A wide staircase led to the level to one below, a large square space with a sunken tile pool in the center. The floors were painted red and scattered with worn red carpets.

The king's concubines gathered around the pool, a hundred women, reclining on large cushions in small groups. Gowns of gauzy fabric revealed the ample charms of their well-groomed, abundant flesh. Their hair was woven into elaborate braided sculptures and their fingertips were stained with henna.

They were far too quiet. Indeed, three women gossiping in the marketplace made more noise than the languid whispers of these hundred. Their silence was a living death more terrifying than the eunuch's threat. I told myself that if my cousin had understood where I was going, he would have struggled harder to save me. He would have prayed to the One God not to abandon me. He would have urged me to cut my own throat rather than to submit to such ruin.

My heart became a torrent of terrible whispers, pushing me to action. I saw my shattered skull on the edge of the pool below. I leaned over the railing to retrieve it.

The eunuch pulled me back by my hair and my hands loosened their grip from the railing. He pinched my neck and slapped my face but I did not dare cry out. I felt other strong hands seize my arms, dragging me to a door along the periphery of the court. It opened into a small windowless room with bare brick walls and a rough stone floor.

Three girls cowered in the center.

"Sit where they sit," the eunuch ordered. I was thrust over the threshold. The door shut behind me.

The stone room was cold and dim, lit by a single oil lamp in the wall. As I tried to calm myself, I examined each girl in turn.

A delicate, olive-skinned girl with long, lustrous black hair was the prettiest of the group. Her large dark eyes sat far apart on her face over high cheekbones. She wept in terrified silence. Her gray wool robe was that of a poor man's daughter and her tiny hand grasped an object attached to a golden chain around her neck. Her trembling lips moved as if to form words, but no sound issued forth. She did not glance up from the floor.

The other two stared at me with expectation. One was a plump girl with a full bottom lip, thick eyebrows, and hair coiled in tight ringlets. Her robe was woven of a costly blue linen and embroidered with red rosettes. I gazed at her round face and dancing curls, imagining that she must have had a cheerful disposition at home. I longed to hear her laugh.

The third girl had eyes the color of copper hidden below a deep brow, thin lips, and hollow cheeks. Her face was unwashed and she was dressed without care, but she wore a robe of soft red wool that only a father with wealth could afford.

I looked from girl to girl and guessed that none had ever known fear. Perhaps they had never been away from their homes for a single night. Only I, among them, had lived through the Babylonian revolt. Only I had lost my parents and traveled a great distance with strangers. Only I knew what it was like to start life afresh in an unfamiliar place.

"We must each be a friend to the other!" My heart quickened by the words that escaped from my throat. I knew, now, that Lamashtu had failed to take all of me. And I vowed to fight her with every breath in my body.

The three girls looked up at me, their questioning eyes filled with fear and doubt.

"We are not forbidden to speak," I replied, as if I had the courage of the king's best soldier and cared nothing for danger. "I am Esther."

Esther! I would teach myself to cherish this name as my own. For though it honored the alien goddess, it was the gift Mordechai had given me, the first and the last.

I sat down on the hard stone and asked each of my new friends what I might call her. The round girl was Vadhut and the copper-eyed one Hutana. From these names I understood them to be daughters of the Zoroastrian faith. But the pretty one would not speak.

"Please tell us your name." I offered her my hand in comfort.

"Sarah," she whispered.

Sarah, descended from the worshipers of the One God, like myself.

"Tomorrow was to be the feast of my betrothal!" She burst into tears. I squeezed her fingers and Vadhut placed a hand on her arm.

"You must forget your betrothal," I counseled, wondering what dangers she might face in the harem if she were known as a Jew. Perhaps she would be sent straight to the soldiers. "Say nothing more of your people and your kindred. You shall henceforth be known as Freni the Persian."

And so I named her for the woman who sold the sweetest smelling rosewater in the marketplace.

"What about this?" Freni whispered, showing me the amulet around her neck, a small gold tube with Hebrew characters etched on one side. It was a charm like the one my mother used to hang over me while I slept, to protect me from the night demon Lilith.

I gazed at Freni and saw my mother's sweet face before me. The well of my eyes rose in grief and joy for all that I had lost and all that I might yet find. But I had to be strong for my new friends and so I held back my tears. "You must hide the necklace along with your true name," I advised. "We will help you, and each other."

And I glanced from girl to girl until each had nodded her agreement.

Eight

We sat in silence until the door opened and a group of servants hurried in. Two women crossed the threshold, their arms piled high with thick towels. Two more followed, each bearing a wooden tray laden with pots, oil jars, combs and tooth picks. Several eunuchs hauled in two large bronze bathtubs and two heavy wooden tables. Servants with steaming brown ceramic jugs followed and then another eunuch with a tray of golden drinking vessels.

Shaashgaz entered last, holding a shimmering silver wine jug unlike any I had ever seen. It was fluted with thick vertical ridges around the body; a circle of lotus blossoms adorned the smooth neck. Handles on each side formed the shape of elongated ibex, their graceful horns curving up and around, far above their little pointed ears. The creatures faced each other across the rim of the vessel as if in conversation. I could not take my eyes from the jug, which shone in the midst of darkness and uncertainty. But the vessel's beauty belied its contents. It would soon became an object of terror.

The eunuchs set the tables down upon the stone floor and dispersed to various tasks. They shut the massive cedar door and lit more lamps.

When the room was bright, Shaashgaz ordered us to rise to our feet. Freni clung to me, shaking in fear. She slipped her hands into mine and my palm closed around her amulet. I had not seen her remove it.

My heart found comfort in her trust , but I was no more able to keep the treasure safe than she. I glanced around the room for a hiding place and edged toward a section of flat wall, keeping watch to make sure no one noticed me. I leaned against the brick, as if too weak to stand without support. With my hands behind my back, I felt for a chink large enough to accommodate the amulet. When I found a space, I pushed in the charm with a single finger, drawing blood as I scraped the flesh along the side of my nail. I slid away from the wall and glanced behind. Nothing showed.

While the servants prepared the baths and the tables for our grooming, Shaashgaz poured the wine and gave each of us a cup. "Drink!" he ordered.

Vadhut and Hutana drank as if they were parched. But Freni held the cup away from her face, her lips moving as if in silent prayer. She caught my eye and I shook my head to warn her against doing anything to give herself away. The sides of her mouth curved in a grateful smile and she began to take the wine in delicate mouthfuls.

Freni's calloused hands and rough clothes told me that she had not led a life of idle luxury. I imagined that her days had been filled with as much housework as my own. But she held herself with grace, like a woman of royal birth. Even the way she lifted the cup to her lips was a pleasure to my eye.

I, too, began drinking the wine after Freni's example. But Shaashgaz soon grew impatient and ordered us to hurry. After we drained the first cup, we were forced to drink another. The thick, sweet wine was much stronger than what I was used to and I soon fell into a stupor.

The female servants disrobed us and threw our clothing in a heap on the floor as if it were refuse. Hutana bent down to snatch her red wool robe from the pile. A eunuch slapped her hand away.

"Nothing that might carry vermin!" Shaashgaz snapped. "Take it to the fire," he ordered one of the women servants. She bowed, scooped up our clothes, and scurried from the room.

We stood naked, our flesh warmed by the wine, while the old eunuch inspected us for obvious defect or disease. I knew by my eyes what was happening, but my vision seemed to belong to someone else. I had no awareness of inhabiting my own body; I felt no shame.

The servants set to work on Freni and me while Hutana and Vadhut were left to doze. Our scalps and hair were doused with olive oil and wrapped in towels, to kill any lice that might be hiding. A eunuch lifted my naked body and laid me upon a towel spread over one of the tables. I heard voices echo in my head as if I was in a deep cave. Someone said it would be many months before we would be soft and round enough to serve the king's pleasure.

Two eunuchs held me down; one at the shoulders and the other at the ankles. My orifices were flushed and wiped clean. My teeth were picked and whitened with an acrid powder. The hair from my most private places was stripped away. Yet I felt no pain.

I was plunged into the warm tub. My flesh was scrubbed and my nails cleansed of dirt. My hair remained drenched in oil.

I was lifted out of the tub, dried with a towel, and returned to the table. I saw Freni lying next to me, on the other table. One maidservant rubbed rich oils into her breasts while another massaged her feet. Freni's eyes were open but she did not see me. She arched her back and moaned with pleasure. My own eyelids grew heavy and soon sealed. I saw a lion monster stalking me, its claws sharper than a knife and its mouth hungering for fresh blood. I knew that the creature was about to attack but I was rooted to the ground like a cypress tree. I could not move. I could not wake up.

I opened my eyes into a stream of sunlight. I found myself on a mattress in a small room with a ceiling window, my head resting upon a soft cushion. The stone walls were bare. I lifted my arm and saw the fabric of a sheer white harem robe. The flesh beneath was whole and unscratched. The lion had not touched me.

A sigh of relief escaped my throat. But when I tried to sit up, my head throbbed as if crushed between two heavy stones. My stomach heaved.

An old serving woman came to me with a bowl. When I finished vomiting, she wiped my face and eased me back down upon the cushion. Uttering soothing sounds, she placed a cool cloth upon my forehead. I closed my eyes and returned to Babylon.

It was a market day and I was walking with my mother on the limestone pavement of the Processional Way toward the Ishtar Gate. I wanted to see the lions on the tiles that decorated the gate. When I held my mother's hand the lions did not frighten me. They were pretty, with their yellow bodies and red manes on the blue background. But the dread name of the king who built the Ishtar Gate was more terrifying than a real lion. Father knew the name of evil deeds and wicked thoughts, and Nebuchadnezzar was that name. The evil king had destroyed the Temple and forced our people to live in Babylon. Jews had to spit on the name of Nebuchadnezzar when it was spoken. But nobody spoke the name of evil unless they drank too much wine. Ninsun told me that too much wine made Lamashtu take you to the house of ashes in Kurnugi, where everyone lived on dust and there was no light. But father warned that if I

55

listened to her Babylonian donkey excrement my nose would turn into a donkey snout and no Jewish man would have me for his wife.

The evil king was long dead and his city captured by the Persians. King Cyrus had been our friend but his successor, Darius, was not. No one knew what to expect from King Xerxes the warrior. He had held the throne for two years and for two years we had lived in peace. But still we had no word of permission for the rebuilding of the Temple.

Father assured the men gathered in the prayer tent and the women in our courtyard that our people would soon return to Jerusalem. But when he spoke of that glorious day, Mother bit her lip. Mother and I liked it in Babylon in our little hut with Ninsun, the Babylonian housekeeper, to do all the work while mother attended her courtyard full of visitors.

I held my mother's hand as we passed through the gate of Ishtar and descended to the bridge. The street was crowded with people buying and selling. Some things always caught my eye. The carpets from Susa were the most beautiful. They were azure with scarlet lotus flowers and yellow elk. There were little wood idols carved in the image of the great Marduk, god of the Babylonians. But I knew to close my eyes when we passed them, because Father said they brought the wrath of God upon the land.

I dragged my mother, as I always did, to see the man who sold ebony and ivory Egyptian boxes. They came in many sizes but my favorites were the small ones with intricate ivory inlay. Every market day I reminded my mother that I wanted one for my dowry chest. She always laughed and asked what I would do with such a fancy little box. "I will keep the treasures of my marriage in it," I told her, though I could not imagine what these treasures might be.

We continued through the market to the prayer tent on the river bank. Father had been there all day and mother wanted him to come home. I held my mother's hand and pulled at her robe. I was bored standing outside the tent and wanted to go watch the weavers. "Quiet, little one," she whispered. And her soft, sweet voice lingered like the warmth of a gentle breeze from the river. "Ezra the scholar is reading the law."

I peeked into the tent through the open door flap. It was filled with many men, all crowded around a youth with wild eyes and an unkempt beard. He wore a small turban and had the white skin of one who never sits in the sun. He was chanting Hebrew from a scroll. Some of the men echoed his chant in a whisper. Others stood with their eyes closed and swayed from side to side.

I did not see my father in the crowd, though I knew he was there.

I woke again, expecting to see the mud brick walls of my childhood home and to smell the scent of a rich Sabbath loaf.

"You can never use too much honey." I heard myself murmur the words my mother spoke when asked for the secret of Ninsun's bread.

"Drink this," my mother replied.

I sobbed with joy for her return and opened my eyes to drink in the sight of her loving face.

But the woman looking down upon me was old and wrinkled. Her skin was as rough as elephant leather. She was not my mother.

And then I remembered all that had happened before I drank the wine. I was in a room in the harem of Xerxes. The woman was the servant who had helped me when I was sick, perhaps only a few moments ago.

I sat up, two rivers of grief streaming down my face.

"You will feel better when you drink this," the servant said, her soft voice filled with concern. I tried to imagine her skin smooth and fresh as a young woman's, her fine straight hair free of gray. She had a proud nose and a graceful neck. Her eyes were the largest I had ever seen, placed with perfect balance on either side of her nose. Her small mouth curved like an archer's bow.

She must have been pretty, once. But now her shoulders were stooped and her flesh hung from her face as if she had known little joy in her life. Perhaps she had come to the harem as I had, her heart torn from those whom she loved.

The servant did not seem to mind my staring. She wiped my eyes with a cloth and once again offered me the ceramic drinking bowl, filled with a white frothy liquid.

I trusted her kind eyes and drank.

The warmed goat's milk and honey eased the knot in my stomach. And when I had finished I thanked her.

"I am better now," I assured her. I glanced around the room, wondering what had become of my friends.

"My mistress was sick from the wine," the woman explained. And I realized that she spoke of me, who had never in all my days been mistress to anyone. "The others are with the hairdressers, being readied for their inspection by Hegai."

And so I first came to know Puah, my comfort and my rock.

Nine

I was taken into the king's palace under the supervision of Hegai, the guardian of the women, the lord of the harem. His understanding of the king's desire was such that he knew upon sight if a girl would bring pleasure to the royal bedchamber. All who arrived without obvious disease were washed and groomed and displayed before him. He inspected them and determined their fate.

Some had known men, though they were not married. Some were young but did not display the beauty of youth. Some bore a blemish that would dampen the king's desire. Some spoke in sour tones. And some were so quarrelsome that even the harem wine would not make them agreeable. Girls such as these were not admitted into the harem, but sent to the army barracks to serve the rough pleasure of the king's soldiers. There they soon grew old and broken.

While I recovered from the effects of the harem wine, the others had moved on to the hairdressers. Puah washed my hair herself, checking my scalp for nits. She spent an hour combing my tresses with slow and cautious strokes, spreading them in a fan across my back until every strand lay in its place, smooth and shining down to my waist. The old servant had no cosmetics at her disposal, no kohl to rim my eyes or perfume to sweeten my scent. But she massaged my feet with almond oil and rubbed pomegranate juice over my cheeks and lips.

She attended me with loving kindness, expecting nothing in return. She knew that Hegai never retained girls who could not tolerate the harem wine. The haoma in it banished rancor and misery from the hearts of the king's concubines. It made them compliant and submissive. It was the strength of Hegai's rule.

A young eunuch appeared in the doorway of the little room and nodded to Puah, who helped me rise. I was yet unsteady on my feet, and clung to her arm as she guided me through the maze of corridors to a large apartment at the far end of the harem.

I entered a receiving room, my eyes tearing at the bright light that shone from the numerous brass ceiling lamps. I lowered my gaze to the floor, covered with carpets of scarlet and blue wool woven into an intricate pattern of rosettes within squares. The fabric on the wall hangings shimmered like stars reflecting on the river at night, but the images they depicted—naked women with heavy breasts and full thighs—made me flush with embarrassment.

Puah urged me forward, guiding my steps toward an enormous man who sat on an ornate armchair of ebony inlaid with lapis lazuli and silver. Male attendants stood on either side of him, some holding jeweled daggers. Two boys hovered over him from a perch on a box behind the throne, one with a large fan of woven reeds and the other with a leather fly whisk.

He was dressed in royal robes woven from violet silk and silver threads. Every finger on his hands sparkled with a ring of gold or silver. His posture, even sitting, indicated someone who held himself to be of great importance. The expression of his face—a mixture of scorn, disgust, and revulsion—made his great bulk menacing.

I stood before this man, not knowing who he was, or why I had been summoned to him. My reason still muddled by the wine, I formed an idea in myself that he must be King Xerxes. And so I fell to my knees and bowed my head.

"Come forward," the enormous man ordered. But the pitch of his voice, higher than my own, revealed that he did not have a man's full vigor. I gazed up at his face: his round, smooth cheek betrayed him as a eunuch, despite the tuft of false beard attached to one of his chins.

This creature—neither man nor woman—could not be King Xerxes. Yet I understood from his manner and position that he wielded great power in the harem.

Puah helped me to my feet. We walked to the edge of the carpet, stopping just short of the platform. I saw by the eunuch's pursed lips and fearsome stare that I did not please him. I glanced to Puah at my side, hoping for some hint how I might win the eunuch's favor. But her eyes remained fixed on her feet.

"So our wine was not to your liking!" The eunuch's shrill voice startled me.

"I could not support its strength, my lord," I whispered.

"You are from Susa?" So great was the pressure of his enormous weight upon his throat, that his words came out as great gasps of sound.

"Yes my lord." I held back tears for my cousin's household and all that I had lost that day.

"What are your parents?"

"I am an orphan, my lord."

"A pretty orphan," he sighed, appraising me with a stare that made me feel like a goat for sale in the marketplace. He sighed again and leaned toward one of the eunuchs by his side. "Such fair skin and shapely form would tantalize the king's desire. Bright eyes the color of ripened wheat, and the shape of luscious almonds. And look at the abundant hair. She would have served him well."

The regret in his voice held my heart like the hangman's noose. I did not want to be an object of the king's pleasure, but I feared a worse fate if I did not cooperate. "I shall be your obedient servant," I heard myself promise.

The eunuch shifted his great bulk back toward me, his eyebrows lifting in surprise. His sharp eyes rose from the flesh of his face like a crescent moon peeking over a mountain.

"What did you say?" he asked.

"I shall be your obedient servant," I repeated, afraid that I had displeased him.

"What are you called?" he demanded.

"Esther, my lord," I replied. The name scratched my throat and tore at my tongue as it escaped, like a difficult birth. I no longer heard the word as Mordechai had said it, with love and concern for my safety. I did not hear it as I had introduced myself to the others, with a show of courage. It was the name of someone I did not know.

The eunuch's thick lips went slack and his mouth fell open as if gasping for air. His false beard quivered. He tightened his grip on the arms of his throne.

He stared at me for some time. I forced myself to return his gaze as if beholding an object of delight.

"Let us inspect her," the eunuch commanded, breaking his silence after a long minute. One of his attendants signaled for Puah to remove my robe. The gauzy fabric fell away from my flesh.

I stood alone in the shame of my nakedness. I felt Hegai's eyes upon me but I could not meet his gaze. After some moments of silence, he raised a finger to a young eunuch who stood beside him. Heaving his great bulk out of the chair, he leaned on the youth like a walking stick and approached me. Each step required great effort. He came so close to me that I could feel the heat of his labored breath on my skin. He circled me, examining every inch of my bare flesh. I held myself very still. I imagined that I was a statue of cool white marble.

After Hegai looked at my skin, he examined behind my ears and in my mouth. He pressed his nose into the hollow between my arm and shoulder. His massive hands cupped my breasts, as if to feel their weight. Then he signaled that I should be laid on my back. With the help of an attendant, he lowered himself to his knees.

Puah draped my robe across my shoulders and chest while a eunuch elevated my hips with a cushion. My legs were spread apart. I was a statue; I felt neither fear nor pain. I closed my eyes and saw my mother.

We were walking on the marble pavement below the hanging gardens of the great ziggurat. Everything was in bloom. She closed her arms around me, holding me close to the child she was soon due to deliver. She wept, thanking the One God for my life and my health. The mid-morning sun warmed us and we sat down to share a piece of honey cake. We watched the boats on the River Euphrates float past like clouds. I turned back to my mother and saw a spasm of pain pass over her sweet face. And I knew that her time had come.

"No man has known her," the eunuch Hegai declared, rising to his feet. Puah helped me with my robe and I sat up. The keeper of the women washed his hands in a basin.

"An apartment shall be furnished for her by the evening," he pronounced. "Attendants shall be provided her as is her due. Whatever her request and her desire it shall be granted to her."

I bowed to the keeper of the women, trying to find the words to thank him. But my tongue was still thick with the wine and my body shivered in shame for all that his hands had done to me. And so I said nothing as he pronounced me suitable for the king's pleasure and instructed Puah to attend me until my apartment in the harem was ready.

We returned to the room where Puah had cared for me. She helped me settle on to some large cotton floor cushions and brought me more goat's milk.

"Thank you for your kindness," I said as I took the familiar cup. I tried to tell myself that I had only imagined the interlude in the eunuch's apartment, but I still felt his hands probing me. I longed to bathe, to rub raw my tainted flesh, to be pure again.

Puah peered down at me, her large eyes blinking as if she unsure of what she saw.

"Please sit with me," I begged.

She lowered herself onto a cushion by my side and raised her hand to smooth my hair. I welcomed her comforting touch.

"You have been spared great suffering," she observed, tucking some hair behind my ear.

"I have not been spared," I retorted, the words bringing a bitter taste into my mouth.

"You would have gone to the soldiers," Puah revealed, an edge of reproach in her voice. "Women who can not tolerate the wine always go to the soldiers."

I put the milk aside. My hands shook with fear for what I had escaped.

"Your beauty found favor in the eunuch's eyes," Puah continued, "but it was something else, too." Her brow furrowed with puzzlement. "Something you said."

"Perhaps he will change his mind," I worried.

"He has bestowed upon you an apartment while you are yet a virgin," Puah replied. "Never has such an honor been given. If you are obedient to him and work hard to please the king, he will not change his mind."

I kissed Puah's hand with gratitude. "I cannot remember all that happened after I drank the wine, but I am glad fate brought you to take care of me."

"It was God who called me to you," she insisted. "When you became ill, Shaashgaz sent a messenger in search of a maid. I, the lowest of the chamber servants, put myself forward for the task. No one expected you to stay in the harem and so I was granted permission."

I kissed her hand again. "You cared for me as if I were your own child."

Puah laughed with pleasure. "When I saw you in your illness, I knew you were the child I never had," she explained. "I thanked the One God for giving me even a few hours to care for you. I prayed for His mercy and begged Him with all my heart to keep you from the soldiers."

"He heard your prayers," I whispered, my eyes filling with tears.

"He heard me," she agreed, drawing me close. "And now we are bound together for all time."

Ten

Hegai hurried to furnish me with cosmetics and rations and the seven maids that were my due. But he would not bring any girl before the king until she had completed a year of beauty treatments. A full year ensured that a woman was soft, fragrant, and free of the flesh-wasting disease, which often took many months to reveal itself. And so I had a year to hope and dream that Mordechai would rescue me.

When I finished the second cup of goat's milk, I felt well enough to rejoin my friends. Puah led me through a dark passageway to the court. I could not anticipate how familiar the stained walls would become, the worn carpet, the lingering odors of perfume, food, and lamp oil. Night after sleepless night I would wander these halls, until I knew them better than my own face.

We emerged into the bright court. Nothing seemed changed from my first glimpse of the concubines that morning. In the harem every hour was much like the one before it.

I studied my surroundings with care: the red floors and carpets, the pool below, and the idle women in sheer white robes lounging on faded cushions. My eyes wandered to the servants, all older women with cropped gray hair, dressed in tunics of rough linen. They hovered over the concubines, offering trays of sweet cakes and bowls of fruit. Whenever a woman raised her cup for more wine, a servant rushed to have it refilled. A tall eunuch stood in a corner with a silver ibex jug.

I did not enjoy the prospect of endless lounging or being waited upon. "I would rather be a servant than be served," I whispered to Puah.

The old woman stroked my head. "The servants were once attended as you shall be. They once hoped to gain gifts enough to leave."

Her voice held such sorrow that I supposed she spoke of herself.

"You must learn to satisfy the king's desire," she advised. "Obtain gold for his gratitude or you will become like them: used by the king until you no longer interest him, with no refuge but to live out your days as a servant to the ones who replace you."

Puah pointed to a concubine sitting alone with her wine cup. Servants hovered near her as if they were her designated attendants. She had a round face made fuller by ample flesh and her smooth ivory skin glistened with oil. Her hair was braided into an elaborate sculpture that stood high on her head and her eyebrows were plucked into tilted arches over her small eyes. Her short nose flared like the snout of a donkey. While the other concubines wore few adornments—earrings, a nose ring, a single necklace at most—her arms, neck, ankles, and ears were laden with gold and silver. When she moved her hand, a ring flashed on every finger.

"Thriti will have enough for a small estate when the king tires of her," Puah noted.

"She has no beauty," I observed, with surprise. I regretted the words as soon as I said them, for they were unkind.

Puah did not spare me the truth. "She pleases him in the bedchamber. He will not look upon her face or endure her coarse manner when his lust is sated, but he rewards her well for the service she gives. I do not doubt that you can surpass Thriti as the king's favorite, for you have a beautiful face and graceful ways. You will not end your days as I am ending mine."

I did not appreciate Puah's confidence in me. I still had the taste of freedom on my tongue and the scent of my beloved in my nostrils. I could muster no enthusiasm for the prospect of serving the king's desire and bearing his children in exchange for a few trinkets of gold and silver.

As I looked across the balcony toward the courtyard door, I imagined how I might escape. I would keep careful watch over the harem gate until a guard left it open. Then I would slip through without being seen and fly home to Mordechai and Aia; they would rejoice at my return. Everything would be just as I left it. My loom would still be whole and I would take up my work as if I had never been to the harem. I would cast out the memory of the eunuch's hand. I would soon finish the wedding belt and be married to my cousin. No other man would ever know me.

My vision returned from this foolish fancy to the women before me. Looking down at my own robe, I realized it was identical to theirs. I was one of them. I would never escape through a gate guarded by the king's best soldiers.

I noticed two concubines whose bellies were heavy with child. Burning bile rose from my stomach to my throat. My heart tore with grief for the loss of the sons I had longed to give Mordechai. I mourned them as my mother had mourned her stillborn children.

Puah put her arm around my shoulders and wiped my eyes with her sleeve. "I am sure your friends will be happy to see you," she told me, offering what little comfort she could. She pointed to the three girls, clustered apart on the edge of the group below, far away from the pool.

In their sheer white robes, sculptured hair, and painted faces, they looked like all the others and I had not recognized them. Now I saw that though Freni's eyes were ringed with kohl, the sweetness of her face was unmarred. Vadhut's heavy brows had been plucked into fine arches, yet her cheeks remained plump and cheerful. And while Hutana's skin shone, her thin lips were still locked in a frown.

I looked from them to Puah and back again. They would want to know I was safe. I kissed the flaccid crevasses of Puah's cheek and descended the steps to join the others.

That evening a servant showed me to my apartment. The door opened from the hall into a receiving room large enough to accommodate ten visitors. The floor was covered with the same worn red carpets in the court and the stone walls were barren of hangings. This room led into the next, which held only a beauty treatment table and a shelf with towels and unguents. Through another doorway I stepped into a small sleeping chamber. Here I found a single mattress and many plain gray wool cushions.

The walls in this airless sleeping chamber, like those in the other rooms, were bare. But when I lay upon the mattress, my eyes detected markings in the stone above the place where my head rested. Looking closer, I saw letters scratched into the wall. I could not read, yet they frightened me. On that first night, and every night thereafter, I could not close my eyes without imagining those lines and triangles floating down from the wall and encircling me with deep and everlasting sleep. The writing seemed to be the work of a demon; it haunted me whenever my foot crossed over the threshold of the apartment.

I should have been grateful for the privilege of my own rooms. Few of the other concubines had more than a mattress in a small space shared with many others. They had no privacy, no place to speak with a special friend in confidence. But I loathed my apartment from the first. It was a prison within a prison.

I grew used to the harem routine, which did not vary. We woke in the morning according to our wish. We were washed, massaged with oil, dressed, and fed. We lounged on the cushions for an hour or two until another meal was brought in. After this, some women went to the hairdressers and others to the colonnade where we could listen to the court musicians practice behind a screen. Some of the younger children were brought in to visit after the third meal, but no one took much interest in them.

I was disturbed to see that none of the women cared to know which child was her own. But I soon understood that they could not afford to give their hearts to the creatures they carried. Many harem infants died at birth or soon after. Many were born with terrible deformities and left to perish on the rock of exposure. Wet nurses cared for the few who survived, lest the mother's breasts shrivel or her interest be diverted from the king. The boy children were sent to the soldiers for training from a tender age and the girls to the cooks and the maids. The concubines never knew what became of them.

I wondered why the king's concubines should be so unlucky in childbirth. Several women blamed the demon Lilith, who found easy access to any place where many women dwelled together. Others were convinced they had been cursed by Queen Vashti who would stop at nothing to prevent another woman's son from advancement. Vashti's children alone were recognized to be of royal blood and given their due as the offspring of King Xerxes. But the queen did not relish the prospect of a concubine's son gaining favor in the king's eyes.

After the children were escorted back to the nursery, we were fed yet again. Voices rose in anticipation during this fourth meal, and a flush came to the faces around me as everyone speculated which concubine the king might choose for the night. But as the meal progressed, tensions rose and malicious words flew from sharp tongues.

"The king takes no pleasure in a female with the ears of an elephant," one woman insulted another, as if this somehow enhanced her own chances to be called upon that evening. Soon the whole group joined forces for or against the concubine accused of having large ears. Several times the women grew so agitated that a fight broke out, leaving someone with deep scratches across her soft white cheek. The eunuchs rushed to break up these brawls and forced everyone to drink the harem wine. But even after calm was restored, the wounded pride and resentments remained. And so I came to understand that coalitions among groups of concubines could be built or destroyed in a single evening. None of the women seemed to take comfort in the refuge of deep and lasting bonds. I had grown up in my mother's courtyard, surrounded by women who loved nothing so much as their time together. I found this indifference to friendship in the harem even more unsettling than the absence of motherly attachment to the children.

After the meal Hegai appeared in the court to announce the king's desire. Once pronounced, the chosen concubine left in triumph to adorn herself with treasures from the harem's vast wardrobe. The rest of the women shuffled to the cushions, finding solace in their cups and in gossip about the chosen woman's flaws. Endless idle hours followed. Some women, I among them, walked up and down the corridors to stretch their legs. The day concluded with a final meal, an oil massage, and sleep.

Once each week the hairdressers washed our hair and wove it into beautiful designs. The hair strippers plucked our eyebrows and removed the hair from our bodies. A henna artist stained our fingertips and toes. After a woman spent six months in the harem, she underwent a weekly perfume fumigation.

At first we knew nothing of the perfume fumigation treatments. One day Vadhut asked one of her maids if we might observe it before our six months of oil massages had been fulfilled. That very day the concubine Thriti came to know of our curiosity and invited us to observe her treatment the next morning.

Vadhut's maid brought us to the perfuming room. We stood in a corner and waited. Soon three serving women entered. The hands of the first were wrapped in towels, to protect her from the cylinder she carried, a perfume burner, filled with hot stones.

The servant placed the burner into a shallow hole in the floor. The other servants stood near the open door. One held a thin ceramic perfume vessel; the other, a golden wine cup. No one spoke.

At last, Thriti appeared. My first impression of her remained unchanged. Heavy features, wide nose, crooked eyebrows, and a sour expression made her displeasing to the eye.

One servant closed the door as another poured the contents of the perfume vessel over the hot stones inside the burner. As a smoky sweetness filled the room, Thriti stepped forward and the maids helped her squat over the burner. They spread the concubine's robe into a tent from her neck to the ground.

The room became thick with the perfume of rose and cassia. Thriti began to sweat and asked for some wine. The cup-bearer held the vessel to her lips and she drained the wine all at once, smacking her lips as she finished. At last she seemed to take notice of us. "Come closer," she purred. "Take off your clothes and dance for me."

We did not dare obey, or disobey. "You with the big breasts!" she called out to Hutana. "Let me see what else you have to offer the king! I will teach you how to please him."

"We should leave now," I whispered to my friends.

"She will be angry," Freni whispered back.

"Bring her to me!" Thriti shrieked at the servants.

Just then the door opened and Puah entered.

"Come," Puah called out to us, taking no notice of Thriti, who hissed. "It is time for your afternoon meal."

As Puah returned us to the court, she warned us to stay away from Thriti. "No good can come from that one," she said.

Word of the incident with Thriti soon reached the other concubines. We endured light teasing about it all afternoon until the mood in the court changed and the women's words turned cruel.

"Can I taste Thriti's kisses on your lips?" an older concubine asked, forcing her face against Vadhut's mouth. Several others came up to us laughing and reached out to fondle our breasts. Another began to rub her hand over Hutana's most private place. When we pulled away they mocked us.

"What you give to Thriti you should give to everyone!" someone called out.

Soon we were surrounded and I felt hands and skin close in on me.

The eunuchs did not take long to disperse the crowd, making sure everyone drank a cup of wine. We rose and fled to my apartment, where I hoped no one would bother us. But soon we heard a knock at the door. When I did not answer, the visitor entered without permission. It was Asabana, the head of the dancing girls.

She comforted us in her rasping voice. "Do not trouble yourself over the teasing. Thriti takes her pleasure with every newcomer."

"We did nothing shameful with Thriti!" Freni objected.

Vadhut's eyes widened with shock "Is it permitted?"

"Hegai says he prefers the girls to save themselves for the king," Asabana explained as a matter of fact, though I heard no warning in her voice. "But he knows Thriti has much to teach."

"They say the king calls for her more often than any," Hutana observed, surprising us with her knowledge. "I have heard she is as skilled as the high priestess of Ishtar herself."

Asabana gazed at Hutana with a smile that sent a chill through my blood. I did not know that she recruited her dancing girls from among the harem women. I did not know that Hegai often gave her the younger ones who engaged in ongoing liaisons with Thriti or any other concubine. But I could not trust Asabana's friendly manner and kind words. Somehow I understood that she had her own plans to lay.

"Thriti is skilled like no other," Asabana agreed.

"What is her secret?" Hutana asked.

Asabana shrugged. "You must ask her yourself. But I have heard that she sits on his knee and gives herself pleasure, causing the king's own loins to burn with desire. Sometimes she brings one of my girls into the king's chamber and pleasures her until the king can no longer stand to watch and takes them both."

I glanced away from Asabana to Freni. She had grown as pale as a corpse and clutched her stomach as if she meant to vomit. I did not doubt that my own revulsion equaled my friend's. But her innocence was more delicate, her spirit more fragile. I wished I could clear her memory of all that she had heard.

"Let us take Freni to her mattress where she might rest," I suggested to the others. "She is not feeling well."

I did not drink the harem wine and so remained free of the lethargy that settled upon the others. But I was required to eat all of the meals. We were fed fattened lamb and rice mixed with thick yogurt, goat stew laden with plums and almonds, and sweets made of butter, honey, and pistachios. We were served dishes laden with plump figs and dates. Servants kept a close eye on our plates when we ate, replenishing them often. If we favored a particular delicacy, we found it set before us at the next meal.

We were encouraged to eat to our capacity and beyond. And so our flesh filled out more each day. In a few weeks we began to look as soft and rounded as the concubines.

Only Freni remained her old self, eating nothing but fruit washed by her own hands. And when Hegai inspected us and offered us rewards—hair ribbons and trinkets—for our progress, Freni received only reproaches.

One day she came to me where I sat with Vadhut and Hutana as they dozed. She was disheveled and weeping. As I wrapped my arms around her, she only wept harder.

"I will be sent to the barracks to be taken by force every night!" she wailed. "My flesh is not fit for a lion's breakfast."

I eased her down upon a cushion. Vadhut opened her eyes, too dazed to understand that Freni was in trouble.

I guessed that one of the concubines had been teasing her. "A terrible threat. But it shall not come to pass."

Freni lowered her head with despair. "The keeper of the women promised me it would be so." Her sobbing grew desperate.

I grew afraid for my friend. Hegai was not one to issue idle threats.

"The hardness of my flesh makes me 'unripe and sour'," Freni continued, her voice trembling as she repeated Hegai's own words. "I cannot even be a dancing girl because 'His Majesty will give no fruit to his guests that he would not care to taste himself.'"

"You must eat more," I observed with quiet determination. I could not bear to see my friend sent to the barracks.

"I cannot eat the food here!" Freni protested, looking up at me through her tears. "It is not prepared in accordance with the laws of my people."

"You are not amongst your people," I reproached her in a firm whisper. But in my heart I envied her. They were my people too, yet I was no longer one of them. I had never known all that she knew of their ways. What little I knew was long since forgotten. All the love that she felt for our people, I had buried with my parents in Babylon.

And so I shrank inside myself with sorrow and shame for the soft and rounded creature I had become by consuming what my mother might have forbidden me to eat.

"I cannot eat," Freni repeated in a dull voice. She looked past me without a spark of recognition, as if I had become a stranger who could not understand her. She looked small and alone.

I longed to tell her the truth of my decent, to link us as sisters and to give her solace. I longed to learn more of my people's ways from her, to know how I might pray for mercy from the One God. But I could not disobey Mordechai.

And I could not admit to her how far my beloved cousin's household had strayed.

"We must find something more you can eat." I tried to recall the kitchen of my childhood.

Freni began listing the dietary laws. "Only certain meat that has been slaughtered in the right way. And no meat with milk."

"Surely you can eat the pastries and rice."

"They might have been cooked with the meat."

I signaled for a servant to bring Freni a glass of wine. Once the haoma took effect and calmed her, I went in search of Puah.

When we returned, Freni was sleeping.

I shook her awake and asked her to describe what she could eat.

Puah listened with great patience and understanding to Freni's explanation, made long and incoherent by the wine.

"The pastries, rice, and cheese are all safe," the old woman assured my friend as soon as she paused for breath. I was surprised by the quickness of her reply. "I know they are made in a different kitchen from the meat dishes. I once worked in the kitchens."

Freni remained unconvinced.

"I too am a daughter of the Jews," Puah confessed, "though I was taken from home at a young age. Shall I go look at the kitchens to be sure about what you might eat? A woman of my age can move with freedom in the palace enclosure," she laughed.

Freni nodded, her face glowing with gratitude.

Puah returned in an hour with a plate of sweet saffron halwa, and declared it safe for Freni along with many other things. She listed the ingredients and explained the way each item was prepared. After this Freni trusted Puah's reports on the food. She ate the halwa, and much more and to my relief she soon grew to be as round as the rest of us.

Eleven

Hegai treated me and my serving-maids with special kindness in the harem. I was permitted to sit in the fresh air of the colonnade whenever I pleased, with a companion of my choosing. I was allowed to request songs from the musicians when they practiced. But I took advantage of these privileges only when an older concubine wished to enjoy them herself. I was always ready to oblige a woman who asked for an invitation to sit with me in the cool colonnade or named a particular melody that she longed to hear.

I had greater difficulty in easing the envy created by two other marks of special favor: the frequent invitations to dine with Hegai and the use of my own apartment.

My first summons to Hegai's quarters came a week after my arrival in the harem. Puah assured me that I had done nothing wrong, but I feared the worst. Still, I was determined to meet him with a pleasing appearance and agreeable disposition.

I visited the hall of the hairdressers for special beauty treatments. I knew that the eunuch admired my hair, and so I insisted on leaving it loose and flowing. But they took great care in washing my tresses, using a goat's milk soap powder and a clove-scented rinse of colorless henna that made every strand shine. They combed and brushed until my hair was as glossy as the mane of the king's favorite horse and as smooth to the touch as the polished stone floor of the colonnade.

After this, the henna artist worked on my fingertips and toes, a process I found more pleasant than any of the other treatments. She began by soaking my hands and feet in bowls of hot soapy water that smelled of mint. A small block of bright red henna was dissolved in brewed chamomile. She stained each fingertip with this paste, using a fine brush and working with as much care as if she were an artist hired by the king to paint the finest details of a wall relief.

Another servant plucked my eyebrows to ensure the fine arches were unmarred by new growth. An old woman who specialized in kohl applications rimmed my eyes, upper and lower, with thick lines of the black powder. She mixed pomegranate juice with turmeric to color my cheeks and lips.

After hours in the hands of these women, I was dressed in a close-fitting robe and escorted to the apartment of the keeper of the women.

I trembled as I came before him, sitting on his throne surrounded by attendants. He smiled when he saw me and dismissed the others with a single word and a wave of his hand. When we were alone, he beckoned me forward until I stood at his feet. He spread his legs, each the size of a tree trunk. Reaching down, he wrapped his massive arms around my waist, and pulled me into his severed manhood. His thick lips smacked together with pleasure and he leaned into me to smell my hair. Then he opened my robe and kissed my breasts until the nipples rose to meet his tongue. My face grew hot with shame.

"Lovely and made still lovelier," he grunted, pulling away from me and adjusting his enormous purple turban. "Fair made still fairer; desirable, made still more desirable." I cast my gaze down on his quivering false beard as he spoke, afraid to reveal my distaste for his attentions.

"Have you heard about the king from the girls?"

"I have heard some, sir," I replied, recalling Asabana's visit to my apartment.

"Learn what gives him pleasure and what does not." The eunuch paused. "Talk to the king's favorites but do not give your sweet fruit to them," he cautioned, as Asabana said he would.

"I shall strive to meet your expectations in everything," I replied, saying what I knew he wished to hear. But I did not relish the prospect of engaging the concubines in sordid conversation about the king's desires.

The keeper of the women grasped my arms to hoist himself to his feet. "You shall dine with us this evening," he gasped as he stood, "rare and exotic delicacies worthy of a goddess."

I thanked him for the honor.

"The honor is ours," he replied, leaning his great bulk on me. He pointed to our destination, a table had been laid for us a short distance behind the throne. I matched his stride with the tiniest of steps. He required many minutes to reach the table and settle himself, a billowing mass of flesh and fine linen leaning against stacks of soft cushions.

The table was long and low, made of brushed lambskin with lacquered rosewood legs. Golden cups in the shape of tulip blossoms were filled with sweet spiced wine from Hodu and shining silver platters were piled high with meat stews and succulent birds I could not identify. A plate of sugared almonds and pistachios was placed close to me on one side, and a sweet of sesame, dates, and honey on the other.

"Please begin," the eunuch urged when he saw I waited for him. "We shall take our enjoyment from watching you. Eat well, and we shall be pleased. The king likes his women soft and round."

And so passed the first of many such evenings. The eunuch would fondle my breasts. He would approve of my progress and urge me to learn what I could of the king's pleasures from the other women but to let none touch me, lest my desire come to be for them instead of the king. Then I would escort him to the table where he would watch me as if he himself took nourishment from each morsel that passed my lips. He would insist that I fill myself to capacity and beyond. Afterwards I would pace the harem passageways all night, unable to lie down for the ache in my stomach and the shame in my heart. I learned to numb myself with a quantity of strong Greek wine before I went to him, that I might appear to enjoy all that the eunuch offered—as if I were someone other than myself—and then forget the encounter soon after.

I sometimes brought sugared nuts from Hegai's table to share with the other concubines, a rare treat that helped soften their envy of my evenings with our keeper. But I struggled for many weeks to devise a plan to assuage their anger about my apartment.

Almost every day new virgins entered the harem, and still I remained the only one to be given her own quarters. Yet I did not enjoy my privilege. I did not like to be alone in the stark apartment, and the marks on the wall continued to haunt me. Father had forbidden the women of his household to believe in the creatures of the night. But when I lay on my mattress I felt them draw near: Lamashtu, Lilith, Azi Dahaka the fiendish snake, Druj Nasu who flies down from Mount Aresura and seizes human corpses, and Allatu, goddess of the underworld whose face is bone white and lips are black. I closed my eyes and saw their demonic forms, flashes of green and red light slithering through my skull, shadows hovering in the darkness. I could not sleep.

Sometimes I tried to protect myself from these monsters by holding an image of Mordechai's kind face close to mine. I told myself that I would rise the next morning to a glorious day, the day of my rescue.

But the sun would climb high in the heavens and still he did not come. One day became another, followed by the same sleepless night. I began to fear that my beloved had forgotten me. The demons grew even bolder then, laughing at my false hopes and squeezing the life's breath out of me until I had to flee the room for lack of air in my nostrils.

The concubines responded to my privileges with annoyance. But Hegai would not permit me to give up the apartment and join the others in the large sleeping room. And so I could only do my utmost to be a good friend to everyone.

I went to the concubines, each in turn, bringing a glass of special sweet and peppery Shiraz wine that Hegai had given me as a gift. I explained that I did not deserve Hegai's special treatment and that I was not the daughter of royalty, as some supposed, but a common orphan. And I offered to help them in whatever way I might be of use. I learned their names and expressed myself eager to hear whatever they wished to tell me of themselves. I asked them of their homes and their gods. The women in the harem did not engage in active worship, though they often spoke of gods and demons. Most worshiped the king's god, Ahura Mazda. Their manner softened when they spoke of their god's goodness, fairness, sweet-scentedness, strength, and power to grant them freedom from sorrow. I listened with understanding in my eyes but bitterness in my heart. Neither their god nor my own afforded us protection from our captor, the king. The only freedom from sorrow to be had in the harem was that of the haoma-induced lethargy.

Of all the women I spoke with, only Thriti remained hostile and refused to speak with me. The rest came to tolerate my privileges and to welcome my attentions to them. But they remained as closed to the possibility of friendship with me as they were with each other. I blamed this on the haoma and the competition for the king's attentions. And I promised myself that I would always work to keep my friends together so that no matter what happened, we would have each other to rely upon.

Though I was able to smooth my relations with the concubines, I could do nothing to ease my restless nights. I dreaded the hour when we retired to our assigned quarters and I longed to join the other virgins in their room, under the supervision of Hegai, who always sent one of his trusted eunuchs to keep watch while they slept. Concubines who had already gone in to the king—whether once or a hundred times—shared another room. The old eunuch Shaashgaz stayed with them.

A few favored concubines also had their own apartments, and were sometimes permitted to have a friend stay with them overnight. But I did not yet dare ask permission of my keeper for this privilege. Servants endured the worst situation of all, sleeping in a room so small that they lay head to foot. Their night guardian was Nusku, a hard-muscled eunuch who took pleasure in beating his charges with a cane and, when he grew mean from excessive wine, raping them with a bottle. I grieved when Puah told me of all that Nusku did and how they said nothing to Hegai in fear for their lives.

"Hegai must be told of this cruel treatment," I insisted. "He will not permit such abuse to continue if he knows about it."

"He does not wish to know," Puah replied, her voice flat and without hope.

But I was determined to confront the keeper of the harem with the truth.

The dancing girls also shared a room, under the supervision of Asabana. She taught them the art of swaying their hips and displaying their charms. She taught them to increase a man's desire before fulfilling it. This much Puah told us, one evening when my friends and I sat in my large receiving room. "They know it is better to live in the harem than the barracks," she explained, "and so they do as they are asked without complaint."

"They do not go in to the king?" Vadhut asked.

"Sometimes the king will take one for his enjoyment," the old servant replied. "But they get no gold from him." The shadow of Kurnugi passed over her long face. "They cannot carry their children to term; a woman big in the belly is not fit to entertain."

"How do they stop it?" Freni asked. She remained innocent even after weeks in the harem. I had long since learned of the wine that induced abortions and the pain it brought upon those forced to drink it. But I did not tell Freni such things. I was strong enough to bear the burden of these horrors for both of us.

I flashed Puah a look of caution, and she understood.

Puah shrugged "They have their ways. Be pure for the king," she added, gazing at Hutana, "and have no fear."

But none of us understood her warning until it was too late for Hutana. The quietest of our group, she pined for her home and grew sullen. She would not accept our love with an open heart. She was lonely and longed for her mother. And so she became prey for the older women and we could not save her.

One evening, a month after we arrived in the harem, Hutana did not return to the chamber of the virgins to sleep. Freni came to my apartment in search of her. Puah was attending me, as she often did before the servants were summoned to retire.

"You should go back to your mattress," Puah insisted. "You can do nothing for your friend."

"Is she hurt?" Freni asked in alarm.

"She is safe," Puah replied, folding her arms and sealing her lips to indicate that she would say no more. But we gathered that all was not well with our friend.

The next morning Hutana appeared at Thriti's side. Her lips were swollen and her hair in disarray.

We crowded around our friend. "Are you hurt?" Freni cried.

Thriti seized Hutana's arm and pulled her away from us.

"I am staying with Thriti now," Hutana replied, her copper eyes burning with defiance.

That afternoon, we sought Puah's advice on how to win back our friend from Thriti.

"It is too late." Puah showed no inclination to elaborate.

"What will happen to her?" Vadhut asked.

"Thriti satisfies the king's desire, and no favor will be denied her while she still pleases him. But Hegai will punish Hutana for seeking comfort in Thriti's arms and pleasure in her bed."

"Asabana told us it was not forbidden," Vadhut objected.

Puah shook her head with disgust. "Asabana would like nothing more than to make a dancing girl of any one of you," she whispered. "A fresh young virgin will bring her rich rewards from the king's guests, who give her gold when they are pleased by the entertainment."

No more than a month after this, all that Puah predicted came to pass. One of the dancing girls took ill and was removed to a quarantined room. We could do nothing to help our friend as we watched two eunuchs drag her from Thriti's embraces and place her in the charge of Asabana.

That very night Hutana was among the dancing girls who entertained at a banquet for the king's advisors. They applauded the lovely young recruit, fresh as a fawn and ripe as the full moon. None noticed her sour face or her eyes, dulled from the haoma wine. The men showered Asabana with coins as they clamored to take a turn with the new recruit. And when Hutana returned the next morning, she had lost her treasure many times over.

Twelve

I did not make known my people or my kindred, for Mordechai had commanded me not to reveal it. But I often shared other confidences with Puah, who sought me out in spare moments when she was not cleaning rooms or doing laundry. She avoided speaking against any of the concubines, lest word get back to Nusku, whom she feared more than God. But she taught me the ways of the harem and lifted my spirit when it waned. Her tenderness for me was that of a mother to her child and I soon came to hold her dear in my heart.

I confided in her about Mordechai, telling her everything of my beloved except the name by which he was known to me. I spoke of him only as Marduka the Babylonian who sat in the king's gate.

I told her of his goodness and wisdom. I praised his loyalty to the king, explaining how he had left his home in Babylon to remain in the king's service. I expressed the depth of my gratitude for how he had taken me, an orphan of ten years old, into his household. I described his kindness, generosity, and fine features.

I spoke as a foolish girl of fourteen.

But Puah understood. She had once been a girl of fourteen, and it was her foolishness that brought her to be a servant in the harem of Xerxes.

I had known her a month when she first told me something of her story, one night when sleep abandoned me. A prisoner of my fears and sorrows, I wandered through the dim and deserted corridors in the night's darkest hour. I gazed up at the smoke stains cast over the stone walls from the oil lamps and down on the threadbare path worn into the carpet. Finding my way into the court, I looked at my reflection in the pool. I closed my eyes and opened them. The surroundings remained the same in my sight, but forty years had passed. I was no longer a young girl of fourteen but an old woman. Forty years had passed since I had said farewell to Mordechai. Forty years since I had come to live in Kurnugi, the house of ashes, the house of nothingness. All the delicacies I had eaten were mud. And all the voices I had heard were a wind blowing through the emptiness.

I turned my heart to weeping and could walk no more.

And so Puah found me in the deep of night, curled up on the floor of the court and crying into a cushion.

"Be brave," she whispered, kneeling next to me.

My heart flooded with happiness at the sound of her voice and the touch of her rough hand stroking my wet cheek.

"Be brave for the sake of those who depend on your strength and wisdom—your friends and me."

I wiped my eyes, and rose to my feet. "But you already have the strength of knowledge and the wisdom of age!"

Puah laughed and rose to join me. "Before your arrival, I was an old woman who had lived long beyond her use to anyone."

And so I came to understand that I was a blessing to Puah in her old age.

"Let us take some cushions to the colonnade and talk ourselves to sleep," she suggested.

"You shall suffer at the hands of your keeper," I objected.

"That one is in a drunken stupor," she replied, her lip turning up in disgust.

"How strange that you came just when I most needed you," I observed.

"I lay on my mattress and prayed to the One God," she whispered. "It came to me that I should seek you out this night."

We took some cushions from the court and settled at the edge of the colonnade. The soldiers at the gate could see us, but they were too far away to hear our voices. We disturbed no one here, and could converse without guarding our words.

For a few minutes we sat in silence. And then at last the old woman spoke. "You have told me of your cousin," she began. "I have seen your face shine with the light of your love for him. But you are here in the harem of Xerxes. And who knows for what purpose you were sent to us? If you hold nothing in your heart but what might have been, and dwell upon what was, you are no different from those who spend their days intoxicated by the haoma."

Such were the hard words she offered. I found them bitter to the taste but filled with truth. And so I resolved to hide from myself all that was in my heart for Mordechai, and continue to use my favor with Hegai for the good of those who might be helped by it.

I looked upon Puah's long wrinkled face. And there I saw reflected my own affections and sorrows. I squeezed her hand and we sat again in silence for some time.

I lay my head upon a cushion and hovered between wakefulness and sleep. Puah began speaking of a land in the east, beyond the deserts and mountains, beyond the River Tigris and the fertile valley and the River Euphrates, beyond the place of my birth in Babylon and the graves of my parents. A place west of the River Jordan, further than the land of my father's grandfather, the land from which our people were exiled, the land to which my father prayed he might return one day. It was west of the ruins of the great Temple, the Temple of the One God. This was the land of the River Nile, where my people were once slaves, upstream to the first cataract on the border of Nubia. In the river's midst lay an island called Yeb, with a mighty military fortress and many temples to the gods of the land. Yeb was rich with date palms and wheat, hoopoe and kingfisher. This was the land of Puah's birth.

"My grandfather was a soldier who came to live on the island at the Jewish garrison," she said. "He was injured in a fierce battle with some Nubian warriors and left with a limp. After he gave up soldiering, he became a glass trader. He loved my grandmother, the daughter of another soldier. When he had enough for the bridal gift, they married in the eyes of the One God. In all my days with them, I never saw my grandfather take a hand to my grandmother. I never heard her complain of being oppressed by his demands, or threaten to divorce him.

"They had one daughter, my mother. I lived in the household of my grandfather because my mother married and divorced so many men that she could not say with certainty who my father was. Once she even married a man who was not Jewish! He was a guardian of the temple of Khnum, the ram-headed god of creation. Grandfather was very unhappy when she went to live with that man and worshipped Khnum, but she soon left him, like all the others.

"My mother was a woman with great beauty and a willful heart. She refused to wear a veil, even when her husbands beat her for disobedience. I was born when she was fourteen. But even ten years later men still desired her. I remember how she would tell them I was her sister. She would go with a man into an alley or a grove and instruct me to keep watch. She would come back with coins to buy herself pretty things at the market. Sometimes my grandfather locked her in the house and prayed for her. But she always escaped.

"The great King Cambyses, son of Cyrus, came to conquer the land of the Nile. He was still in Memphis when we had word of it on Yeb. It was said that Cambyses worshiped at the temple of the holy Apis bull and paid tribute to the Apis with gifts of gold and ivory. It was said that a king who would honor the Apis of Memphis would honor the ram-god Khnum. It was even said that the son of Cyrus would be tolerant of the Jews on our island, just as the worshipers of Khnum were. And it was said that the Persians would hire recruits from the island soldiers to help them conquer Nubia. So the Island of Yeb did not fear the arrival of the Persians.

"When their big cedar wood boats drew near, my mother took me to the harbor. We sat in the sand watching them row to shore. Soon my mother was surrounded by Persian soldiers. They were large men with short tunics and cropped beards. She laughed and teased with them, even though she could not understand their language and they did not know ours.

"A handsome warrior, who seemed to be their leader, walked right up to my mother and touched her breast. The other men laughed. She laughed back and slapped him across the face. The handsome soldier grew red with rage but mother did not seem to care. She said: 'Bring me the head of a Nubian and cover my arms in gold. Then I will be yours.'"

Here Puah broke off, searching my eyes with a voiceless question. I understood her to be asking if the story held my attention.

"I am eager to hear more," I replied.

She resumed her story.

"My mother made that gruesome demand in her sweetest voice, but the soldier did not understand Hebrew or Egyptian, which were our tongues. He turned to the men behind him and called out a question. I did not yet know the Persian's language, but I supposed he was looking for a translator. And soon a Jewish soldier made his way through the crowd. The Jewish soldier asked my mother what she wished to say and she repeated her conditions. When the Jew told the Persian warrior my mother's price, the warrior laughed with delight and agreed.

"Mother threatened to sell me to the Persian soldiers if I dared to tell Grandfather. When I asked her how she and her new lord would talk to each other, she kissed me and said 'in the language of love.'"

Puah paused once more to catch her breath. She stared at me for a moment with a strange smile.

"My mother did not doubt the soldier would come back for her. She waited for him, two months at least, and took no other husband. She spent all her days in beauty treatments or asking about her Persian at the garrison. She learned that he was Darius, a son of the royal family and a bowman of great strength and skill. After that, she would boast to me of how she would be a woman of great wealth and power in Persia. And even when she learned that Darius had a wife with him in Egypt, she continued to imagine her future as the wife of the great warrior. "Can you guess who this Darius was?"

"The father of Xerxes was King Darius," I replied. "I know of no other."

"Darius was a member of the royal family," Puah confirmed, "but not a direct heir to the throne. That would come to him later when he defeated the false Smerdis. In the days of my childhood, Darius was an expert bowman of the Immortals. He was the finest figure of a warrior anyone had ever seen. Later he took me as he had my mother before me."

Puah noticed the look of astonishment on my face and clicked her tongue. "I never had your beauty," she said, "but my body was not always so withered. I was once young and longed for a handsome man to fill me with the seed of his desire, just as you do now."

I turned my head from her in embarrassment. The first light of dawn crept across the courtyard toward us at the edge of the colonnade. Nusku would be looking for her. She would have to resume the story later.

"Do not forsake the One God, though he must remain hidden in your heart," Puah whispered, patting me on the knee.

I turned back to her with great dismay, unable to fathom how she had discovered the secret of my people and my kindred.

"You understood my mother's words," she explained.

"Your mother's word were…immodest," I recalled. But nothing more.

"I said them in Hebrew," she laughed.

Later Puah confessed that it was my concern for Freni's diet that first caused her to wonder. And so she tricked me into giving myself away. But she promised to keep my secret, and I knew she would.

Thirteen

After that night in the colonnade with Puah, I slept as if the demon Lilith had taken possession of me. For the third or fourth day in a row I did not rise until the morning was gone. Hegai had word of it and came himself to inquire if I was ill.

He passed through the harem like a king on a visit of state, dressed in a magnificent robe of white with a mantle of purple. His fleshy feet were shod in leather sandals with gold studs. His chamber attendants stood at his side when he came upon me in the hallway near my apartment.

"I am honored sir," I said to the eunuch, bowing low and kissing his bejeweled hand.

"We are concerned for your health."

"Rather should I be concerned for your health, sir," I replied. "May the goddess continue to serve you and guide you, and the lord Ahura Mazda, be with you in greatness, goodness, fairness, sweet-scentedness, victorious strength, and freedom from sorrow."

The eunuch's face was flushed with pleasure at these words, though they were no more than a formula I had often heard from the worshippers of Ahura Mazda in the harem. But I was happy to find in my knowledge a means to please him.

"We understood you to be sleeping as one who is not in full health."

"Sleep often abandons me in the night, sir," I confessed.

Hegai turned to the maids who attended me. "Sleep abandons the old and the troubled," he reproached. "It darkens the face with shadows and causes a mournfulness of disposition that does not serve the king's desire."

I saw fear in the faces of those who waited upon me.

"The maids are not to blame," I announced, surprised as anyone at the bold words coming from my mouth. "It was the sound of Nusku beating them that robbed me of my rest."

And so I caused Nusku to be removed from his post and sent to wait upon the keeper of the king's chamber pot. Word of what I had done spread amongst the servants and they rejoiced to be free of their tormentor. Many expressed their gratitude to me.

Puah avoided me for more than a week, fearing punishment for being seen with me. "I am only a servant to the servants," she whispered in the corridor as I passed her. "When Nusku's spies me in your company, they will come to me in the night with a knife."

And so I determined to secure Puah's safety by asking Hegai for the favor of her service.

When I next saw Hegai, I invited him to dine with me in my apartment the following evening. He accepted with pleasure, as if I were a queen and my modest rooms a palace to which only the privileged were admitted. I enlisted Puah's help in securing a modest feast from the kitchens. She brought baskets of plump black grapes and dates oozing with sugar. She asked the keeper of the wine, who had known her when she worked in the king's kitchens many years ago, to send a special bottle for Hegai's pleasure. He offered a sweet white wine, made in the land of my ancestors.

Once the feast was prepared, I bathed and instructed my maids to massage me with oil of roses and almonds. I asked the hairdressers to do all they could to beautify my appearance and I dressed with as much care as if I were going to see the king himself.

Hegai arrived at the appointed hour with a single escort, a young eunuch. He settled into the shabby cushions and craned his neck to examine the room around him. The thick folds of his flesh rippled like water on the river.

"The room has changed for the worse," he pronounced.

"I am sorry it is not to your liking," I replied with some distress. I had cleaned the stone walls and the carpets, but the rooms were barren and I did not feel it was my place to ask for decorations.

"Queen Vashti used to hide here, to escape the king. It was a delicious secret and she paid us well to keep it," he confessed. "Of course the king paid even better to reveal it."

I could not help but join in his laughter.

"She appointed the room from her own rich collection. Fine wool hangings and cushions of Tabari silk. And the carpets…" He broke off, his little eyes staring past me at nothing, as if recollecting the past. And in the silence I wondered why no one had told me that these rooms had been used by the banished queen. It was she who would not let me sleep.

The keeper of the women returned to the present and his bloated cheeks rose in a smile. "No matter," he chirped. "We shall see that the walls are covered in silk and your luscious breasts with gold.

I poured the sweet wine into his cup and watched him drain it. He sighed with pleasure and indicated by the flicker of a finger that

I should refill the cup. When he was lighthearted with the wine, I sat at his knee and fed him succulent fruits from my own hand.

As he finished the last date and licked the sugar from my fingers I knew I could delay my request no further.

"Sir," I began, "if it be your pleasure I have a request to make of you."

"Queen Vashti would ask for a young eunuch to warm her bed," he smiled. "The king never knew."

I saw that his sense had been drowned in the river of wine and his discretion with it. "My request is for Puah the chamber servant to attend me in the evenings and during the night," I blurted out.

Hegai laughed. "She is an old Jew good for cleaning the chamber pots and washing the servants' feet. What would you want with her?"

"She knows the incantations against Druj Nasu and Azi Dahaka," I replied, turning my eyes full upon him.

The eunuch sighed. "We find you deserving of your request. In exchange for certain favors," he added.

"Your humble servant offers no special skills," I observed with false lightness. For I feared what he might ask of me.

"To be served by one of your beauty and charm is a favor no other can offer."

And so Puah became my night maid. And in exchange, when I went to Hegai's apartment each evening he dressed me in the fine robes and jewels he kept for those who went into the king. I fed him fruit and massaged his feet with oil. And sometimes he put his head in my lap and I stroked his cheek.

Such, I learned, were the pleasures of a man without his manhood.

When Puah arrived to attend me on the first night, I rose to help her prepare my mattress. She objected with alarm. "You must not treat your lowest servant as an equal!"

"But you are my friend and I wish to be of use to you."

"It is I who should be of use to *you*," she replied, plumping my mattress cushions.

"Then tell me more of the girl from Yeb," I suggested. "I am eager to hear what became of her."

And so we sat on the mattress and Puah finished her tale.

"The soldier Darius returned to the island with all that my mother requested. I do not know which she preferred: the head of Nubian in a basket or the arm bands of gold. She kept the grizzly token with her on the journey to Memphis, but when it began to smell, the men on the boat threw it overboard.

"Darius took my mother that afternoon in a chamber of the temple of the ram-god Khnum. I waited in the temple gardens, to see what would happen. A soldier of the retinue, a friend of Darius, was keeping guard. When he saw me sitting alone, he asked me to join him on patrol. His name was Gobryas, and he taught me the mix of Persian and Aramaic that was the language of the soldiers.

"In an hour, after Darius had used my mother for his pleasure, he wished to leave the Island of Yeb and return to Memphis where King Cambyses awaited his return. When my mother realized the soldiers were gathering on the river bank to leave, she feared she would never see her soldier again. She ran after Darius and clung to his tunic. She wept and begged. He understood her meaning and agreed. I would have run home to my grandparents, but Gobryas swept me up in his arms and carried me on to the boat. And so I went to Memphis.

"We lived with the king's concubines and soldiers' wives on an estate near the great Temple of Ptah. The temple gate was guarded by a statue of a pharaoh named Ramses. I had never seen anything so big and frightening. And even though Ramses had lived many hundreds of years before me, every night he came alive and frightened me in my sleep. But I prayed to the One God, just as I had heard my grandfather do, and I found some comfort in that.

"My mother did not like to be confined. She caused trouble among the wives and other concubines. Whenever Darius asked for her, she made sure his wife knew. If he did not ask for her, she complained that she was being held a prisoner. When he asked for her less often, she began to accuse the other women of plotting against her. She had no friends or allies. Soon Darius stopped asking for her altogether.

"Gobryas came to play the game twenty squares with me almost every day. He had a daughter my age and he had not seen her in three years. He told me that when I went to Persia I would be able to visit his family and we could all play twenty squares together."

Puah's voice faded and the furrows on her brow relaxed. Her lips turned up into a smile, as if once again she knew the hopes and joys of her young heart. I did not wish to take these from her. And so I remained silent some minutes until she resumed.

"One day my mother saw Gobryas in the garden with me. She came to us in a rage, and threw over our game board. She shouted at the soldier that he should stop playing with little girls. He did not understand her words and I refused to translate. My mother crawled into his lap and began kissing and touching him. But he would not take a woman who belonged to his friend. This was the code of honor among the Immortals. He pushed my mother aside and left.

"The next morning was one of great confusion. King Cambyses received word of a usurper to his throne in Persia. A magus by the name of Gaumata had proclaimed King Cambyses dead and declared himself to be the king's brother Smerdis, inheritor of the throne. The people did not know that the real Smerdis had died by Cambyses' own hand before his departure for Egypt. And so they pledged allegiance to this false Smerdis, who had suspended all taxes to make himself popular.

"King Cambyses commanded everyone to leave for Persia at once, and all the women hurried to pack. There was great confusion and chaos and I could not find my mother anywhere. Gobryas came upon me and took me to the boats with him, assuring me that his wife would be my new mother and his daughter would be my sister.

"I never learned what became of my mother. But King Cambyses died on the journey back to Persia, and Gobryas became involved in the plan to put Darius on the throne. And so my soldier friend left me with the concubines and I became a servant to them.

"Within a few weeks Darius and his six closest companions—Gobryas among them—overthrew the false Smerdis. Darius divorced his wife and married Atossa, daughter of Cyrus, and became the new king. He moved to Cyrus's capital city of

Pasargadae, and I was sent there to the kitchens. Not long after this, Darius began building the great city of Persepolis and this palace, here at Susa. His reign lasted over thirty years."

Puah broke off as if she would say no more. But I was eager to hear how she had come to the harem and if she had ever again seen her friend Gobryas. I did not hide this curiosity from my face.

"I have little more to tell of myself," she sighed. "One evening I was sent from my work in the kitchen to wait upon the king's banquet. Gobryas was one of those I served, but I had changed from a child to a woman and he did not know me. I tried to catch his eye, but he was much occupied with his cup and the dancing girls.

"I had not seen the king for many months, but he was handsome and retained his soldier's vigor. My heart blossomed in his presence, for he was a man of great power and beauty and I was a foolish young girl. I dared to look upon his face with the light of my love and desire. And though I was just one of many servants, thin and rough, he noticed me.

"That night he took me in lust as he had taken my mother, and he sent me with sweet words to live in the harem. But he never asked for me again. Nor did any of the concubines believe that he had called me to him even once. I was a kitchen girl sent to serve them, and no more. And so I have been for forty years."

The night closed in on us as Puah finished her tale and the silence came to be filled by the wind whistling through chinks in the stone roof. I wept.

I wept because the king had forgotten Puah. I wept because Gobryas had not recognized her. I wept because the woman who gave her life had abandoned her.

And I wept because she herself was not weeping.

"Do not cry," Puah urged, handing me a cloth to wipe my eyes. "We must see that you win the king's highest favor, and then I will end my days in joy for your success."

Fourteen

When the turn of each girl came to go into King Xerxes—after she had completed the twelve month treatment prescribed for women—she had her choice of costume and adornments from the harem's vast wardrobe. In the evening she would be presented to the king, and in the morning she would return to the harem, under the watch of Shaashgaz, the keeper of the concubines. She would go to the king again only if he asked for her.

I had come to accept this as my portion in life. A year had passed since my arrival in the harem and with it, my dread of going in to the king. I hoped I would find my place among his favorites, and so avoid being sent to the soldiers. Perhaps I might even advance Mordechai's career in the king's court. I no longer allowed myself to hope for rescue from the harem, or that the light of my cousin's eyes would ever shine upon me as his wife. I knew I might never see him again.

As our year of beauty treatments drew to a close, Vadhut began to look with anticipation to her night with the king. Freni, too, became excited. She no longer spoke of her family with a heavy heart and seemed to have forgotten the young man she was to have married. This change was the effect of the haoma wine: it calmed the spirit and dulled the memory.

For days I listened as my friends spoke of the jewels and fine clothes they would wear, the elaborate hair weaving, rich perfumes, and cosmetics that would secure the king's desire. The other concubines—most of whom had ignored us during our year of preparation—took great interest in these conversations. They recalled their own dress and hair, their hopes, desires, and every detail of their preparations before they went in to the king. They did not dampen the enthusiasm of the virgins with the truth of their own experiences. Rather they seemed to take great pleasure in reliving their own first night with the king, encouraging my friends to look forward to it as the moment of their greatest glory. They never mentioned the trials to follow. But I understood that a concubine was subject to the desire of a master who cared little for her comfort, and was accorded even less honor than a bride in the household of her husband's mother.

These women had forgotten the sorrowful truth of their own initiations. But I did not challenge them or contradict anything they said. I did not remind my friends of the lifetime they would face upon returning from the king's embrace to the harem. I said nothing of the children they would never know, the constant fear of the king's displeasure and neglect, or the likelihood of ending their days in poverty as servants. I saw no benefit in shattering what little time of innocent pleasures remained for them.

Vadhut was the first of the virgins to go in to the king. We embraced her and offered our best wishes. She left in a flurry of excitement to prepare for her night with the king. Freni mumbled prayers for her well-being.

The next morning, Freni and I sought her in the room of the concubines. We found her alone and unattended on her new mattress, drinking a cup of harem wine.

"She looks unchanged," Freni whispered to me as we approached. But I could see from the heaviness of our friend's head that she was not joyful in her heart. I had heard much of the king's ways with women, which had grown worse since Vashti's banishment. He was rough and restless in his regret for the beautiful queen. He had found none to heal his pride, wounded by the hand of the traitor Themistocles. "Only Ishtar herself can help him," Hegai had said to me.

"Good thoughts, good words, good deeds," I greeted Vadhut, fearing what I might find when we reached her. Our friend did not look up from her wine.

"My heart was empty in your absence!" Freni exclaimed, throwing herself down next to Vadhut. "Your jewelry is a wonder!" She touched one of the many thick gold bands encircling Vadhut's arms.

Vadhut raised her head and glanced from me to Freni. The kohl that had lined her eyelids was now smeared in dark circles under her eyes. Streaks of dirt darkened her cheeks and her lower lip appeared swollen and scabbed, as if she had bitten herself. Her hair, once woven and pinned into a crown, fell loose in a tangle of small braids. She wore enough gold to purchase a year of wheat for the whole harem: large gold bands on her arms and neck, gold hoops dangling from her ears, a golden ring in her nose. Her robe, a fine rose linen embroidered with silver lotus blossoms, was torn from her neck to her chest. The bangles around her wrists and forearms moved, revealing some discoloration on her skin beneath. I looked closer and saw that the flesh was chafed and bruised.

Freni's eyes grew wide with fear and concern. I saw that questions would bring Vadhut further distress, and shook my head at Freni, pressing a finger to my lips.

"He did not offer me wine or any refreshment." Vadhut drained her cup. Her voice was dry, despite the wine, and she spoke too loud, as if she had gone deaf, or did not realize how close we were. "He held me down and hurt me. He laughed when I cried out for my mother and struggled to get free. And now I have no maids, or any servants of my own."

I took a deep breath to steady myself, and hid my anger at the king I had never seen. Vadhut needed our comfort now. "Our hearts are joyful in your return," I said, sitting down and taking her hand. "And there are servants to assist you."

But I saw none, though Vadhut needed a bath and fresh clothing. I could not endure the cruelty of sending back a girl to the harem, a virgin no longer, with none to attend her that first morning.

"What is done is done!" a voice called out from the doorway. And I did not need to look up to know that the old eunuch Shaashgaz, keeper of the concubines under Hegai, was hobbling toward us.

"This gold must be returned." He pointed a withered finger toward Vadhut's arms.

"I will help," I whispered in her ear as she slumped even lower. I began to remove the arm bands.

Freni gasped. She did not know that the adornments a girl wore when she went into the king were not hers to keep, unless the king wished to make a present of them. I could not believe that she had never heard talk of a subject that so occupied the concubines.

"My friend is in need of the bath," I told the eunuch as I handed him the jewelry.

"It is where it is," he replied, indicating that Vadhut could go to the bath if she wished.

I reached over to remove her earrings.

"The earrings stay where they are," the eunuch announced.

Vadhut looked up. She dared not ask if she had found favor in the king's eyes.

"The king is pleased," the eunuch confirmed.

Freni threw her arms around our friend, to congratulate her but my heart foamed with fury. Vadhut had been forced forever from her family to live as a prisoner and a slave in the king's harem. The earrings were not worth the smallest portion of the life she had lost.

"They are my property to keep?" Vadhut asked Shaashgaz, shrugging Freni away.

"From the king's to what is the king's," the eunuch said.

Freni and I accompanied Vadhut to the bath and brought her more wine and a warm stew of chicken with pomegranates and peaches. We rubbed salve into her wrists. Despite our attentions, she did not speak.

We returned Vadhut to the room of the concubines late in the morning, laying her on the mattress and placing a soft cushion under her head. We covered her with blankets and urged her to rest. We kept guard outside the room so she would not be disturbed.

After the morning meal, many of the women, virgins and concubines, gathered before us to hear Vadhut tell the story of her night with the king and to see her rewards.

"She is worn and weary," I explained. "Let us leave her to rest."

"Did he give her anything?" one woman called out.

"She would be here to show us if he did," another speculated.

An angry concubine shouted at me. "It is our custom here to tell each other of our first night! Who are you to change our ways?"

A rumble of discontent rolled across the growing crowd.

"It is our room," someone called out. Several woman began to push me out of the way.

"Friends!" I cried, raising my arm to ask for their attention. "Vadhut is in need of sleep for she had none last night."

A chorus of tittering rose to my ears.

"What did he give her?"

"Tell us!" many demanded.

I did not feel this was my place to reveal. But Vadhut would get no rest if I kept silent. "A pair of golden earrings," I announced.

The women murmured approval and I smiled in relief. Later, Vadhut could tell them whatever tale of triumph she cared to invent. I waited for them to leave but I had done no better than whet their appetites for more. Instead of leaving, they hurled further questions at me.

"Was he rough with her?"

"Was she with him the entire night?"

"Did he take her to his chamber?"

"Did he praise her beauty?"

"I am sure she would rather tell you everything herself when she wakes," I replied with false certainty.

The women scowled at me and others groaned with disappointment. But no one challenged me further and the group

111

dispersed. After a few minutes, Freni and I left Vadhut sleeping and withdrew to a corner of the court.

"I would be happy with such earrings," Freni observed with cheerfulness. She spoke as if the gift was all she knew of Vadhut's night with the king.

I looked into Freni's eyes. They shone like rays of sun in a cloud-darkened sky. And I saw that her youthful heart was unchanged from the day of our arrival in the harem. She remained without cunning or guile, saw nothing ugly, and felt no despair. She seemed to have forgotten the shock of her abduction and hold no dread of the future.

I knew Vadhut would recover. She would stand in the court and tell everyone of the costume she had chosen, her adornments and cosmetics, and all that she had done, real and imagined, to entice the king's desire. She would display her new earrings with pride and enjoy the admiration of the crowd.

And I knew that I, like Puah, would endure.

But Freni would be broken forever.

I had to prevent her from going into the king, to preserve the sweet-scentedness of her youthful bloom .

Freni returned my gaze with curiosity. And I searched for something I might say to fill the silence. "I would like to learn a prayer," I whispered.

Later that afternoon I sought Puah and found her washing soiled rags in the bath. I told her of Vadhut's condition but she was not surprised.

"Vadhut lay beneath him as if she were a statue," the old woman explained. "When he took her, she struggled. He was soaked

112

with wine and did not like her fear. But he found her pleasing to look at."

I did not doubt the truth and accuracy of Puah's words. Hegai often sent her to the kitchen or the wine cellars where palace servants told her all that they heard from the attendants to the king's chamber. In exchange, she told them what she knew of the concubines and the virgins yet to come into the king.

"He is still longing for Vashti," Puah continued. "The queen held his interest and he valued her counsel. He has not forgotten her."

"Hegai should teach us to be like her," I suggested, in jest.

"May God strike him first!" Puah exclaimed. "The day of her banishment was a day of rejoicing for all at court."

"I have heard she was cruel to her maids."

Puah clicked her tongue in disgust. "She was good to her maids: she left *them* with their faces."

When she saw that I did not understand, she took her hands from the washtub and sat down to tell me the story of Artaynta.

"Artaynta is wife of the eldest son of Xerxes. But she is also the daughter of the king's brother Masistes, who perished as a traitor. Long before Xerxes came into the kingship, he fell in love with her, though she was his niece and promised to his son. But Xerxes set his eyes upon the girl when he joined his brother to put down a rebellion in Egypt. The future king was smitten by the beauty of his brother's daughter, whom he had not seen since she was an infant.

"Vashti remained in Babylon because she was expecting a child. And so Xerxes offered the young virgin anything she wished in exchange for her treasure. She asked only for the robe on his back. Maybe she knew that Vashti had woven this robe herself, and so schemed to undermine Vashti's hold on her lord. But a girl of her age and inexperience was a fool to fancy herself a match for Vashti.

"Xerxes was filled with desire for Artaynta. So he gave her what she asked for, and she kept the robe hidden in her tent. Each night she went in secret to the king. She flattered and admired him, asking for nothing other than to let her please him. And soon he began to talk of making her his queen when the throne came to him.

"Vashti had spies everywhere, and she learned about Artaynta's design even before the girl's mother and father knew about their daughter's affair. On the very day that Vashti's child, a girl, was born and died, she dispatched two messengers to Egypt. One carried news of the child. The other carried a knife. He was instructed to retrieve the robe from Artaynta and warn her to stay away from the king.

"When the messenger sought Artaynta in the camp, he found Masistes' wife in her daughter's tent. She was looking for Artaynta, who was with Xerxes.

"The mother was still young and beautiful herself, so he mistook her for the daughter. But the mother knew nothing of the robe and could not satisfy the messenger's demand for it. Artaynta returned to the tent just as the messenger delivered Vashti's warning, intended for her, to her mother. He slashed the woman's face and cut off her nose."

Puah paused to savor the effect of her words. Her skill as a storyteller had improved in our many months together.

"The mother was more fortunate than the Greek doctor who attended Vashti's children. He gave a diagnosis that the Queen disputed. When he would not change it, she had him executed as a traitor to the king. And woe to any concubine that the king favored!

If he asked for a girl more than once in a week, Hegai found her poisoned or mutilated. The eunuch did not dare tell Xerxes the truth, for fear the queen would seek revenge on him.

"She did not have a single supporter at court. From the highest advisor to the lowest eunuch, everyone prayed, each to his own god, to be rid of her. And then the king's advisor Memuchan succeeded with a foolish argument for the queen's banishment. Do you recollect that?"

I nodded.

Puah laughed. "Memuchan argued that the queen's refusal to display herself like a dancing girl threatened order in the state. And the king had drunken enough to forget himself and so agreed to banish her. Now she sits in Chaldea on her father's estate, unable to return to court in the king's lifetime. But her son Artaxerxes will return, I am sure of it. She favors him over Darius, the elder, and will see him king, whatever she must do to achieve it."

Puah's words burned in my ears.

"I hear little of the queen in the harem," I remarked after a moment. "But Hegai once told me that she had the use of the apartment which is now mine."

"We were forbidden to speak of her after she left," Puah replied.

"I shall tell no one," I promised.

Puah looked at me with laughing eyes. She seemed to enjoy my curiosity, which had grown bolder over my months in the harem. "When the queen was banished, she came here to remove all her fine possessions. She clutched her infant son, shrieking like a madwoman and vowing revenge upon us all, from the lowest servant to the most favored concubine. She grabbed a knife from one of the fruit trays

115

and threatened Hegai himself. Then she ran to the apartment. Everyone feared for the child but only Asabana dared follow. She found the baby safe on the mattress and the queen carving strange symbols into the rock on the wall of the sleeping chamber. I have seen it there still, but I do not know what it says."

"I am astonished that you have kept this story from me!" I exclaimed. "I have often wondered about the writing and you have held your tongue. We must find someone who can read what it says."

Puah shrugged. "Hegai ordered us to forget that evil woman. I have no wish to recall the days of her rule or torment you with the shadow of her presence."

A chill running through me. "I feel her there still," I confessed.

"She is gone," Puah insisted. She plunged her hands back into the tub and wrung a rag full of water so tight that I was reminded of how Aia used to slaughter a chicken. "The hour of Queen Vashti's banishment was one of relief and joy," she continued. "And so will be the day that King Xerxes names you his favorite."

"Your storytelling runs away from you like a wild horse."

"We shall soon see!" the old woman smiled.

And I knew from the tone in her words and the curve of her lips that Hegai would come for me next.

Fifteen

After my conversation with Puah, I returned to the court. I found Vadhut and Freni with two of the children, a girl and boy of about four years old, who sought their company whenever they visited. I always took great delight in watching Vadhut crawl on the carpet, tossing a soft ball made of goat skin into the little hands, playing clapping games, and telling stories. But I did not feel at ease with children and when asked to join, I always excused myself by saying I did not know how to play. My reluctance did not discourage Vadhut, who never stopped trying to include me. On this day, when I longed for nothing so much as to be a child again, I sat with them.

Vadhut told a story about a brave child who had to get medicine for her mother in the middle of a dark night. I looked at the little girl, whose name was Anatana. She had dark curls, round pink cheeks, and wide eyes that seemed to take delight in everything they saw. She sat on a cushion next to Vadhut, her tiny legs tucked under and two dimpled kneecaps peeking out beneath her short yellow tunic. She clutched a soft cloth doll in one hand and sucked the thumb of the other. If this child was mine, I would hold her dearer than my own eyes.

But Anatana did not know her mother. She was being raised in the care of servants and treated with indifference by the concubines, one of whom had brought her into the world. Though I had lost my own mother at a tender age and the image of her face had long ago faded from my memory, her love for me filled my heart. Anatana's heart held no such treasure.

My eyes grew damp and I looked away from the child. Anatana must have sensed my sorrow, for she rose from her cushion and threw her arms around my neck, kissing my cheek. I smiled as she climbed into my lap. Holding her close to my breast, I stroked her soft curls. Together, we listened to the story and then another. I would have held Anatana forever.

When it was time for the child to return to the nursemaids, she clung to me. I told her that I would play with her the next day if she was good. She promised to do all she was told and gave me another kiss. But As she was leaving, Anatana broke away from her nurse and ran back to me. "Here!" She held out her doll. "You have to take care of her."

I sat with Vadhut and Freni while they refreshed themselves with a cup of wine. We said little, though I knew that Vadhut had been pleased by my attentions to Anatana. Freni and Vadhut soon fell into a stupor from the wine and I left them dozing on the cushions.

I paced the corridors of the harem for several hours, holding the doll in my arms. And for the first time I regretted that I would never have a child of my own to love and cherish. No child would ever call me mother or find in me the comfort that I had known from the woman who gave me life.

My friends came for me when it was time for the evening meal. I did not want to go, but I knew that staying away from them would not prevent Hegai from taking me to the king. We stopped in my apartment to lay the doll on my mattress.

"You are good with the children," I observed to Vadhut, not for the first time.

"I have four younger siblings," she reminded me. "It was always my task to look after them."

Hearing the tinge of sorrow in her voice, I realized that though she never spoke of her family, she missed them and the life from which she had been taken. The haoma dulled the pain of her torn heart, but did not erase her memories.

"I wish I could be one of the children's nurses rather than a concubine," she whispered to me. "I do not care about the gold."

I found no words of comfort and so I squeezed her hand.

When we entered the court, the room was ringing with excitement. I soon understood that the king had called for Thriti rather than another virgin and that though Thriti was a good friend to no one, each concubine took the king's choice as a complement to herself.

"He prefers us!" a woman shouted as we walked by the tables to take our place among the other virgins.

One of the concubines laughed as she stuffed a handful of almonds into her mouth. "He likes a girl who knows what to do."

"The virgins have no advantage in the king's favor," someone agreed.

"They think they hold a special grace above us," another woman pointed out, "but they know nothing."

A woman pinched me as I walked by. "It takes more than what you have between your legs to please him."

I was so relieved, I laughed to be the target of their taunts.

After I finished eating, my maid bent low behind my back and whispered that Hegai was asking for me to join him. Since I spent some portion of every evening in the company of the keeper of the women, I did not wonder at his summons, though it came an hour before the usual time.

When I arrived at Hegai's apartment, he asked me to sit at a dressing table and began to comb my hair. I heard a rustling noise from the wardrobe and realized that Thriti was still dressing.

Hegai permitted no concubine, even one of Thriti's experience, to go in to the king without his inspection and approval. Because Hegai had called for me early, it happened that my visit to the eunuch's apartment overlapped with Thriti's presentation.

She appeared before me wearing a long, thin white garment with many pleats and a heavy gold belt around her thick waist. Her earlobes hung low from the weight of large gold earrings, shaped like eagles in flight. A collar of precious beads in many brilliant colors swallowed her neck, and her hair was shaped into a sculpture that reminded me of the great ziggurat in Babylon.

Thriti stamped her foot for attention. Hegai sat behind me, running one of his jeweled ivory combs through my long hair. He must have known that the concubine was waiting for him. But he did not turn his attention from my hair.

The concubine noticed me looking at her and hissed.

"You may go," Hegai announced, as if he did not care whether she went or stayed.

"You have not approved my costume!" she objected.

"Go," Hegai commanded in his shrillest voice.

And so she left.

Hegai put down the comb and laughed. I turned to see a smile blossoming over his bloated face and realized that the keeper of the women had roused Thriti's fury for a purpose.

"Send word to Asabana and her girls," he called out to one of his attendants, gathering some of my loose hairs that the comb had removed. "Tell her the king would like a taste of their sweet fruit tonight."

"They will fight!" I exclaimed, sure that neither Thriti nor Asabana would enjoy a competition for the king's attentions.

"They will fight like wolves," Hegai agreed. "And the king will not have a woman tonight. So much the fuller will his desire be for you tomorrow." He rolled the strands of hair into a ball and pushed it into a small pouch of white linen that was on the dressing table. He kissed the pouch and turned it over, revealing a sixteen-pointed star, embroidered in silver thread. I could not imagine what he intended to do with this keepsake. But as I stared at the star, I came to recall Aia's high priest. A voice of warning whispered to me from the shadows of my hidden self.

"Shall you dress like Thriti when you go into the king?" Hegai asked, as if in jest.

"I shall wear whatever you advise." I had long ago decided to rely on Hegai's skills. Many of the women enjoyed dressing themselves, the endless hours of discussing robes, jewels, and hair adornments, but I could summon no enthusiasm for the task. The keeper of the women knew what pleased the king, and I would defer to him.

The eunuch smiled with deep satisfaction and tapped my arm to indicate that he wished me to rise. I helped him to his feet, watching his brow grow damp from the effort.

"We have a gift for you." He signaled for me to wait and passed into his private sleeping chamber, where none but one close attendant was permitted to enter. The door was never without a guard; I had come to imagine a horde of personal treasures stored within.

Hegai's great bulk brought slowness to his steps. And even after I had braided my long hair and tied it out of the way, I waited for many minutes. At last he returned, holding something in his hands.

It was an Egyptian box of glossy black ebony, with ivory inlaid to form an intricate pattern of rosettes. The box was no bigger than my two hands put together, just like those I had so often admired in the marketplace with my mother.

It was the box that should have been in my dowry chest.

But she was no longer alive. And I would not be my cousin's wife. I would not be a wife to anyone.

Hegai gave me the gift as if it were the king's own turban, presenting it in his upturned palms. And the River Euphrates rose and rushed through me. And the tears of my heart were the waters of Babylon, but I held back the flow.

"You are a gift to us from Ishtar herself." He declared this as if he believed in the truth of his own words.

"I am only a poor orphan," I protested.

"She foretold your coming," he insisted, motioning to his throne. "Let us sit and we shall tell you the story."

I helped him settle into the chair and perched myself on a cushion at his knee.

"The king had returned from Salamis to the jewels of our toil. Any man's passion would have been inflamed by the delights we

122

had readied for him. But by the evil work of Ahriman, the enemy of Ahura Mazda, the king's wish was for none other than the disobedient Vashti, the one banished from him by his own decree.

"We had seen a servant lose his ears and nose for no worse crime than spilling the king's wine. How much greater the punishment for causing him to spill his seed in vessels that did not fit his desire?

"We prayed in the king's own fire temple. And that very night we were blessed with a visit from the great goddess Ishtar.

"Her skin was like cream and her hair like the sun. Her lips were the color of rubies and her eyes like ripened wheat. She wore a lion skin tight across her wide hips and her uncovered breasts were as full and firm as two ripe pomegranates. A star pendent hung between these luscious fruits and her ivory arms held out to us an offering of choice dates.

"Already tasting the sweetness on our tongue, wet with desire for the delicious dates, we reached to take one. But the goddess snatched away her treasure and vanished. Nowhere in the entire royal city were there to be dates such as those which we now craved.

"All that following day we wondered what it could mean. Why this cruel punishment? But she came again that next night, extending her fingers, gleaming with thick honey for us to suck. 'I am your obedient servant,' she said as our mouth sought out her delights. And again she was gone, having aroused in us a great hunger that could not be satisfied.

"A magus skilled in dream interpretation was summoned. 'The goddess requires an offering,' he said. His words were good in our eyes and that very morning two concubines were sent by our hand to serve Ishtar in her great temple at Babylon, where the king himself had often gone to refresh his vigor. The gift was pleasing to the goddess and by her inspiration, the king declared the gathering of the virgins. Before nightfall, she had sent you, her namesake."

"Esther," I whispered to myself. The name my beloved Mordechai had given me.

"The name was a sign," the eunuch replied, "and the color of your eyes, for they matched the goddess's own. But it was your words that revealed your lineage."

I looked at him, trying to remember what I had tried to forget, the day of our first meeting.

"'I am your obedient servant,'" he quoted. His fleshy hand reached down to caress my breasts. "Your words were taken from the mouth of the Great Goddess herself."

And so at last I knew why I, who could not drink the harem wine, was spared from the soldiers. I looked at the box, wondering what was inside.

"Open it," Hegai commanded.

I lifted the lid. A sixteen-pointed silver star as large as my hand, shone from within. A silver lion of Ishtar sat in its center.

"This was consecrated by the goddess herself through the high priestess at Uruk," Hegai explained to me, fingering the silver chain attached to the star. "Is it not the most beautiful object you have ever seen?"

With a slight nod of my head, I gave Hegai the answer he expected. Then he called for a guard, who appeared at once from behind a curtain at the far end of the room. He was a big eunuch with a jeweled dagger.

"She must kiss it in the name of the goddess three times when she retires. Make sure she does this with her lips upon the center of the star and places it beneath her cheek cushion." He looked back at me again. "The great goddess will enter you with the ripe fruit of her desire to serve the king's pleasure. Tomorrow we will dress you in the skin of a lion, and make your hair like the sun. You will go into the king—as Ishtar herself."

I thanked the eunuch for his kindness to me and promised to do as he instructed.

But the beautiful box burned in my hand. And I fled from his apartment in pain.

I could eat the food of the harem. I could submit myself to the authority of a eunuch. I could go into the king as a virgin and return to the harem as a harlot. I could live a life like Puah's, with little joy over the generations.

But I could not worship the gods that were an abomination to my father. I could not betray Avihail, whose living seed remained in none other than me. I could not crush the memory of his righteous ways.

I had hoped to fulfill my days in Mordechai's household and to give him strong sons. Mordechai was a stranger to his people's ways but my father would have lived on through the generations of our children's children. For Mordecai was still a Jew in his heart. He would walk among the idolaters but he would not worship a stranger's gods.

And I could not do so now.

I ran through the dark corridors of the harem. The box was a horror in my hands, an abomination to be destroyed. I would throw it where the chamber pots were emptied. I would tell Hegai that the goddess herself had come to claim it. I would sleep in the valley of bones. And in the morning I would rise on the road to Jerusalem.

I could not see through the veil of my tears. I could not hear through the clamor in my head. I could do nothing but run like a hunted doe.

And then I fell. The box flew out of my hands and I lay with my cheek upon the ground.

I sat up. I was in the court and saw I had stumbled over a sleeping concubine. My own sorrows slid away in pity for her abandonment. Shaashgaz had not sent someone in search of his missing charge.

When I rose to help her, I saw it was Hutana. She had not spoken to me since she had joined the dancing girls. I shook her and she moaned, but she would not open her eyes. I tried to lift her and staggered; she was too heavy. When I lay her down again, her robe fell open, revealing a swollen belly.

Asabana had given Hutana the abortion wine. Hutana would soon wake in a burst of pain, and might not survive the bleeding. I knew then that I could not refuse any part of Hegai's plan for me. Because if I displeased the eunuch, he would hand me over to Asabana, or worse. And Avihail's grandson, like Hutana's child, would be slaughtered in the womb.

I gathered up the box and the star, which had fallen out. And then I sought Asabana in her quarters, waking her and explaining that Hutana was in the court. Asabana roused a eunuch and they carried Hutana back to her mattress.

As I returned to my apartment I caught a glimpse of the big eunuch waiting for me in the passageway. I had no choice but to obey

Hegai's instructions. And so I formed a plan to seek the protection of my father's God.

When I came at last to lay my cheek upon a cushion over the burning box, even Puah did not know that Freni's amulet, rescued from the wall, was entwined with the star of the goddess. And only the One God Himself could hear the prayer in my heart, the words that Freni had placed there: *Who is like you among the heavenly powers, God! Who is like you, mighty in holiness!*

Sixteen

When my time came to go into the king, I requested nothing other than what Hegai suggested. I trusted Hegai to know what would be most pleasing to the king's eye. And now I understood that he planned to dress me as the Ishtar of his dream. From the hour of our first meeting he had regarded me as a gift from the goddess. He had imagined that her spirit would enter my flesh and win the king's heart away from Vashti.

I knew a little of this goddess who ruled over love, procreation, and war. Desire drove her to take many lovers. She hunted for men in taverns, at the marketplace, and on the roads at night. She could turn men into women and priestesses in her temple prostituted themselves in her name.

This was what Hegai wished me to become: a goddess of impure lust, a goddess of idolaters.

I lay my head upon the cheek cushion and remembered how I used to imagine my wedding night with Mordechai, as if I were Rebekah and he Isaac. I would close my eyes and see the weary stranger by the well, Abraham's messenger, and his parched camels in need of watering. I quenched their thirst with bucket after bucket and in return, the servant gave me lavish gifts of gold and gained my brother's favor. My heart swelled with joy to be called to my cousin. No longer would I give offerings to the idols of Aram in my brother's tent. I was not afraid to go.

The journey was swift on Abraham's fine camels and I saw a man in the field before us, approaching in his fine white robes and tall turban against the evening sky. He was a man of the One God and his eyes were turned to heaven. I blushed to see him, and I pulled my veil forward over my face. That night he took me into the tent of his mother in the sight of his God. My heart was his and his heart was mine. We became one.

I closed my eyes and drifted into sleep, praying that Freni's amulet would protect me from the goddess. But Ishtar came to me nonetheless, seducing my nostrils with the sweet scent of jasmine. I saw her face beside me glittering like a star in the dark heavens. Her lion was as tame as a newborn lamb and I was not afraid.

We wandered through the night in a garden of fruit trees, flowers, and fragrant grasses. I followed her flowing robe as a ring rippling over smooth water from her center. Men held out their hearts to us in the moonlight.

And then the wellsprings of the abyss burst forth from below.

And the floodgate of the heavens opened up from above.

And there was darkness.

The goddess rose over the deep to pull me from perdition. She placed me as a sacred vessel on her altar of desire, a blossoming flower, full and fragrant. A hooded worshiper mounted me and I took his torrent of pleasure into my flesh until it became my own. I writhed with desire until his hood fell away, revealing the face of Mordechai.

And I was the priestess of shame.

I woke in a sweat, unsure of the hour. The sun streamed through the window high in the wall and a eunuch from Hegai's retinue stood over me.

"The keeper of the women requests that you rise."

Puah appeared by my mattress wringing her rough hands. "A little time," she begged, "for me to attend my mistress in private."

"A few minutes," the young eunuch allowed. "The keeper is waiting."

I watched him leave the apartment. But I found no relief, knowing that he was stationed just outside the door.

Puah stroked my cheek, her old eyes filled with hope. "Be proud and yet kind," she whispered, "as others before you have not been. Your beauty will enchant him, but it is the quiet warmth of your grace and charm that will hold him."

I did not believe that I could do as Puah advised, but I knew no other choice was left to me but to summon all my strength to try. I sat up and glimpsed Anatana's doll on the floor; the little creature had fallen from the mattress in the night. I stooped to retrieve the bundle of rags, kissing the doll and then handing it to Puah. "Please take care of her for Anatana," I asked. Then I reached under my head cushion for Hegai's box and removed Freni's amulet. I rose to fasten it around the old woman's neck.

Puah opened her arms and I melted into her embrace. A voice cried out from the wilderness of my heart. "Whatever I become, I will never abandon you."

I was taken to the hairdressers where Hegai awaited me. The keeper of the women sat upon a chair near a washing basin, issuing instructions to two women. One, an Athenian I had never seen, was an expert in hair coloring. Hegai had sought her for many months and paid a high price for her purchase. The women of the Persian Empire only colored their hair with henna but Hegai intended to transform me into the golden-haired goddess of his dream.

She labored long hours over me, smearing substances of a foul odor into my hair, rinsing it, and then smearing again. I was hungry, having eaten nothing since the evening before, and the smell burned my nostrils until I grew faint. When she finished, Hegai's full face flushed in pleasure. I looked down on the hair that fell over my shoulder, unable to believe that the gilded tresses were my own.

The henna-dyers worked on my fingertips and the hair strippers went over all my skin until it was as smooth as the day I was born. When they had finished, two servants came to rub oil into my tortured flesh.

The sweet-scented almond oil soothed my spirit. I closed my eyes to imagine my mother preparing for her wedding day—rubbing her skin with fragrant wedding oil, hooking the golden engagement hoops into her ears, donning the white linen robe embroidered with all the colors of the rainbow. Her own mother pinned the coin covered veil in place. It sparkled in the sun.

And then I remembered our last afternoon together.

We walked by the waters of Babylon, to find my father. Her belly was so big that I was sure she would burst if the baby did not come soon. All morning her face had filled with spasms of pain. But she would not send a messenger to summon Father. "He would not want to leave when Ezra is reading the law," she explained. "We will just catch a glimpse of him and go home again."

I saw no madness in her plan: I was only a child of ten.

"I was once a small girl, just like you," she told me, as if searching for a subject to distract herself.

I laughed to imagine her the same size as me.

"My heart had turned toward my cousin even then," she admitted, a secret smile spreading over her face for anyone to see. Father would sometimes scold me about it. 'You should hold your heart behind the veil of modesty,' he would say. But I could not hide my love for him.

"Avihail was a scholar and a pious youth. I would watch him with the other men, offering wisdom beyond his numbered years. Sometimes, when he sought the cool evening air to study, I would watch him from the roof of my father's house next door. When he came to visit his uncle—my father—I would wait upon him."

"I am sure you were prettier than his own sisters," I said.

"He did not seem to notice me," she laughed. "But when his beard grew full and his desire for a wife awakened, he came to my father and said: 'She is pleasing in form and gentle in speech. And if her desire is for me as mine is for her, we should be wed in the sight of God.'

"That was the day of my greatest happiness," she sighed, her voice dancing over the river like the song of the spring winds. "Our families rejoiced and offered their blessings: 'May you have myriads of children. May you live to see our return to Jerusalem.'"

But I was their only child to survive. And their days came to an end in Babylon.

The servants finished and helped me rise from the table. Hegai hoisted himself from his chair to inspect my naked body, circling from back to front. He placed his hands upon my flesh, my breasts and my buttocks. He had the head of a man and the claws of a

132

lion. But I did not cringe with the shame of modesty. I was proud of my glistening flesh, the beauty of my form and its power to unleash desire. The goddess Ishtar had claimed me and I no longer knew myself.

"She is ready for the king!" Hegai declared. "And the king is ready for her," he added in an undertone. "Let us eat."

The servants wrapped me in a thick cotton robe and took me to Hegai's apartment where he fed me figs and sugared flowers and strong honeyed wine. I surrendered to the sweet wine and when the keeper of the women advised me to enhance the king's desire by giving free reign to my own, I lay back on the cushions and laughed. *Does the goddess of pleasure need instruction from a eunuch?*

And the eunuch laughed too and I opened my robe to suckle him.

When afternoon faded into evening I arose from a stupor, and trembled as Hegai approached me with my costume. I longed for more wine to numb my senses. I begged for Ishtar to possess me again, to give me courage. I cursed Mordechai for condemning me to relinquish my most precious treasure to a man who would not honor the gift. But I remembered all the others who had gone before me. I resolved to be strong in memory of their suffering. I would heed Puah's words and face my fate with grace and kindness. I would turn my heart to the king alone, to win his favor through my devotion to him.

I saw Hegai wrap the lion skin around my hips and laced fine doeskin sandals around my ankles. I did not object that my breasts were left bare beneath my flowing golden hair. I did not flinch when

133

the silver star slipped over my neck and the cool metal lay flat against my chest.

Hegai covered me with a dark cloak and veil. He called for my escorts, two eunuchs dressed like the king's Immortals in tunics of fine silver-flecked linen, and sandals of white leather. But their breastplates were solid gold, embossed with an emblem of a lion.

The eunuch murmured to me, an Avestan prayer to the king's god, Ahura Mazda. "Bestow on him riches and good things. Bestow on him a healthy body, noble offspring, and a long life."

He handed me the golden vessel of honeyed wine.

The eunuchs took me to the king's palace through a door hidden behind a tapestry at the back of Hegai's apartment. We walked down a long narrow corridor and reached a heavy door with an iron ring. My escorts grunted as they pulled, until last it opened to reveal a soldier posted in the courtyard outside.

"Evidence of permission to move forward?" he demanded.

One of the eunuchs handed him a papyrus scrap with Hegai's seal. The soldier waved us on.

I had not been without a roof over my head in more than a year. The courtyard air was fresh, as if after a rainfall, and cool. The thick veil obscured the sky, yet standing under the stars after a year of confinement felt more intoxicating than ten cups of Hegai's honeyed wine.

The winged disc swooped down from the apadana cornice, crying close to my ear: "The spirit rushes and sits near the skull. The spirit tastes as much suffering as the whole of the living world can taste."

But I was not afraid.

Seventeen

I was taken to King Xerxes in his royal palace, in the tenth month, which is Teveth, in the seventh year of his reign.

But I did not go to him that first night in my own flesh.

I was a goddess, a high priestess of Ishtar, a statue, a virgin. I spoke much, I was quiet. I was eager to serve him. I was reluctant. I was prepared to be whatever the king wished me to be. But my flesh was not my own. And I did not betray Mordechai as myself.

We walked a brief distance from the harem, across the court, and through another guarded door into a passageway. The opulence of the king's palace exceeded that of Hegai's apartment many times over. Rich tapestries of violet wool hung on the walls by silver rods the length of two men. The carpet beneath my feet felt as soft and thick as a mattress stuffed with feathers. Statues of polished white marble, most in the form of unclothed women, kept watch at regular intervals. Many of these, I later learned, were the spoils of war against the Greeks.

We paused at the edge of a large inner courtyard. I brought out the vessel of wine from my cloak, the wine Hegai had given me to steady myself. One of the eunuchs raised my veil so I could drink, then took the wine and placed it on a table.

Hundreds of tallow rushlights lit the courtyard with such brilliance that I might have mistaken the time of day for morning. I could see the pavement, a mosaic of rich blue lapis lazuli and shimmering mother of pearl. White lotus blossoms floated in a large pink marble basin in the center of the courtyard. Couches of gold and silver were tucked into shaded corners. And tendrils of creeping jasmine wound around the alabaster columns.

Laughter and music hovered in the night air, coming from an open doorway across the court. When the musicians rehearsed for our entertainment in the harem, their practice sessions were filled with stops and starts. Now I could hear the music continue on and on, like clouds floating across the sky, the rippling flow of a river, the flight of the falcon.

I stood listening to the tombak, nay, and kamancheh, but the vibrations of the santur rose above them all, sweet in its sorrowful tones. It was the song of my heart and I longed to lose myself in it.

One of the king's attendants emerged from the portico across the courtyard. He was a Greek youth, clad in a linen loincloth and little more. When he signaled to my escorts, they snorted to each other and whispered derisive epithets, foreign to my ears. As they guided me over the slippery mosaic, I came to understand that the king kept such boys for the benefit of visiting Greek dignitaries.

We stepped into the king's banquet hall, a room so vast that several hundred could recline in comfort amidst the low tables and cushions. Gold-flecked glass jars glowed with candle light. Across the room, the musicians played from a dais and the men clustered close to them on cushions, each with a golden drinking vessel in his hand. Servants stood by with wine and others with towels and basins for those who wished to wash.

The gathering that evening was small; I counted fifteen to twenty of the king's companions. I could not discern the king himself from his company. When the men turned their attention to us, the cloaked figure and her gilded escorts, the music stopped.

"*What maid are you, the fairest maid I have ever seen?*" a deep voice called out.

"*White-armed,*" replied one of the eunuchs by my side in a ritual exchange. "*Strong, tall-formed, high standing, thick breasted, beautiful in body, of a glorious seed, as fair as the fairest things in the world.*"

A man rose from the midst of the gathering; the others followed, staggering to their feet. The first to rise towered above the tallest of his companions. He was steady in his stance, though no less affected by the wine.

"Let us have a look!" the king called out. A chorus of men echoed his cry, adding lewd suggestions. I understood why Queen Vashti had refused to obey her husband's drunken command. No woman would choose to endure such shame.

Vadhut too had been paraded before the company in her rose robe. The men had bid for first use of her as if she were destined to be a dancing girl. The king had laughed at his lively companions and ordered that Asabana's girls be provided for their use. He had not prolonged his pleasure with the virgin Vadhut, taking her in an adjoining room, before returning to his cup and his companions.

"Let us have a look!" the king called out again. But my escorts did not obey his command to uncover me. Instead, their voices rang out, high and clear, reciting familiar lines from the Hymn of Ishtar.

"Ishtar is clothed with pleasure and love,
She gleams with vitality, charm and voluptuousness.
She is glorious; veils are thrown over her head.
Her body is beautiful; her eyes are brilliant."

The men grumbled at the delay of my unveiling but the king motioned for them to sit and be silent. As he approached, I gathered courage by telling myself to be strong for Vadhut, Freni, and Puah. I did not tremble as he uncovered my bare breasts and my golden hair, but my bones were as brittle as a dry leaf.

I looked up into his eyes as if I were his equal. And I saw him soften before me as if he were a simple shepherd and I, the goddess, held him in my hand.

Ishtar herself would have been pleased with the beauty of this majestic mortal: his wide brow, dark, deep-set eyes, his strong nose and resolute chin. Each of his legs was as thick as a cedar of Lebanon, and his shoulders were as broad as the rivers of Babylon. His beard was a forest of fragrant juniper.

With his eyes he kissed every crevice of my flesh. The other men disappeared from my vision. The king raised his fingers and caressed my bare breast as if it were forbidden fruit. My bones melted into honey.

He broke away from me. "Bring her to my chamber," the king ordered. As the eunuchs covered me, cries of disappointment rose from the drunken company.

"Give us a taste!"

"Let her dance in my lap!"

But the king did not even pause to appease his guests by calling for the dancing girls. He cared nothing for another man's lust in the urgency of his own. He dismissed their clamoring with the flick of his hand and hurried to his private rooms to receive me.

The two eunuchs escorted me through the banquet hall and the adjoining throne room, through the wide marble-paved corridors and the gardens obscured by the darkness of night, through porticoes of alabaster and over carpets of fine wool. We stopped in a vestibule before the king's sleeping chamber, crowded with servants, officials and guards. Two fierce soldiers stood on the threshold before the closed door. The others were assigned to wait, should the king require something in the night.

The soldiers opened the door and my escorts drew back to let me pass into the king's gilded chamber. The room was almost as large as the court in the harem, and gleamed with silver and gold. The carpets were woven of purple wool and the cushions of shimmering blue linen. A gold curtain screened the wardrobe, and low ebony chests ornamented with gold lions lined the walls. The moldings were covered with writing composed of lines and wedges, just like the script Vashti had carved on the wall of my room.

The king reclined on a high mattress in the center of the room. A gold fluted column flanked each corner of the mattress and a molded relief of the winged god hung over his head. Ebony tables sat by either side. One table held a silver wine vessel and several golden cups; the other supported a marble head, a life-sized sculpture of a woman with high cheekbones and full lips. This was Queen Vashti, the woman against whom all others were to be compared.

I stared for a moment at Vashti, the queen of cruelty, blessed with more beauty than any woman known to the king. Her face was a perfect flower, yet cold as the marble from which it was carved. And though her almond eyes were empty, they flashed at me in defiance and I felt her hot, poisoned breath upon my cheek. *I shall not heed you*, I told her in my heart. *I shall win the king in ways you never imagined. I will find a way to hold his interest and use it well.*

Your blood shall drain like a slaughtered bird, she replied deep inside my ear.

"Let us have a look!" the king called out again.

I removed the veil to reveal my head and face. But my other treasures remained hidden beneath the cloak. I moved toward the king in steps so slow that he grew pained in anticipation. But I held his eye with an enticing smile and he did not hurry me.

I poured wine for him into a golden cup in the shape of a horn. Leaning over the king, I held the horn to his lips. He took some liquid into his mouth and motioned that I, too, should drink. I took a delicate mouthful, imagining that I had all Freni's grace and charm. But I did not know what to do next. What would bring special pleasure to a man who already had a harem full of women to satisfy his warrior's lust?

Looking into his eager dark eyes I recalled how much enjoyment Vadhut took in spinning stories for the children. The king himself must have tales to tell of his exploits; he had once been a warrior who inspired awe and fear. Surely, I reasoned, any man would relish a request to relive his days of glory.

"What are you called?" the king asked. He touched my cloak.

"Servant to the victorious," I replied, hoping to please him with a warrior's epithet. I returned the cup to his hand and uncovered myself as if plunging into a rapids.

He toyed with the necklace between my breasts. "You are as voluptuous as the day of victory."

"It is said the Great King Xerxes is a fighter of victorious strength."

The king snorted. A sorrowful memory spread over his face and his eyes drifted away from me. I feared my plan was a mistake.

"It is said the victory at Thermopylae is a tale worth the trouble of telling," I pressed, pouring the king another cup.

He drank a deep draught. "The Hot Gates," he recalled.

"Great is the god Ahura Mazda," I observed. "Great is the god Ahura Mazda who set wisdom and strength down upon King Xerxes."

The king sat up and laughed. "By the grace of Ahura Mazda it *is* a tale to tell."

"Our ears are on fire with eagerness," I urged, stroking his thigh. He was a different man from the lustful brute of Vadhut's encounter.

And so the king began to recount his greatest glory, the battle of Thermopylae.

He spoke all night until the crest of the dawn. And when the last of the Greeks had been defeated, he took me in his arms.

I slept in the valley of the bones.

Eighteen

I carried my grace and kindness before the king. He did not know my name, my people, or my decent. He did not care. Desire seized his senses and roused him from lethargy and indifference. He tasted life again as his old self, the man he was before the loss of Vashti and the defeat in Greece. For this, King Xerxes loved me more than all the other women.

I woke and find myself alone in the king's private chamber, covered with a linen blanket and nothing more. My head ached from the wine and my face flushed with shame for all that I remembered of the evening before. I sat up and saw that someone had removed the wine, cups, and clothes. My necklace was gone. But the marble head of Vashti remained. I stared at her for a moment but she was silent.

A door across the room stood ajar, opening into a court I had not seen. I could hear loud voices arguing just beyond the threshold.

"Ahura Mazda has sent her to be our queen!" The king was a warrior, and brandished a warrior's anger when crossed. I would soon learn that his spirit changed from calm to fury without warning, like hot lightening scorching the night sky.

Another man's voice replied. "But she is not of royal blood."

"Fool!" the king shouted. "Was it not you, Memuchan, who said we should bestow Vashti's place upon one more deserving?"

Memuchan replied with deference. "I beg the forgiveness of Your Majesty. I meant that one other than the disobedient Queen

Vashti should be queen of His Majesty's heart. Surely Your Majesty knows that a queen must be of royal lineage. The rules for selecting a queen to bear the royal heirs were long ago established by Cyrus the Great, Your Majesty's own grandfather."

"You dare speak in clever contradictions to me? I who by the favor of Ahura Mazda smote the men of Egypt and Babylonia? *She* shall be my queen and none other: I hereby proclaim it!"

I found no comfort in the king's words. I trembled to remember all that I had said and done. But I was myself again. I was a girl in her sixteenth year—a virgin no longer—with a head that ached from too much wine and the stale odor of an unwashed and unperfumed concubine. When the king returned to look at me in the light of a new day, he would be disappointed.

And so I wrapped myself in the cotton blanket and rose to my feet. I moved with quiet steps through the chamber in search of an escape.

The room appeared to have two exits—through the door that I had entered the night before and through the courtyard. The king and his advisor stood together in the court, so I went to the other door and pushed it open a finger's width.

I saw the glint of a soldier's knife and moved away, berating myself. Any entrance to the king's private chamber would be guarded. But I could not wait in the middle of the room like sheep before slaughter. I crept toward the curtained wardrobe.

I slid behind the curtain into a small, dark space. And I saw that it was not a wardrobe but an alcove for the king's chamber pot. I crouched low in a corner and wrapped the linen blanket over my head.

The sound of footsteps filled my ears.

"Where is she?" the king demanded. "Call the door guards!"

"Door guards!" Memuchan shouted.

And I heard the clatter of armed guards in the commotion beyond the curtain.

"Where is the concubine?" the advisor demanded.

"She is my queen," the warrior king raged. "I shall have you hung for this!"

One of the guards answered, his voice shaking in fear. "Your Highness on my life she has not passed though the door."

"Might it be a trick of the magi?" the advisor asked.

The king did not answer. The room grew silent. And then the walls shook from an explosion of royal laughter. I heard the king approach my hiding place and I looked down toward the crack of light at the bottom of the curtain. The king's bare toes poked through under the edge, but he did not pull the curtain back.

"What is your name, sweet girl?" he asked in voice so gentle it could coax the shyest gazelle.

"If it please Your Majesty, I am called Esther."

"By Ahura Mazda, you shall be Queen Esther," he pronounced.

My heart rose with such force in my chest that I was sure it would tear through my breast. I took a breath to compose myself. "Your Majesty does his servant too great an honor."

He raised his voice so the others could hear. "Some say a queen should be of royal birth. But they would advance their own daughters."

The king paused to confirm that Memuchan understood his displeasure. "What is your lineage, my lovely bird? What mortal man could have planted a creature so perfect from his seed?"

And he spoke to me words of such tenderness that I forgot he had threatened his guards. I forgot that he had suppressed the revolt of Babylon and caused my father's death. I forgot that his lust had dragged nubile virgins from their families and confined them to the prison of his harem. I forgot that he had crushed my heart's hopes. The man who spoke to me was not that man. This was the lord of my heart, the awakener of my desire. King Xerxes might have chosen anyone to be his life's companion, but he had chosen me. I was his wife and there was no shame now in the pleasures of the marital bed.

"Have you lost your tongue?" the king teased, an edge of impatience in his voice.

I longed to answer his question with the truth. But I could not betray my promise to Mordechai.

"Your servant is the daughter of a scribe." And I hoped he would ask no more. "She is an orphan of Babylon," I added.

"Would the orphan of Babylon permit her lord the pleasure of gazing upon her beauty again?"

I feared his disappointment, but I could not deny his request. I rose from my crouch, hoping that what he had seen at night with wine-soaked eyes would still please him by the bright light of day.

Before I could step out from the curtain, I heard new footsteps scurrying into the room.

"Hegai the keeper of the women enters!" the booming voice of the eunuch's attendant announced.

"Your Majesty!" I could hear that Hegai had walked too fast; he struggled for breath.

"Do not kneel, you old woman! You can never get up. You have scared my bride into the closet of the chamber pot," the king complained.

"We shall leave," Hegai deferred. "But perhaps…" Hegai hesitated, as if the interjection was unplanned.

"What?" the king snapped.

"The lady might be desirous of the opportunity to refresh herself before she came to His Majesty again."

The room grew silent. My heartbeat echoed in my ears.

"A lady of refinement is reluctant to reveal her ripe fruits without adequate preparation," the keeper of the women continued. "A lady of refinement is accustomed to her bath and her cosmetics after a night of passion."

The eunuch said no more. After a moment, the king laughed. "By the will of Ahura Mazda!" he conceded, "the keeper of the women is right."

"Let me bring her to His Majesty again tonight," Hegai proposed, "and He shall have a bride more radiant than the sun itself."

Behind the curtain I exhaled in relief and considered what words of gratitude I would offer Hegai.

"She shall be taken to the queen's chambers," the king commanded. "Let only the best serving-women wait upon her."

"Your Majesty is great in his wisdom," Hegai approved.

"Tonight shall be the feast of Esther!" the voice of my lord rang with excitement. "Tell the cooks to prepare their finest delicacies! Tell the wine stewards to bring forth the best bottles! And Memuchan, summon all the men of the court and their wives to see my bride."

I thrilled to hear the king's deep and powerful voice refer to me as his bride in tones of soft affection. His hands had caressed me with this same sweet mixture of vigor and gentleness. Perhaps he would enter my heart as my father had come to possess my mother. But how long would I hold his interest? What could he find in me that another could not provide? Would I still be queen in a day or a year?

I waited behind the curtain for the king and his attendants to depart, my heart a torrent of questions. But I did not once wonder about the feast to come that night or if the king's company might include Mordechai.

Nineteen

The King proclaimed a great feast for all his officials and courtiers, and called it "the feast of Esther." I heard him shout orders and instructions to his chamber attendants. But I remained behind the curtain until he left.

Hegai called to me when the king and his attendants had gone. "Reveal yourself, great goddess." When I emerged, his massive flesh shook with excitement.

"We are victorious!" he proclaimed. "Tonight we shall seal the triumph and show the world by dressing you in the harem's finest."

"Thank you, sir." I longed to see my friends again. But my home was no longer the harem.

Hegai snapped his fingers at his two youthful escorts. "Take her to the queen's quarters," he ordered. "You!" He gestured toward one of the king's chamber servants. The servant flinched but I did not know enough to understand the liberty Hegai took in appropriating one of the king's servants for his own use. "You shall return with us to the harem. We must go at once for bath attendants and wardrobe."

I remained wrapped in the linen blanket so that only my feet and eyes were visible. The eunuchs and one of the king's guardsmen led the way through the door to a colonnade.

The polished marble of the floor felt cool beneath my bare feet. I did not remove my gaze from the stone.

We wove our way around rows of columns, following the king's soldier to a guarded door, which another soldier opened for me.

I stepped over the threshold. The brilliant morning sun shone on a garden more beautiful than any I had ever seen, though it was small with a simple brick walkway. My eye was drawn to the pool in the center, which held a profusion of pink lotus blossoms. Each corner of the basin was marked by a tall pomegranate tree in bloom. Patches of fragrant grasses waved in the breeze. My eye feasted on clusters of red and yellow tulips and I saw that lilies would take their place when they were spent. A bed of Persian roses was planted far to one side of the courtyard, away from the path. And I noticed that the garden had only one bench, in a shady alcove. But when I looked up to the balconies, I understood that this was a garden designed to delight viewers from above.

A servant emerged from a door across the courtyard. He wore the short cotton robe of a chamber attendant, but held his head high as one of greater importance. This was the eunuch Hathach, the keeper of the queen's apartment and servants.

Hathach was neither young nor old. In build he resembled a soldier more than a eunuch. He was beardless, as all eunuchs are. But he carried no excess weight on his bones, and the muscles of his arms and legs were well-defined, like a man of combat. He was dark-skinned, as one from the land of Ethiopia, and he looked upon me with kind eyes.

"Would the lady bathe first? The water is ready," he added, "but the attendants have not yet arrived."

"Thank you," I replied. He smiled, knowing I would welcome the chance to bathe alone. I did not wonder that the eunuch had known of my impending arrival in time to have a bath drawn. I later came to understand that both Hegai and Hathach bribed the king's youthful attendants to bring them news and in this way the two eunuchs kept well-informed of the king's disposition and desires. They spied on one another too, each paying informants to let him know what the other was doing.

Hathach dismissed Hegai's escorts and offered his arm to assist me.

I entered the queen's bath through a garden door. Sun flooded in from high windows, and the colored floor tiles glistened like jewels. Hathach pointed to a large brass basin, towels, and a thick cotton robe. Then he left me alone.

I unwound the blanket and lowered myself to the bottom of the basin. The tub was so deep that all but my head was submerged. I sank into the silence and the warm embrace of the water.

I remembered the bath that Aia had drawn for me on the day of my arrival in Susa. I pictured the old woman taking care of a dirty little orphan. Aia had aged since then, and so had I. My beauty and youth were fresh enough to arouse the king's interest, but my heart was ancient and withered for all that I had lost.

I closed my eyes and remembered walking to the tent of the Jews with my mother. It was my last afternoon with her.

My mother was so big with her unborn baby that she walked like the crippled old woman who washed the dead. I grew impatient and skipped ahead until she called me back to her side. We were going to look for Father in the tent where Ezra the scribe was reading the law. When Father went to the tent on market days there was always a large gathering and he never left until late at night. But mother knew that the baby would be born before sunset.

We hovered on the edge of the tent but Father did not see us. I wanted to run in and find him, but she held my hand tight and forbade me to move. "He will not want to leave the men," she said. A spasm of pain passed over her face.

"But you are not well!" I argued.

"He has written the protective prayer." She spoke as if choking back tears. "He has hung it over my mattress. He can do nothing more. It is all in the hands of God the Almighty."

And so we trudged home by the banks of the Euphrates. I offered my arm to my ailing mother who whispered words of tenderness to me as we walked. I did not know she was afraid. I was a girl of ten and did not know how much she had to fear.

I opened my eyes. The water had cooled, but I was still alone in the bright room of the bath. I thanked God for the new day and prayed for my continued success with the king. I rose from the water renewed.

I dried myself with the towels and put on the robe. I wondered when someone would come for me, but soon heard raised voices beyond the door.

"Where is she?" the great gasping voice of Hegai demanded.

Hathach remained calm. "She is in the bath."

"She must be attended in the proper way!" Hegai declared in angry tones.

"You are keeper of the women, not keeper of the queen," Hathach returned.

My heart filled with chaos and confusion. Hegai had permitted me to stay in the harem and so saved me from serving the soldiers. He had favored me above all the other women and created in my appearance a figure of desire. My success was his victory and his triumph. I would be a vessel of bitter waters to deny him that tribute.

But I had obeyed him in all things as a slave obeys a master. I was glad to be free of his authority.

"We are her keeper," Hegai thundered. "We made her queen!"

My heart divided as I listened to the two eunuchs argue, each in his own manner. And then I understood that I must flow as a gentle river between them.

"If it please the king's servants," I called out from behind the door, "I have need of them both."

And so Hathach asked a servant to take Hegai and his retinue to the room for dressing. They waited for me there, preparing all they thought necessary for the evening's presentation. While they worked, I walked up a grand staircase with Hathach to see the rest of my new home.

The queen's quarters had stood empty for four years. But all was spotless and unspoiled as if Vashti had been absent only an hour. I dared not tread on the beautiful carpets nor touch the silver vases, the ebony chests and benches, the molded reliefs of lions and ibex colored with lapis lazuli and golden glaze. I dared not taste the sweets laid out in ivory lotus blossom bowls.

For I knew Vashti was watching.

We passed through a room for dining with cushions and low tables to seat twenty in comfort. Painted finger bowls lined a shelf against one wall, and tapestries with pictures of ripe fruit hung on all the others. I could not imagine sitting in the place of the hostess here.

The room for dining opened into a music room. I admired the selection of instruments resting on a carpeted dais—the santur and the kamancheh—and I ventured to rap my fingers on the skin of the tombak.

"Would the lady wish to play herself?" Hathach asked.

"I do not have that skill," I laughed, plucking the string of the santur.

"You have only to ask," he replied, "and I shall summon an instructor." I felt my heavy heart lift with joy, as if a pinpoint of sunlight had found its way through a cloud-covered sky.

I entered the queen's gilded chamber, astonished to see it appointed with a splendor equal the king's chamber. The violet and azure carpets, the golden curtain rods, ebony furnishings and carved moldings washed with a glaze of lapis and gold leaf, the glided posts at each corner of the mattress, satin cushions that shone like jewels, a washing basin of gold-flecked black marble: the room lacked no item of luxury anyone could imagine.

I stepped through an open doorway, just beyond the mattress, into a wast wardrobe room. Here the eunuch Hegai awaited me. The flesh of his face burned red with rage.

He held in his two hands a gathering of glimmering fabric so delicate, it looked like stars caught in a net of spun sugar.

"The king himself sent this!" Hegai stamped his foot and pointed at Hathach. "You planted the idea in him!"

I looked at Hathach for explanation.

"The king has sent his mother's veil," he offered, without revealing if it was by his own suggestion.

"You wished to cover her beauty!" Hegai accused, his small eyes narrowing into thin slits. "So that none could admire the work of our hands!"

I looked upon the eunuch who was king of the harem. His station was slighted in the sight of Hathach. Though I did not understand the situation, I knew that Hegai must be calmed lest the blood burst forth from his great bulk and end his days.

"Sir," I intervened, gliding across the scarlet carpet to where the keeper of the women stood. "The king himself has admired the work of your hands. If His Highness has decreed that I be covered by this veil, he must have some purpose for the request. You are weary and worn. I would be pleased for you to rest on this mattress while I am readied for the feast. And I would be pleased if you would make a request of some wine and other refreshment while you take your ease."

I had never spoken at such length to Hegai in all my days with him. I had never spoken at such length to anyone. I smiled at each eunuch in turn before moving into the wardrobe where the attendants waited.

I was fed and oiled, my hair brushed and decorated with jeweled ornaments. I was dressed in a robe of amethyst silk embroidered with gold lotus blossoms. Golden pins in the shape of pomegranates held together a cloak of thick violet velvet encrusted with a thousand pearls and precious stones. They placed the golden

154

crown of the kingdom on my head, over the flowing veil of the queen, which allowed me to see without being seen.

After many hours, I emerged from the wardrobe. I presented myself for Hegai's approval as he reclined on the mattress with a bowl of sugared pistachios. Hathach had left the room and Hegai was himself again.

He summoned his attendants, the two young eunuchs, to help him rise from the mattress. He clung to them, first bowing low and then kneeling before me. My heart cried out in objection to such obeisance. But I sealed my mouth shut and received the reverence due to a queen.

"Do not forget those who have seen you to this day," he whispered. "Do not forget those who may continue to serve you."

Hathach waited for me in a small receiving room attached to the bedchamber. Two of the king's guard stood with him, assigned as my escorts to take me to the banquet hall.

I went to the king this second time without wine. I was no longer a concubine in the costume of Ishtar.

I was the queen.

And I was not afraid.

Men and women crowded the banquet hall, all dressed in rich garments and eager for the king to distribute the wedding gifts. The company grew silent at my entrance. The king rose from his place, a table elevated upon the dais where the musicians played the previous night. He wore a short tunic beneath a gold embroidered white robe that was open in the front. I looked at his massive legs, as strong as tree trunks, and his powerful arms, as muscular as those of a quarry worker. His face was as beautiful as the full moon and his fingers as long and sensitive as a master sculptor. My heart pounded and my flesh stirred to be near him again. He came to greet me and took my hand.

"Behold!" the king declared to the company. "I am Xerxes, the great king, the king of kings, king in this great earth far and wide! I am king by the favor of the great God Ahura Mazda who created this earth and made Xerxes king. And now I, Xerxes the son of Darius, proclaim this woman my queen: Queen Esther who is both beautiful and obedient and a fitting consort for the king of kings."

He bowed to me and I to him. The crowd clapped and called out their good wishes. The king bent his head to my ear.

"Your beauty must remain veiled to all but me. This is my wish and command."

"I am your obedient servant," I replied, taking my place next to the king and casting my gaze over the crowd.

There, in the midst of the court officials, I saw the face of Mordechai.

His beard was sparse and the turban of fine white linen had grayed. His brow had paled and his cheek was hollow. He sat among many yet he sat alone.

Our eyes could not meet through the veil. He did not dare glance in my direction. But I felt his heart look at me with longing. My flesh began to crawl as if a thousand vermin fed upon it. I wept bitter tears my cousin could not see. I whispered words of love he could not hear.

Twenty

When I gained the king's favor, I did not disclose my relation to Mordechai. He had not forbidden me to speak of him as my foster father. But my face had revealed my heart to Puah, who had shown me how easy it was to guess the truth of my people and my descent. And so I held my tongue, lest others come to know that Marduka the treasury official was a Jew.

During my year of beauty treatments, Puah often told tales of my glorious future with the king. I listened with only one ear until she pointed out that the king's favorite would be permitted to summon friends and family to visit my quarters. I imagined a reunion with Mordechai as the occasion of my greatest happiness. We could not be bound in marriage, but our hearts would be as one. Even if I slipped in my discretion and our heritage became known, surely none—I reasoned—would penalize the king's favorite and her relation, a loyal servant to the king.

I was a foolish girl in those early days, never considering how we might shrink away from each other in the knowledge that I belonged to another man. But once I became queen, I saw that I could not face my beloved. I could not bear for him to look at me with eyes that knew my flesh had given and received pleasure in the arms of another. And so I chose to keep my relation to Marduka the treasury official a secret, fearing that if the king or my servants knew, they might try to surprise me with a visit from him. Queen Esther could have no reason to request a private audience with Marduka the treasury official, and Marduka—should he choose to keep a secret of our kinship—had no authority to request a private audience with the queen. I did well to hide the truth, because in doing my cousin was shielded from potential enemies who might have sought to do him harm if his status was elevated.

The eunuch came to me one morning during my second month as queen. I was alone in the music room practicing the santur, when Hathach approached with great distress on his face.

"Do not stop!" he urged, as my fingers grew still. "Keep playing so none can hear me," he added in a whisper.

I plucked the strings in no particular pattern. Playing even a simple tune required my full attention as I was not yet accomplished.

"I have just spoken with a treasury official," Hathach began. "His name is Marduka the Babylonian."

My heart fluttered like the wings of a wild falcon trapped in a hunter's bag. My face flushed and my throat grew parched. I struggled for air, and my labored breath echoed louder in my ear than the vibrating santur strings. Sorrow and longing pressed behind my eyes like a gathering storm. But I summoned all my courage to remain calm, and wrapped myself in the shroud of a queen's dignity. As the eunuch spoke, I bent my head toward his whisper, avoiding his eye so he could not read my secrets.

"This Marduka sits in the king's gate all day and half of the night," Hathach continued. "I have made inquiries and learned that he has been at court as long as the King himself: he came to Susa when Xerxes was crowned. He is one of the king's most trustworthy servants."

I feigned indifference. "I am sure the king's servants are all trustworthy."

"They are not." Hathach's whisper sank even lower. "The treasury official told me of a plot. A plot to take the king's life, and yours."

I heard the eunuch's words before I understood them, the bile burning in my stomach as I came to comprehend. My life was in danger and Mordechai, my beloved cousin, once my betrothed, had sought to save me. I gazed into the eunuch's dark eyes, waiting to hear more.

"Bigthan and Teresh," he whispered. "Do you know them?"

The names were not familiar. I shook my head.

"They guard the king's threshold until the soldiers come for the night."

At once I formed a picture of them in my eye. They looked as if they might be brothers, with their straight dark hair, high cheekbones, and small eyes.

"Marduka overheard them in the king's gate. They did not know he was hidden in another room and never guessed that someone in the king's court understood the language of Tarshish in which they spoke. But this Marduka seems to be a master of all the languages in the empire.

I was shocked to learn something about Mordechai that I did not know. But I realized that he had never spoke to me about his work. I was foolish to assume that because I held Mordechai in my heart, I knew everything about Marduka.

"He heard the two plotting death to King Xerxes," Hathach explained.

"Such a thing cannot be easy for two lesser eunuchs to accomplish," I observed.

"Marduka understood from what they said that one of far greater authority at court sat behind this scheme. The traitors referred to him only as the Elamite."

"Many of the king's court must come from Elam," I whispered.

"That is why Marduka sought me out. He could not go to the officers of the guards or the king's advisors: any one of them could be involved. But he followed the two in the night, to the house of Dumza, the perfumer, who is known to sell poison. Marduka fears the traitors intend to harm you and the king in the royal chamber."

I held my breath and saw a vision of the king's cup before me. "The king's wine!"

Hathach placed a finger upon his mouth.

"The day guards bring the king his wine before he retires," I whispered. "Sometimes he will have me share it."

Hathach nodded.

"But I cannot warn him," I lamented. "We both know I am forbidden to go to him unless he summons me."

When I had first learned of the strange rule I did not care. I could not imagine wanting to go to the king for any reason. I wondered if Vashti, who did as she pleased, went before the king whenever the mood took her.

But she was of royal descent. She was mother to the king's sons, his heirs. I had nothing to recommend me for a second chance if I displeased the king. If the king did not call for me, Hathach would have to find a way to prevent him from drinking the wine. Yet we both knew that saving the king this once would not be enough; the king would not be safe until the traitors were apprehended.

"If the plot is revealed when the wine is already poisoned," I suggested, "we would catch the traitors in their guilt." A thousand pins of fear stabbed my stomach. Anything could go wrong with this plan.

Hathach smiled, as pleased as a teacher whose student is making good progress.

I do not know how I endured the rest of the day. I could not eat. I could not sit. I could do nothing but wander from room to room, imagining all the flaws in my plan. The eunuchs could poison the king before he retired. The king might return to his chamber early, before I could warn him. He might not summon me at all that evening.

But none of my fears came to pass. Bigthan and Teresh had access to nothing other than the chamber wine. Hathach sent a servant to keep watch on the king's movements, to ensure he did not retire early. And the king had not grown weary of me in a month.

The day turned to dusk and it came time to prepare for my visit with the king. I summoned Hegai to assist me, and sent him a message that I wanted to appear as fresh and dew-kissed as the spring dawn. For I felt as old and dry as the dust from which my bones were made, the dust to which they would return.

The keeper of the women brought a robe woven of rose silk. The hem was edged with a border of silver flowers, embroidered in a thick brocade. He placed a gold ring in my nose and matching hoops in my ears. He arranged my long golden hair to flow behind my shoulders and placed a garland of pink roses on my head.

The ritual of dressing restored my calm and refreshed my courage, until Hegai asked me for the silver star of Ishtar. Apprehension crept into my heart. I was not sorry to lose the necklace and had not concerned myself with it since. Now I realized that if a thief could gain access to the king's chamber while we slept, a murderer would find no difficulty in doing the same.

"I have not seen it since my first night with the king," I confessed. "I left it on the table beside the mattress and when I awoke it was gone."

Hegai spluttered in anger. "One of the servants has stolen it! We shall insist that the rooms of the chamber attendants and guards be searched!"

Before Hegai could enact this plan, Hathach appeared to convey the king's summons.

I bade farewell to Hegai, assuring him that I would enlist help to find the star without raising an outcry throughout the palace. "It is better to keep such a matter as private as possible," I suggested, as he kissed my hand.

Hathach accompanied me down the stairs to the garden. He opened the door for me and the night air sent a tremor through my spine.

"The king will never seek to replace you after you render him this service," Hathach whispered. "Be sure to give credit to the treasury official. Marduka the Babylonian is deserving of the king's notice."

I grasped the eunuch's hand for a moment before turning to the guard who would take me to the king.

King Xerxes greeted me in the court outside the chamber. He wrapped his powerful arm around me, and complimented my appearance. He guided me through the door, speaking of dignitaries visiting from Egypt. And I already knew him well enough to realize that he looked forward to spending an hour or two recollecting the glory of his campaign in Egypt.

When we entered the chamber, my eyes fixed upon the wine jug at once, placed on the bedside table as it was every night. I began to tremble.

The king noticed my distress. "What troubles you, Queen Esther?"

I had to reveal the plot at once. "Your Majesty, word has come to me of a threat to your life."

The king's face flooded with darkness.

"A treasury official by the name of Marduka the Babylonian has overheard a plot to poison Your Majesty this night in this chamber."

The king followed my gaze to the wine vessel and grasped me. His grip on my shoulders was so tight, I feared he would crush my bones. "Who would do this!"

"The eunuchs who guard the threshold during the day," I replied in a whisper. "Bigthan and Teresh."

He turned and shouted towards the door. "Immortals!"

The two night guards rushed into the room, followed by four chamber attendants and one of the king's lesser advisors—the people positioned to attend the king, should he call for someone in the night.

"Seize the eunuchs Bigthan and Teresh!" he ordered, drawing himself up to his full height. His beard seemed to grow in length and even the locks of his flowing hair appeared to quiver in fury. "Bring them to me."

No one dared ask the king about his request, but I read fear and questioning in all their eyes.

The guards returned in a moment, each with a eunuch in his grasp. The king's advisor followed, a tall dark man in a cloak of white linen and a matching turban.

"A fine evening," the king observed to the eunuchs. They did not answer. "Would my loyal servants care for a cup of the king's choicest wine?" He strode to the table and poured the poisoned liquid into a golden cup. "Here," he said, thrusting the cup at one.

The eunuch slumped against the soldier who held him. The king grabbed a fistful of the eunuch's hair and held the wine up to his mouth until he begged for mercy.

I could not watch.

As I turned away, I saw the face of the second eunuch, pale with anger. I followed his glare to the king's advisor who did not appear to notice the eunuch's fury. His small dark eyes darted everywhere and seemed to see nothing.

The advisor pushed to the front and presented himself to the king with a low bow. "Your Majesty, might I be of assistance? Have these servants wronged you?"

"I have reason to suspect them of poisoning my wine."

One of the eunuchs began to protest. "It was not…"

"Seal their mouths or cut out their tongues," the advisor commanded, his jaw tight with controlled rage.

The guards drew their daggers and held them to the captives' mouths. The other followed suit.

The advisor turned back to the king, relaxing his face into a mask. As he bowed again, I noticed his stiff posture, strange in one who was not older than my cousin. He spoke in soft tones, but his measured words carried force.

"If it pleases Your Majesty, your servant requests a live chicken. We will get to the truth of this matter."

The king seemed relieved to have the advisor take charge. He nodded to one of his youthful chamber attendants, who ran from the room.

The attendant soon returned holding a chicken by its legs. It squawked and flapped and struggled to be set free. The advisor took the chicken and held it out to the king.

"Would Your Majesty care to do the test himself?"

"Let us see how this bird enjoys the king's wine," the king laughed. The advisor forced the chicken's gullet to open while the king poured in the wine, spilling much of it on to the precious carpet. In a minute the chicken shuddered and went limp. I ran to the alcove of the chamber pot to vomit.

"Lock away the traitors," the king commanded. "Tomorrow they die."

That night his lust was urgent and forceful, like a victorious warrior seizing the spoil.

Twenty-One

The two were to be hung from the gallows. When the king insisted that I watch the execution in his company, I did not dare object. But I wore a veil so I could shut my eyes without being seen.

Hathach escorted me to a balcony that overlooked the main court. I stood at the edge against a stone parapet, gazing down upon the place where I had first entered the palace a year ago, as a virgin of fourteen. But I no longer knew that girl and had already mourned her passing from my days.

The gallows rose high from the center of the courtyard. Several soldiers secured the ropes under the supervision of the lesser advisor. He was dressed in fine robes of somber gray and dark blue, and his turban stood almost as tall as the king's.

A clamor broke out behind me. I turned to see the king entering the balcony in the company of a loud group. Soldiers protected him from all sides and his seven chief advisors clustered around them. Attendants followed, carrying wine and cups, platters of fruit, fans against the heat of the day, blue-glazed ceramic finger bowls for washing, and towels. Several youthful attendants clad in loincloths—young Greeks, beautiful in form and swift of feet—stood ready to do the king's bidding.

The king did not notice me as his advisors made excuses for why they had not known of the plot. Each in his turn insisted that he could not be held responsible.

"We would need a spy to follow every attendant, soldier, and advisor at court!" one protested.

"And spies to follow the spies," added another.

The king's expression remained troubled as he walked to the edge of the balcony. "If you cannot be entrusted with the king's safety, we shall have to find others who can!" he rebuked. "Now there is a reliable man." He pointed to the advisor below. "While the rest of you dallied with dancing girls, he took action. He apprehended the traitors and proved their guilt."

"Haman son of Hammedatha is a man of action," one advisor agreed, looking over the balcony.

"He holds himself a stranger to us in our revelries," commented another.

"Not a man to enjoy his wine," a third laughed.

"Bring him here," the king ordered. "And call for the scribes who keep the record-book of the days."

A young attendant ran from the balcony to Haman in the courtyard below. The two hastened to the king's presence and the king welcomed Haman with exaggerated ardor.

Haman bowed low and then dropped to his knees. When he lowered his head his mouth spread in a strange expression as if his teeth clenched in pain beneath the surface of his smile.

"The king is grateful for your service to him," Memuchan said.

"It is my honor to serve," Haman replied. But his lips did not move and his voice was muffled. His face seemed no more than a molded relief.

"I suppose the men are all known to you?" the king asked.

Haman bowed to each of the higher-ranked advisors, one at a time, before casting his small, dark eyes upon me. Soon the entire group turned to me.

"My beautiful Queen Esther." I could not tell whether he greeted me or offered an introduction to the others. "But she has no lady companions to attend her," he observed, as if surprised. "A queen must have lady companions!"

I wanted no other companions than Freni, Vadhut, and Puah. But I held my tongue for fear the king would not look with favor on such a public display. I wished he had not raised this subject at such a time. But he was not one to restrain his tongue if he felt the urge to speak.

Haman bowed. "I would be pleased to offer the service of my own wife."

My heart groaned. I longed for my old friends; the wife of this man could not take their place.

"Send for her!" the king ordered as the ram horns sounded from the courtyard below. "Pour the wine."

The attendants on the balcony began filling the golden cups as soldiers led the two pale eunuchs across the courtyard to the gallows.

"They do not cry out," the king observed. 'So great is their guilt, they do not beg for mercy at the final hour."

"Haman had their tongues cut out," one of the Greek boys explained, "last night."

A smile spread over the king's face. He lifted his cup as if in a toast and laughed. "A fitting end for those who plot against me!"

"A fitting end!" several men echoed in agreement. I felt no sympathy for the traitors, yet my stomach churned at the brutality.

The king moved forward to the edge of the balcony and stood by my side. He placed one hand on my shoulder. His other hand held a wine cup that he lifted high, as if to signal someone below.

The two eunuchs were hoisted on to the platform and a rope was placed around each of their necks. My knees grew weak.

"This is their reward and their recompense," the king announced.

The advisors murmured in agreement and the king turned to me. "Let us ask Queen Esther what she would wish for those who deceive and disobey their king!"

The men grew silent as they waited for my response.

I knew that the king's question was not what it seemed. I could hear that his laughter reflected neither amusement nor drunkenness. He laughed in fear and in warning.

And so I came to know that however much this king favored me, I would always have to be watchful and wary of him. I must never give him reason to doubt my devotion.

"Your Majesty, I am only a woman," I began.

"And a good thing!" he roared to his men.

I waited for the laughter to stop.

The king raised his hand to them and silence reigned.

"I am only a woman," I continued, "and I know only this: my loyalty is to my king and my concern is for his comfort."

The king seemed surprised by my answer. For a long moment he said nothing, and then he raised his cup. "By Ahura Mazda," he proclaimed, "here is a woman fit to be queen!"

He drank deep cup and drained his cup. His men nodded in agreement and followed his example.

169

The ram horns blew again. I turned away and closed my eyes. But the king lifted the veil from my face and held my chin between his fingers, forcing me to look upon the courtyard. His soft laughter fell into my ear, as if he enjoyed the violation of a woman's heart more than that of her body.

I will never cleanse my memory of what I witnessed that morning in the courtyard. When I recall the limp heads and twitching legs, I feel the rope burning on my own neck and my throat closing shut. I did not doubt the justice of the punishment. But I could not stand the sight.

When the two traitors lost their last breaths, the king kissed me. He removed a gold ring from his little finger and placed it on my middle finger. I never learned to cherish this gift and removed it whenever I was not in the king's presence.

The king turned to those assembled on the balcony: the advisors, attendants, and the scribes. Haman hovered behind them in the doorway with a woman who I guessed to be his wife. She looked much older than her lord and her long face was covered with fine lines. Her robe appeared to be as shabby as a kitchen servant's. When she saw me looking at her, she folded her arms over her chest and bowed her head.

The king cleared his throat and stood erect.

"I, Xerxes the king, proclaim this day that Queen Esther has saved my life. To those who insist that a royal consort must be of royal lineage, I command that they bow down to her as royalty."

The group clapped. The king raised his hand to silence them. And then he continued.

"By the favor of Ahura Mazda I smote the traitors and put them down in their place. Those who follow the law that Ahura Mazda has established will be happy in life and blessed in death. Attendants, pour the wine!"

The drinking continued for many hours. And when the king grew tired of the balcony, he moved the party into the banquet hall. He commanded that I sit near him with the scribes, and that I retell the events as they happened, so that the scribes might record the incident in the record-book of the days.

And so I told the story as I knew it then, excluding the truth of my kinship with Marduka the treasury official. But the king was too merry with wine to notice that it was he who had uncovered the plot.

Twenty-Two

After these things, King Xerxes promoted Haman son of Hammedatha. That very day he joined the ranks of the king's most trusted advisors. I stole glances at him throughout the evening after the execution. He seemed unlike any of the other advisors in manner or disposition, for he was quiet in the king's presence and did not partake of the wine. His posture was stiff and his face immobile, yet he listened with rapt attention to every drunken utterance from the king's mouth. I saw him offer the king delicacies from the table, but he exercised great restraint in filling his own plate.

"Your lord eats with moderation," I observed to his wife Zeresh who sat by my side at one point toward the end of the evening.

"He is not one to lose himself in gluttony or lust," she agreed. "His greatest pleasure is to serve the king." She folded her arms across her body and held her frayed black robe from either side. "Not all of the king's servants are so loyal."

My throat grew tight with fear. "Your lord must not hesitate to inform the king. If he knows of others who would betray the king, he should identify them at once!"

"Do not let worry wrinkle your pretty face," she assured me, her expression softening. "My lord Haman will protect the king with his own life."

"I am sure the king is grateful," I replied, as a servant slipped between us to offer Zeresh a cup of wine. She hesitated for a moment and bit her lip before shaking her head in refusal. Her hands, rough as those of a house servant, tightened their grip on her robe. I followed her eyes across the room to Haman, who gave a single nod in approval. Her drooping lips curved up into a thin smile.

I observed this exchange with interest. But she offered no explanation and I was soon distracted by the king. The room grew silent as rose. Too intoxicated to stand unaided, he steadied himself upon Haman's shoulder.

"This is a worthy advisor!" he announced, his words slurred but comprehensible.

The crowd began to murmur.

"Some of you may say he is not rich enough to sit at my table!" the king thundered. "But a man who knows how to serve his king is richer than all the princes in the land!"

The king's words were met with polite applause. Scanning the faces of the other advisors, I saw that they felt slighted by this praise of Haman. The king's implication was clear: while they had filled his ears with excuses for their failure, Haman had shown himself concerned for the king's welfare and made himself useful.

The king snapped his fingers for a cup and lifted it high. "In reward for your service to me, Haman the Elamite, I grant you fifty talents of silver, pepper from India, and an estate in Ecbatana!"

At this, the company cheered. The advisors made an effort to participate, lest the king's opinion of them fall any further. Haman rose in the midst of the commotion and bowed. I wanted to cry out that it was Mordechai who deserved such rich rewards. Haman had helped capture the traitors and supervised their hanging, but Mordechai had uncovered the plot! Yet I could do nothing more than applaud with the others. Such a protest would not advance

Mordechai's position and might cause me to lose favor in the king's eyes. I told myself to be patient, to wait for a more auspicious opportunity to speak on my cousin's behalf. I had another, more urgent concern. For I knew if I did not help Freni soon, it would be too late.

The king summoned me that night, not long before the dawn. He stood naked in his chamber holding the marble statue of Vashti in his hands. Raising the sculpture high over his head, he hurled it with great force against the stone wall. It smashed into a shower of rubble and dust. "She was disobedient and sour," he declared, waving his hand toward the fragments. "You are the true queen!"

My heart warmed at his declaration, but I remained uneasy. Even as Vashti's likeness lay shattered on the floor, her presence continued to haunt me.

The king flung himself on to the bed and reached for his cup.

"Enough with treachery and disobedience," the king cried. "Haman is right: I must rid my court of all traitors!"

"Your Majesty enjoys the loyalty of many," I observed, trying to temper his drunken misery.

The king sat up. "I can trust no one!" he shouted, and threw his cup across the room.

I sat on the bed and kissed his hand to soothe him. His anger turned to lust.

"Her beauty was nothing compared to yours," he murmured, toying with my hair. "I would give you half my kingdom for your favor."

"Half is not enough," I teased. I pulled away from him and rose to stand over him like an imperious goddess. It was a foolish game I played to fuel his desire and give him greater pleasure for his conquest.

"Name your price," he returned.

It was my custom to answer that I desired nothing more than the pleasure he gave me. Such were the words he loved to hear. But on this occasion, as I gazed upon his splendid form, I summoned my courage to ask for something more.

"The gift that shall win my favor is the freedom of a virgin in the harem."

Drunken laughter spilled from his throat and resonated throughout the room. He was amused to have a woman ask for something other than gold and silver. "Come cover me with your beauty," he said, running his powerful hands up and down his bare chest, "and I shall grant your request in the morning."

I went to him my heart filled with joy and my flesh with desire.

When we rose the next day and the attendants entered the chamber, I fell to my knees and thanked the king for his kindness in granting the release of my friend. His baffled expression revealed that he remembered nothing of his drunken promise. But he did not deny it in front of the others. And so I asked one of the servants to make sure Hegai was informed at once, requesting only a brief farewell for myself. I knew Freni would not be safe until she left the palace.

I saw Freni for but a moment's embrace, in the courtyard garden in the queen's quarters. She was wild-eyed with joy, and her beauty blossomed like a tulip in the sun. I put my arms around her and promised that I would always hold her thus in my heart. "May God's light shine upon you all your days," she replied. And then she was gone.

In the weeks following the execution of Bigthan and Teresh, the king's spirits fell. He was suspicious of anyone who claimed to serve his interest, save Haman. I heard an endless flow of praise for the Elamite's wise advice, competency, and lack of self-interest. The king had granted permission for Haman to build a network of informants throughout the palace, to catch traitors before they could reach the king. He bestowed upon Haman the authority of judge and executioner, and granted permission for the gallows to remain standing as a permanent fixture in the courtyard.

The king's new advisor disturbed me, though I did not see him often after the execution. I could not discern any tangible reason for my dislike of Haman. But I feared the king had placed too much of his authority into the hands of one man. Yet because it was not my place to question my lord on matters more important than his choice of wine for the evening, I held my tongue.

While the king grew more distrustful of everyone around him by day, at night his ardor for me only increased. He summoned me to his chamber every evening and pierced my flesh with his passion. Three or four times he would come to me like a lion upon its prey. And I learned not to cry out, for my fear and pain only increased the heat of his loins.

When he was spent, he became a different man. He undressed me and brushed his lips over my breasts until I moaned with a pleasure I had never known. His hands caressed me in long, gentle strokes like a sculptor smoothing clay. My body opened to him like a rose in bloom, each soft petal unfolding until the final burst of color and fragrance.

After, I would close my eyes and return to the days of quiet contentment in Mordechai's household. I drifted from what was to what might have been. In my imaginings, Mordechai was my husband, but he gained the king's muscular form and resolute manner. He made me his and allowed no other man to look upon me.

To ease my shame I turned to memories of Freni, who I longed to see again almost as much as Mordechai. I had received no word of her since she had left the harem, but I guessed that her father had given her in marriage soon after her return. I pictured her, a treasured wife with a wife's work to occupy her hours. I saw her lips plump from her lord's kisses, her wide brow smooth with contentment, her large dark eyes sparkling with joy for the child growing inside her. I knew she would love her child as my own mother had loved me.

Certain of Freni's happiness, I would drift into sleep. I slept deeper in those days than I had since I was a young child.

But one night, the king embraced me and did not let me go. I suffocated in his grip, my head crushed to his chest. I breathed deep breaths and waited for his arms to loosen with sleep, but he held me firm for many minutes.

My blood ran cold and my body began to tremble. I tried to imagine I was a child again, seeking comfort in my mother's arms. But all that came to me were long-forgotten memories of my last hour with her.

She lay upon a mat in heavy labor. The midwife and our house-servant, Ninsun, knelt by her legs to assist her. I was allowed to stay and wipe the sweat from my mother's streaming brow.

We sat for hours while she struggled. She bit her lip to hold back her cries until blood trickled down her chin. She panted and groaned while the midwife examined her. I saw the fear in the midwife's eyes and heard her whisper to Ninsun.

"The baby's feet are pushing into the birth canal first," she said.

"We must find her lord Avihail," Ninsun replied.

I did not know then what they did not tell me: that a woman and child cannot survive such a birth. I did not know that they sought my father so that she could die with the prayers of her lord in her ear.

I became aware of a great noise from the street, a thousand horses, an uproar like that of the Babylonian New Year's celebration, when the people paid homage to the great golden statue of Marduk. I looked from the midwife to Ninsun, wondering if we had forgotten a festival. The two women seemed to grow even more fearful.

"Go see what is happening," Ninsun told me. "But do not leave the gate."

"See if your father is coming," the midwife added.

I ran out the door and across the courtyard. The noise was deafening and the sky was dark. Dust filled my lungs and settled in my eyes. I opened the door of the gate just enough to squeeze through without letting go of the handle.

The street was a river of blood. Bodies lay stabbed and trampled in the wake of Xerxes' army. The Persian horsemen were gone, but several soldiers remained behind, picking over the corpses for spoil. A man lay at my feet, blood and tissue spilling from his crushed skull onto our gatepost. It was my father.

I saw and I did not see.

I lay in the king's suffocating arms and wept for all that had remained hidden in my heart. I wept with the eyes of a ten year-old girl who could not save her parents.

The king's chest grew wet from my sorrow, but he continued sleeping and soon rolled away from me. I could not close my eyes all night.

Alone in the garden the next afternoon, I recalled all that I could of my father's strength and goodness. And I pledged, in his memory, to be a daughter he would have been proud to claim. Calmness came upon me and I closed my eyes.

I woke to see Hathach arriving from the king's palace. He always took care to leave me undisturbed in the garden, as if he understood my need for a place of solitude. And so I was surprised to see him approach.

"Come sit." I tapped the golden bench.

"Queen Vashti required me to kneel before her," he observed.

"I have no royal blood," I reminded him.

Hathach smiled.

"You have been a good servant," I said, gazing at his large, truthful eyes and his ageless dark skin. I knew he had long since forgotten his people and his descent. They had removed his manhood and sold him into slavery. I was his only family now.

"I am sorry to disturb you," he apologized. "You are looking unwell; might something be ordered for your relief?"

I declined his offer and he leaned toward me. "Haman has accused Memuchan of treason with the Greeks," he explained in a low voice. "The advisor is to be executed."

"Memuchan has been a favorite in the court many years!" I objected, a chill running through my heart. I did not know Memuchan well, but I could not believe him capable of deceiving the king.

"The king begins to doubt the trustworthiness of all his courtiers except Haman son of Hammedatha," Hathach whispered. "Some say he would sit on the throne himself, but they dare to speak thus only because they do not value their lives."

I had known Hathach for no more than two months. But I trusted him. He held no faith in anything he could not see with his own eyes. He did not overstate matters. He watched and listened with an open heart. He repeated nothing that he did not believe to be true and necessary.

I was sure that the suspicion he had voiced was his own. And I could not dismiss it.

We sat in unsettled silence. The summer had gone but the heat remained. Servants carried large jugs of water to cool the plants and trees each morning, and still the edges of the jasmine vines grew brown with thirst. The birds hid from the midday sun. I heard nothing but Hathach's breathing and my own. We might have been the last two creatures alive in the world.

But the specter of the king's weakness sat between us.

I remembered Puah's story of the false Smerdis and Darius, how a man who was not the rightful heir might aspire to be king through force and cunning. I believed that Haman would accuse the innocent to promote his own advancement, and even remove all who stood between him and the throne. But Xerxes was the king of the Persian Empire, grandson of the great King Cyrus, a fierce warrior and a resolute leader, a man with little tenderness in his heart, the man whose army had crushed my father. Such a man, I reasoned, could not fall prey to a schemer.

The door leading to the king's palace began to open. Hathach jumped to his feet. He could not be seen sitting next to the queen, as if he were her equal.

The guards moved forward but the visitor pushed past them: Zeresh, the wife of Haman. She was followed by an escort, a soldier from the king's personal guard.

Hathach bowed to the guest and nodded to the king's guardsman and the soldier, indicating that Zeresh was welcome to remain. The men withdrew from the garden and Hathach stood, waiting for me to dismiss him.

The king had urged me to accept the companionship of Haman's wife. Since the execution, not two days passed without a visit from Zeresh.

She was woman of forty with small squinting eyes that looked upon everything with suspicion. Her thin lips were always pursed with displeasure and the deep grooves running from either side of her long nose to her chin spoke of a life ruled by hardship and suffering. She clutched herself, her arms folded beneath her sagging breasts, whether she was sitting or walking. I knew she he had ten sons and one daughter but she never spoke of them. I pitied her, for she always seemed worn and unhappy.

I smiled as she approached, indicating that she might sit beside me on the golden bench. She bowed to me and then gave a pointed look at Hathach. I knew that she wished him to leave, but I did not dismiss him.

"May Ahura Mazda protect you," she declared, dropping herself down next to me. She smelled of camphor and stale goat's milk.

"I hope the day finds you well," I remarked, gazing on her profile.

"How can anyone be well in the midday heat?" she complained.

I knew that I should ask Hathach to send a servant for a cooling drink. But I did not wish to prolong her visit, for I was tired and troubled by the news of Memuchan's punishment. And so I remained silent.

"The king is well?" Zeresh asked, after a moment.

"His Majesty is well," I confirmed.

"Praise Ahura Mazda. My Lord Haman is well too."

"May your good fortune continue."

"Does the king speak of my lord?" she asked with more guile than pride. "Does he tell you that my lord works from dawn to dusk in his interest?"

She hoped to hear me speak of her lord's favor in the king's eyes. But since the king had fallen into a deep melancholy, he spoke little to me. I could not reveal the truth of his condition.

"Are you still warming his bed?" Zeresh probed when I did not answer. "They say his thirst is unquenchable."

My face grew hot with embarrassment. I gazed upon her hands which grasped her elbows. Her fingernails were broken and ragged. Her withered breasts sagged, sucked dry by eleven children.

Her black wool veil was so thin, she looked more like an ill-used servant than the wife of the king's chief advisor. I pitied her.

I could not know why she asked such bold questions. Perhaps she envied my youth and wished to fill her weary spirit with some of my vitality. Or maybe she was no more than her husband's agent, sent to gain my trust and knowledge of the king's mood and intentions. Perhaps Haman considered me a foolish girl that he could use to increase and solidify his power in the kingdom.

I was not that girl. But I decided to play the part for Zeresh. I would pretend to take her into my confidence, to admire her lord, and thereby learn more of his intentions. And even as I used her, I would lavish kindness and gifts upon her. I would bring some joy into her life.

"The king is very grateful to your lord for his services," I replied at last. And then I sent Hathach for a drink to cool my guest.

PART II

Twenty-three

It came to pass that the king commanded all the servants who sat in the king's gate to bow and prostrate themselves before Haman. From one year to the next the king grew to rely on Haman above all others. He never questioned the tales of treachery that Haman told or denied permission for any punishment that he recommended. Haman was said to have spies in every corner of the court and barracks: anyone might be in his pay. The gallows had becomes a permanent fixture in the courtyard, and Haman permitted none but himself to secure the ropes.

In matters of state, too, the king relied upon Haman's advice. When the Spartans sent an emissary for peace, Haman encouraged the king to reject the overture. When the Egyptians began to grow restless, Haman urged the king to appoint a new governor to employ brutal measures against those who spoke of sedition and their families. Haman cared nothing for building projects or agricultural improvements but each year urged the king to raise taxes still higher to enrich the coffers of the kingdom. In the king's nightly drunkenness I saw how little engaged he was with affairs of state or the intrigues of the court. He held more interest in his cup than his kingdom and it seemed he had relinquished the kingship to Haman in all but name.

And so the weeks and months passed from the eighth to the twelfth year of King Xerxes' reign.

In the four years since the king had taken me as his queen, I had learned much about court life—who should get gifts of coin, wine, and almond cakes, whose wives must be invited to parties, and how often such gatherings should be held. I became an expert at appeasing the king during his worst moments of gloom and, in happier times, at casting myself upon the waves of his joyful spirit. I learned to be watchful, even as my perfumed body succumbed over and over to the king's desire and grew familiar with his chamber. For it was not only Haman who frightened me. I could feel in my bones, in the lurking shadows, in the wind that blew over the marshes and across the wide plain from Chaldea to Susa, that the rage of Vashti never slept.

I remained, year after year, cloistered in the queen's chambers like a prisoner of the state. I was treated well, and remained the king's favorite. But I came to rely on others to be my eyes and ears. Hathach knew much of the king's daily disposition and charted his weakening authority. The eunuch often found excuses to speak with courtiers and officials, to learn who was in favor and who was bound for the gallows. Zeresh told me her version of her lord's triumphs. Puah, who lived as a servant in my apartment, kept me abreast of what was happening with the women of the harem and the children. Hegai watched the concubines who the king summoned from week to week, determining how they differed from me, in case I should consider some adjustment to my appearance or dress.

But even the most attentive informant could not reveal what my own heart neglected to tell me about the king.

One late winter afternoon in my fourth year as queen, I sat with Anatana on the balcony of my chamber. Looking down upon

the dormant garden for signs of the spring tulips, I recalled the yellow
tulip I had picked for my cousin Mordechai, so long ago, and how it
had been trampled in the dust. I wondered why, if God had wished
me to be my cousin's daughter instead of his wife, I still remembered
my hopes with such regret and longing. I found comfort in telling
myself that Mordechai and I had a sacred love. Ours was a love that
rose above the darkness of drunken nights, above the pleasures of my
hungry flesh yearning for the king's hot passion to work its will upon
me. Ours was a love as pure as Anatana's untainted heart.

And it was a love as barren as the garden below.

Anatana soon grew impatient with my silent contemplation
and began to sing. I turned back and looked at her with fresh eyes.
She was almost ten years old: in a few years she would be a woman.

I found great diversion in my visits with Anatana, who came
to my quarters every afternoon. I dressed her in clothing fit for a
king's daughter and braided jewels in her hair. We played games and
I indulged her fondness for honey cake, feeding her morsels dipped
into sweet wine as if she were a newborn chick. She climbed into my
lap and showered me with kisses. Her dark curls danced like Vadhut's
and her big eyes reminded me of Freni. Her laughter was sweeter
than the sound of the santur. I no longer wondered who Anatana's
mother might be and gave that title to myself.

But the king frowned when I spoke of her, often changing
the subject to that of his son, Artaxerxes, whom he had not seen since
Vashti's banishment. He did not forbid Anatana's visits to me, but he
did not listen with favor when I hinted of my desire to remove her
from the nursery to my quarters as my adopted daughter. The child's
position could not change without the king's approval, yet I did not

dare ask his permission outright for fear he would deny it. Perhaps, I reasoned, he would look with more kindness on my love for Anatana if he knew her. Perhaps he might even come to be fond of her, his own daughter.

And so one evening, when the king summoned me to join him for an early meal, I brought the child to meet her father.

We dressed with care in matching robes of yellow silk, pink slippers on our feet, and pearls around our necks. I tied gold ribbons into the child's hair and instructed her to say little and defer to the king in everything. We were a picture of charm and grace, according to both Puah and Hathach, and neither foresaw any harm in taking the child with me. No one knew what the king himself did not admit.

Anatana and I left the queen's quarters hand-in-hand. She skipped over the smooth stone floor of the colonnade between my apartment and the king's. I could feel my beauty renewed through her youthful charm. I was young again, and joyful in the child's exuberance. When I saw the king waiting in the distance, my heart skipped like Anatana's little legs. But before I could draw close enough to meet his eyes, he turned in haste and retired. He sent a guard to tell me that his inclination had changed and he would seek the company of a concubine instead.

I wept in Puah's arms that night, not for myself, but for the child whose father did not care to know her, who would condemn her to a life of servitude. Puah suggested that the king was jealous of my affections and did not wish to share them with anyone, even a child. And so I never again spoke of her to the king.

A year passed and as I sat with Anatana in my chamber, I saw that she would soon be put to work as a harem servant or a kitchen hand. Perhaps I might keep her from laboring under a hard taskmaster by requesting that she wait upon me in my quarters. The king could not object to that, I reasoned.

I gazed upon her pretty face and began focusing on her song. The words described a woman's longing for a lover well endowed by the gods and able to satisfy her desire. My face burned with shame for the person who had taught a child such lyrics.

Anatana interrupted herself, sensing my discomfort. "Do you not like my new song?"

"You have a lovely voice," I replied, avoiding any criticism of the song. But as I looked upon her innocence I knew I must say something more. "I am surprised to hear you sing such a grown-up song," I added.

Taking my words as a compliment, her face blossomed with pride. She jumped up from the cushion and continued the song, accompanying herself with a suggestive dance. I watched as she swayed her hips, ran her palms over her chest, and then began touching her most private parts.

"Stop!" I cried out, in fear and fury, pulling the little girl's hands away from herself.

"But Asabana taught it to me!" She began to weep, distraught by my displeasure.

I held the girl close to me and then kissed her tears away. "Asabana should not be teaching such a dance to one who is only nine years old," I explained as we sat down on the cushions again.

"She wants me to be a dancing girl," Anatana boasted, "but the keeper of the women says I should be a priestess in the temple of Ishtar and the king would like that best."

The child's words tore at my heart like a lion ripping the life from its prey. Anatana was the daughter of my heart and I the only mother she had ever known. I could not consign her innocent body to a life of serving lustful men. I could not lose her.

My eyes grew dim and everything faded before me but the memory of my mother's white face in the darkness of her passing.

She stared up at me in wide-eyed terror, as if I were Lamashtu or Lilith. "Mother," I wailed, warm tears bleeding from the wells of my eyes as matter oozed from my father's skull. I saw she did not know me anymore. Her body shuddered and quaked as if a strong poison was rushing through her veins. Her eyes rolled up in her head. She began to shriek like a druj.

"Ishtar! Save the child!" Ninsun called out, her hopeless prayer swallowed in the vortex of my mother's deafening cries.

"Curse your useless gods!" the midwife retorted, her hands deep inside my mother's body as she tried to tear the monster free. "They are both lost: the head is trapped in the womb."

"No!" I shouted at the midwife who had forgotten me until that moment. "You have to save her."

"Hadassah! Go into the alcove and do not come out!"

And so I did not see my mother at the end, but I heard her cries grow weak and shallow, until the last whimper, her final plea for God's mercy as she passed from this world.

"I cannot lose you to such a fate!" I clung to Anatana, who had found her way into my lap. I would not let her go, even when the nursemaid came to fetch her. Hathach sent for Puah to soothe my fears and coax the child from my arms.

"She is not a baby," Puah observed. "You are upsetting her."

I pulled away from Anatana enough to see that Puah was right. The girl had not struggled to free herself from my grasp, but her face was stained with tears and she looked at me in fear.

I wiped my eyes and kissed her cheeks. "You are a brave girl," I told her, "and I promise to be more cheerful tomorrow."

Shaken, Anatana tried to smile. I held her hand for a moment longer than I should have, and then she was gone.

"Asabana is planning to take her," I explained to Puah and Hathach when all the others had left. I stood and paced the chamber, the golden bands around my ankles chinking like a songbird. But I stiffened at the melodious sound of these gifts from the king, the shackles of my bondage. "If Hegai does not give her up to Ishtar first!"

"Much worse could happen to her," Puah observed.

I stopped my pacing to stand before the old woman, stooped from so many years of labor. She had grown a little rounder in my service and the grooves of her face had softened. But she had long since been broken beyond repair.

"I would rather she work in the laundry than lay her body upon an altar for strangers to use," I declared.

"She is not your child," Hathach reminded me in gentle tones. "The king can do with her as he pleases."

I looked into the eunuch's troubled dark eyes and read in them the king's own despair. He had never spoken of a desire to have a child by me. He had never asked me why I remained barren. I had always assumed that he preferred to use me for pleasure rather than breeding. I had been content in this belief. Once, while I was yet untouched, I had longed to give Mordechai strong sons. Now I wanted no child other than Anatana.

"I have turned the king against the child," I realized aloud, growing weak in my knees. "I have turned him against her," I wept, "because I have not given him a child of my own."

"Perhaps it is time," Puah suggested.

I gazed from one expectant face to the other, unable to comprehend how my two closest servants could not know that I was barren. I sunk to my mattress in shame and buried my head in my hands.

"I have done nothing to prevent it," I confessed.

"Nothing?" Puah gasped.

"Hegai has told us otherwise," Hathach explained. "He has said it is your own will. We believed he had provided the means."

"I am not the goddess he imagines me to be," I wept. The room was silent.

"It can be fixed," Puah announced after a few moments, coming to my side and putting her arm around my shoulders. "And when you have a child of your own, perhaps he will give you Anatana too."

I looked up at the old woman, always so ready to comfort me. And I smiled at her, thanking God in my heart for what He had allowed me to keep.

"We must get to work," Puah told Hathach. "We need a mixture of equal parts frankincense, oil of northern olives, fresh dates, and barley beer. She must squat over the perfume burner. After that she will be as fertile as the black earth and the king's seed will take."

We followed Puah's treatment for a week, telling the king that I was indisposed. Puah spoke incessantly of giving the king an heir. Once or twice Hathach reminded her that the king would face opposition in naming a successor borne to a woman who was not of royal blood. But I did not listen to either of them. I did not even imagine a child of my womb as a creature I would cherish and love. Night after night I sat over the perfume burner for one purpose alone: to retain the king's favor that I might save Anatana from her fate.

When I returned to the king's chamber, I told him of my desire to bear his child. My words echoed in the shadows of my heart and I was not sure if I had said them. But the warrior's face softened with pleasure and his passion rose as if renewed. I lay beneath him and imagined other things: a field of yellow tulips, the wind rippling through river reeds, my mother's shawl, the waters of Babylon.

Soon my monthly bleeding failed and my breasts swelled. The king rejoiced at the news.

Twenty-four

When I came to be with child, the creature gnawed at my insides and broke my spirit. I never knew if I was hungry or sick and I kept down little of what I ate. Fevered dreams filled my sleep. Night after night a lion monster tore through my womb and devoured my flesh, leaving only my bones in the dust of a barren valley. Melancholy and exhaustion filled my days. The santur rested untouched in the music room, and I did not call for Anatana to visit me. Once, I asked Puah to take her some cakes and explain I was not well. When Puah returned with no greeting of good health or token of affection, I told myself that the plan to save Anatana was foolish: she was already lost to me.

The king was happy about the child, but he found little pleasure in my lethargic company. He called for me less often and then not at all. I doubted that he had ever loved me, and condemned myself for caring. I wondered if Mordechai knew of the pregnancy and assumed that I was content with my lot, or that I forgotten him. I longed to be a young girl again, innocent of desire and darkness. My courage faltered and I wished that I had perished with my parents.

One afternoon I sat in the courtyard garden with these sorrowful reflections. The tulips were ready to blossom, their heavy heads supported by long slender stalks that stretched up toward the light. I turned my face to the sky, imagining that I, too, was a flower nourished by the sun's warmth. My eyes closed for a moment and then fluttered open again as if I had woken after a sleep of many weeks. I saw everything in great detail: the henna-colored fingertips of the hands clasped in my lap, a tiny water stain on the sleeve of my blue silk robe, a fissure in the carnelian glazed tile at my feet, the beads of perspiration on the smooth upper lip of Hathach's dark skin. I saw the taut raised muscles of the eunuch's cheeks, his puckered frown, furrowed brow, and the fine lines of concern ringing his eyes.

"Puah has prepared a meal for you with her own hands," he told me.

"Tell her I am too ill to eat."

"You will harm yourself," he protested.

"Let me sleep in the sun a little longer," I begged. "I need rest more than food."

The eunuch rose, bowed, and left. He returned a few minutes later with cushions and a blanket.

I slept a dreamless sleep. When the courtyard grew dark, I woke refreshed. I asked for a bath and two servants to attend me. They washed my hair and oiled my skin until I glistened. After this I dismissed them so that I might examine my body for signs of the child. It did not yet show, but as I looked down at my swollen breasts, my loins grew warm with desire. Hungry for the king's passion, against my will and without shame, I knew the goddess still stirred in me.

Puah knocked at the door, urging me to come eat. I covered myself with a soft cotton robe and followed her without complaint to the dining room where she had spread a feast on a low table. The odor of the food caused my stomach to rise in rebellion. I could not sit.

Puah frowned. "The child may be from the king's seed," she observed, "but it is a gift from God. You must care for him and for yourself. It was not for starvation that you were brought from Babylon and made queen."

Her harsh words brought hot tears to my eyes, but I did not reproach her for speaking the truth. I had indulged in my sorrows too much and too long, like the king and his cup.

I took my place before the feast and began with a morsel of salted flat bread. Puah looked on with satisfaction. But before I could swallow the first bite, a eunuch entered to announce an unexpected call from Zeresh. She had been away visiting a sick relative somewhere in the west and I had not seen her in two weeks. I nodded to the eunuch.

The years had brought no relief to my discomfort in the company of Haman's wife. I had long suspected that she came at her husband's bidding, to learn what she could from me. But the abuse she suffered at the hands of her husband seemed so terrible, that my pity for her grew with each tale of woe. Even after amassing great riches, Haman allowed her no more than one robe at a time. All of the household cooking and cleaning fell to her, with help from no one but her own daughter. She had borne eleven children, getting up after each birth to serve her lord his meal. He and their ten sons never left her enough to eat and she was forbidden to drink wine because it was too costly. Sometimes he beat her.

I tried to bring some comfort to her life, to ease her heavy burdens. But Haman did not let her keep any pretty thing I gave her, even a simple veil, insisting that it be sold or given to one of her sons' wives. She did not dare accept my offer of a beauty treatment for her parched skin, lest her husband's anger be roused, and she would take no refreshment from me other than a cool drink in the heat. I was cautious to say nothing more than I would want repeated before Haman, but I was sorry for her misery.

Zeresh swept into the room, her black robe and long veil swirling around her like a cloud of dust. She dismissed her escort with an impatient wave of her hand, indicating that she took offense at having to stay below while the eunuch sought permission for her to enter.

"I hear the king is well," she commented, lowering herself to the floor cushions without waiting for an invitation. She squinted at the untouched meal spread over the table between us and then fixed her eyes fixed on a silver wine vessel.

I filled an alabaster cup with wine and held it out to her. Though I did not expect her to accept, I did not want to appear inhospitable. "I hope you found your kinswoman in better health."

To my surprise, Zeresh snatched the cup and brought it to her thin cracked lips, hesitating for a moment before she drained the contents in one thirsty gulp. "That one is no kinswoman of mine." Her jaw protruded as she frowned. "I made the trip at my lord's bidding. He threw the pur before the fire and the magi told him I should go."

"It is an act of special kindness to visit the sick," I noted, trying to soothe her anger and resentment. I refilled her cup and again she drank all that I gave her without pausing for breath, slamming the empty cup on the table.

"Sick in spirit, not in body." The old woman smacked her lips and folded her arms over her stomach as was her habit. Her hollow checks seemed to rise as if she would smile, but her mouth did not lift from its downward curve. "You are not eating," she remarked, jerking her sharp chin toward a succulent stew of ostrich meat and rice.

"I am not well," I confessed. "But please be my guest and partake."

"You have the sickness of early pregnancy." She removed a little glass jar of red liquid from her sleeve. "A friend sends this to you: it will help."

My eyes widened in astonishment for her knowledge of my condition. She curled her lip in disdain for my ignorance.

"The king confides in my lord as if they were brothers," she explained with pride.

"Yes, of course," I whispered. I should have known that the king kept nothing from Haman. Still, I was troubled that Zeresh knew of my discomfort, which I had never expressed to the king or to anyone other than Hathach and Puah. Perhaps she had made the assumption from her own experience.

I changed the subject to regain my composure. "Please have something to eat,"

"Just a little more wine to ease my thirst." her voice was hoarse with longing as if she had gone long days with nothing to drink. "Just a little more," she repeated, "but first let me see you drink this gift to restore your appetite."

Her eagerness caused me to hesitate. "Please tell me who I might thank for this considerate gift, if it is not from you."

Her eyes narrowed even further. "A friend," she muttered. "Someone who is concerned about you from a distance." She raised the cup to her lips.

As I took the jar, an image of Hutana, ill from the abortion wine, floated before me. The liquid grew hot in my hand and the smell of burning flesh rose into my nostrils. I put the jar on the table and inspected my fingers, untouched though they smarted in pain. My baby cried out from the womb: a long, low wail of despair.

I would not harm my child, my gift from God. I would cherish him for the sake of my parents, so their memory could be honored from one generation to the next, from me to their grandchild. It was time, too, for me to bury my regrets and melancholy, to find my way back into the king's heart. This I knew I must do for the sake of the women in the harem and my baby, if not for myself.

Zeresh looked from the jar of poison to the wine. I reached for the silver vessel, but before I could pour another cup, she snatched it from me and poured her own. I watched in silence as she poured and drank, poured and drank. Soon the corners of her eyes seemed to soften and her arms fell slack by her sides. Slurred words came spilling from her mouth like grains of sand shaken from a traveler's cloak.

"I saw my lord tonight," she whispered, as if confessing a secret. "He had a purse of silver for the magi…always running to the temple…I followed him."

I nodded, hoping she would continue.

"The temple keeper took his purse…knelt before the fire basins. I watched in the shadow of a column…no one knew I was there! A magus lit the fire basins…flames shot up. Another drank haoma…chanted incantations over a jar of pur stones marked for months and days…drew a magic circle in white powder on the ground…blessed my lord's hands…hands that would beat me if he saw me there…a sight they keep us wives from that I saw…his white robes glowing red in the firelight…my lord took the pur in his fist…kissing his fingers more than he kissed me in all our days…threw the pur into the circle…threw and gathered and threw and gathered ten times until the magus named an auspicious combination…almost a year away…I ran to you before he caught me to deliver…

The stream of words faded into senseless sounds, flickered, and then stopped like a candle flame snuffed by the wind. She slumped against the cushions, her chin on her chest. A loud, gasping snore escaped from her nose, hidden beneath the veil that had fallen forward over her face. I understood, now, why her husband refused her wine, why she had always taken nothing but fruit juice.

I rose to my feet and crept toward the shrouded black form, intending to lay her on the cushions where she might sleep in comfort. I had seen the king after a drunken sleep when he could remember nothing of what he had said or done the night before. So, too, I told myself, might Zeresh forget her indiscretion in revealing that she had spied on her lord. But I could not send her home in a drunken stupor, knowing she was sure to receive a beating.

I eased the shrouded black form on to her back. Her veil fell away from her neck and I noticed a glint of silver. Curiosity took hold of me; I unpinned the top of her robe, pulling a pendant out from its hiding place between her sagging breasts. Once again I held the star of Ishtar.

Twenty-five

While Zeresh slept, I tucked the silver star back into her robe. I stood for a moment, trembling as fear flooded my heart. Haman had stolen the necklace. He could have gained access to the king's chamber through a eunuch, or even bribed a night guard and entered himself. But why would he have taken such a risk to obtain this gift for a wife he despised? I had always been wary of her company and her constant questions. From the first I had suspected that she came to me on her lord's bidding. But perhaps the bond between Haman and Zeresh was closer than I had imagined.

Yet if the necklace was her price for delivering the red liquid, he would punish her for returning without evidence that I had taken it. And so I poured the liquid into a wine glass and tucked the empty vial back into her sleeve. Then I went to search for Puah.

I could not find her anywhere in my quarters, from the servants' rooms to my wardrobe. None of the other servants had seen her. Hathach, too, had disappeared. I could not recall a time in my years as queen that I had been without one of them nearby.

My imagination raced with terrible possibilities. Haman had sent for them to ensure that neither interfered with his plan for me. Perhaps he had even imprisoned them on false charges. No one was safe from him.

I left the cup in my chamber and fled to the courtyard, my heart pounding with fear. "Haman's wife has collapsed in my dining chamber," I called out to the door guard. As I hoped, the guard was more afraid of Haman's displeasure than the king's. He thanked me and abandoned his post to attend Zeresh. I slid through the open gate and closed it behind me.

I stood unsupervised for the first time in many years, my heart pounding. Should the king learn of my escape, the consequences could be severe. But no one yet knew and I rejoiced to stand alone and unencumbered, with none to remind me of my role as queen. I was free to go anywhere my feet might take me.

The colonnade was dark, but for a ray of light from the door to the king's chamber. I heard people talking, but saw no guards. And then I recognized the king's voice.

I had not looked upon him in a month and the sound of him drew me closer, as if I was tied to him by a line, reeled in a little closer with each word. He was my lord, the father of my child, a man so resplendent in beauty and stature that none could help admiring him. He had been brave, once, and wise in his willingness to accept counsel. But his withdrawal from the affairs of state had caused him to fall in the eyes of many.

I reached the door and put my eye to the crack. Peering inside the chamber I saw him again, sitting on his mattress wearing nothing but hunting breeches. His powerful broad chest, as muscled as a Spartan wrestler's, might have been a model for a Greek statue of a demi-god. His long hair flowed loose and his beard remained uncurled. He had spent the day lion hunting, a pastime he often enjoyed.

Haman stood near him. He wore a white robe, tall turban, and a silver breastplate with a picture of the winged God, Ahura Mazda, molded in relief. He stood as erect and confident as one of the king's elite soldiers, though he himself had never served in the military. Nor did I hear any hesitation or subservience in his speech.

"I have but one other matter to discuss with Your Majesty this evening," Haman said.

The king clicked his tongue with impatience. "State your business and be done with it!"

"There is a certain people, scattered and dispersed among the provinces of your kingdom, who do not keep the king's laws. They are of no worth to His Majesty, and they inspire others to disobedience. I have consulted the magi in this matter and they have advised me. Let it be written that these people be destroyed."

The king shrugged with indifference and motioned for his youths to remove his hunting boots.

"Your Majesty," Haman continued, "I shall myself weigh out ten thousand silver talents from my own coffers to be brought into the king's treasury, so His Majesty need not regret the loss of taxes and tributes."

The king waved his hand with irritation, though I knew him well enough to see that he was not indifferent to the silver. "The people are yours," he said. "Do with them as you see fit and cease to bother me with this matter."

Haman bowed without ceremony, his pale mask revealing no emotion. But he hesitated to leave.

"Would you ask more of me?" the king bellowed.

"May Ahura Mazda strike me dead if I displease my king," Haman replied, his voice without fear. "It is only the matter of a seal on the written decree. I do not wish to disturb His Majesty on this again when the scribes have completed their work."

The king removed his signet ring and dropped it into Haman's outstretched palm.

I watched Haman's fingers close over the ring as the king called for his cup. My heart tore with grief. I knew King Xerxes was once a glorious man. I believed he could still be a great leader, if only he allowed reason rather than wine to be his master.

I wanted to run to him and demand that he take back his ring, his authority, his rule. I wanted to remind him of the days when he first came to Susa, when he built his palaces and ruled with wisdom. But even as I gathered courage to step forward, a heavy hand clapped me on the shoulder from behind. I cried out in fear.

"Here she is!" the soldier called to his companions.

The noise drew the king's attention to the door just as I was being led away. My eyes, filled with tears, met his. He looked at me with displeasure and turned back to his chamber.

When the soldiers returned me to the queen's quarters, Hathach and Puah were waiting at the gate. I felt their displeasure but offered no word of explanation for my escape until we had reached my chamber.

"I could find neither of you," I wept, ashamed for the trouble I had caused and wounded by the king's scorn.

The two servants looked at each other.

"Zeresh insisted that I drink a strange substance and I feared that it would harm the child. I was afraid…"

Puah put her arms around me. "We will be more careful in the future," she apologized. From her voice I gathered that this was not the first time she and Hathach had left the queen's quarters when

Zeresh was with me. They did not consider her to be a danger. Perhaps, I told myself, she had fooled us all.

I pointed to the cup on my side table. Hathach took it and sniffed.

"It seems to be a small quantity of wine," he observed.

"Dumza the perfumer will be able to tell us what it is," Puah suggested. "Shall I take it to her?"

Both Hathach and I nodded. It was better to know the truth.

Puah returned within an hour, her face flooded with darkness. "It is a drug that induces contractions of the womb, far more powerful than the formula Dumza sells to Asabana. You were right not to trust a woman whose lord has snatched the king's power."

"The king has given him the signet ring," I whispered.

Hathach gasped. Puah's face went pale.

"I heard Haman request a terrible edict, to exterminate a whole people for disobedience. The king consented without requesting evidence or witnesses. I cannot understand how he can be so indifferent to his subjects."

"He will change when you present him with an heir to the throne," Puah insisted. "His love for your child…"

She stopped as a servant entered the room to help me undress for the night.

I smiled at Puah's ancient face, knowing that it was filled with false hopes. The wisdom of her years had served me well, and the gift of her loving care had been my greatest comfort during my imprisonment. But even she could not spread enough perfume on the corpse of the king's reign to keep the decay from reaching my nostrils. He had given away his ring. There was little more to lose.

I slept late into the morning, waking only when I woke only when I heard a crash in the hallway outside my room. I ran to the door where two servant girls squabbled about a tray that had been dropped. When I opened the door to tell them that they should not fight over such a trivial matter, I saw by the light of day streaming in through the ceiling vents that it must be well past morning.

The servants greeted me by bowing their cloth-covered heads low and dropping to their knees, a show of subservience to which I had not yet grown accustomed, even after four years. One of the girls, I noticed, had the king's dark beauty. Black curls escaped from beneath her gray wool head scarf and her large eyes glittered. I guessed that she must have been his daughter by a concubine. I remembered Anatana with sudden longing.

I smiled at the two who knelt amongst the ruins of my breakfast, and took comfort in knowing that they were better off serving me than the soldiers in the king's barracks. "Some rosewater with plain bread will be enough for me."

I turned back toward my room. The dullness of sleep lingered and as I tried to recall all that had happened the previous day, the memory of the king giving his ring to Haman returned to me like a hundred needles stabbing at the hollow of my stomach. When I reflected back even further, to the meeting with Zeresh, my knees buckled and the walls began to spin. Soon the light fled from my eyes and I remembered no more in the darkness.

I awoke on my mattress with one of the serving girls fanning me. Puah came rushing in. "The chamber has no air!" she scolded the servants, motioning for one to open the heavy curtain that blocked the door to the balcony. Then she bent over me and kissed my limp hand. "I am not well," I whispered to her.

"You need to eat," she replied.

"I must see Anatana again," I insisted. "And Vadhut. I have not seen my friend for many weeks."

Vadhut, too, was expecting a child, though much sooner than me. I invited her to my quarters every few weeks for a visit and Hegai did not object. But he had advised me not to request her removal from the harem, for the king enjoyed her from time to time and would not look with favor upon the loss.

"First you shall have your breakfast," Puah instructed. "Then we will call for visitors."

I ate with a hunger I had not known since my journey to Susa. Bread, honey cake, goat stew and almonds, ripe grapes and olives, salted fish and dates cooked in sweetened pomegranate juice, fried lentils and sheep's entrails: I ate everything they set before me and called for more. Puah cautioned me to slow down but I was like a woman possessed by a demon and I ate without pause. I stopped only after an hour or more, no longer able to ignore the throbbing pain of overindulgence, far worse than the gnawing pangs of emptiness. I ran to the vestibule of the chamber pot.

Puah stood with me while I vomited. She used a cool wet rag to wipe my face and clean my hands. Each time I imagined I was done, I would find the waves of sickness rising in the sea of my stomach. Relief never lasted more than a moment.

When I had rid myself of everything I had eaten, I heard arguing at the door in the chamber. My throat and nostrils burned. My eyes stung. The robe that I wore for sleeping was drenched in sweat and I shook from sickness.

"A new robe and some sleep will ease your discomfort." Puah helped me back to the chamber, her arm around me for support. I knew from the fear on her face that she wanted to send for the midwife. I did not have the strength to reassure her.

We made slow progress toward the mattress. I looked up and noticed an unwelcome sight in the doorway of the chamber: Zeresh. The old woman was arguing with a eunuch. It seemed that she was trying to push past him into the room.

"I am sure the king would want me to see her." She craned her neck over the eunuch and then pushed past him into the room. She was clutching herself as always, wearing the same ragged veil and robe. The slits of her eyes squinted even narrower and she seemed to have recovered from the evening before. Her eagerness to enter confirmed my suspicions: she knew the truth about the liquid she had given me and sought to confirm that it had taken effect. I resolved to say nothing about it.

"Please leave us," Puah requested. "My lady is not well."

"Send the filthy Jew servant away," Zeresh demanded. "I know how to help your illness."

My sickness turned to anger as Zeresh's ugly words echoed in my ears. She might have delivered poison to me in fear of her lord, but her hatred for my people was her own. Yet I did not express the contempt I held in my heart for her, lest she set her husband against me further or decide to harm Puah.

"I thank you for your concern," I said to Zeresh as Puah helped me on to my mattress and covered me with warm wool blankets. "I only need some rest."

"I will speak to my lord about this," Zeresh threatened. "The queen should not be attended in her chamber by Jews."

My heart raced in desperation. I had lost my father and my mother. I had lost my cousin. I could not lose Puah.

"Please leave us," I asked Puah.

An expression of fear and worry crossed the old woman's face but I raised the corners of my lips, enough to reassure her.

Puah bowed to me and to Zeresh. She left the room, though I knew she remained just behind the door in the passageway. When she was gone, I summoned all my strength to sit up. And though I felt hot knives searing through my loins, I spoke to Zeresh as the queen, with firmness and conviction.

"Her people are the Jews," I conceded, "but sometimes their God gives them the gift of soothsaying. I dare not lose her visions. They are more frightening than those induced by haoma, more true than the Delphic Oracle."

"What has she seen?" Zeresh asked, drawing closer, her eyes widening.

"Just two days ago she told me of a danger," I whispered as if to a co-conspirator. "She told me of a woman in black rising above the acropolis like a cloud. A demon of evil, an agent of Azi Dahaka, who meant to harm me and my baby."

Zeresh clutched herself even tighter. "What more did she say?"

"I do not know what it means. But you must tell no one." I leaned back upon the cushions behind me.

"You have my word," she replied, eager for my secret.

I paused to heighten her impatience. "The demon wore a silver star around her neck."

"A star?" Zeresh echoed with a gasp.

"It was hidden in the depths of her darkness," I elaborated. "And a poisonous red fluid oozed from her fingers like blood."

Zeresh grew as pale as the white linen of her lord's turban.

"We must beware of the Jews," I added. "They have a powerful God."

Twenty-six

The king removed his signet ring—the symbol of his authority—and gave it to Haman. When I witnessed this final act of weakness, I fell into a darkness of uncertainty and fear. The wind rushed through the collonade as if it were the voice of the Delphic Oracle herself, foretelling a future of horror and destruction. But I lived a secluded life and could not yet put together the pieces of the story: the ring, Haman's edict, his throwing of the pur in the fire temple, the necklace of Ishtar, the vial of poison. I wanted to speak with Hathach, to lay everything before him and determine what course of action I might take to help the king recover his authority. But Puah insisted that I was not well enough to do more than rest, and I did not argue with her.

I slept for several hours after Zeresh left but awoke feeling no better. Puah appeared at my side in an instant when I called for her. I asked for Vadhut and a servant was sent to summon her at once.

When Vadhut entered I sat up, happy to see my friend again. Her dancing curls were as merry as ever and her smile lightened my heart. Many months into her pregnancy, she had grown so big that she moved with less ease than Hegai. But she was livelier than any time I had known her, and seemed more like Anatana in years and spirit than me, though our age was the same. I was glad she did not comment on my poor appearance as she lowered herself on to the mattress next to me, eager to tell all the harem gossip.

"The king has not called for Thriti in a year!" she exclaimed. "We are told she will have to leave her apartment soon and even the harem."

"She should have enough gold to return to her family without disgrace," I observed.

"Thriti wants to be queen of her own estate somewhere. She wants to purchase Hutana to go with her. I did not know dancing girls could be purchased!"

"I do not imagine they can be," I sighed, recalling Hutana's sad fate. "Poor Hutana."

"She is worn out," Vadhut agreed. "And nothing to show for it. I am afraid she will soon be sent to the barracks."

"Let us speak of other things." I suggested this even as I considered whether I might have enough influence to gain permission for Hutana to leave with Thriti. I did not care for Thriti, but Hutana did. She would have a much better life with the concubine than she did as a dancing girl, forced to submit to four or five rough men every night.

"How are you feeling?" Vadhut said, turning shy. "Does your baby move yet?"

"It is still too early," I replied. "I am often sick."

"It does not last too long," she assured me. "Imagine how happy we will be to watch our girls playing together!"

I did not tell her that the king would prefer a son.

"Do you want to hear my secret?" Vadhut leaned closer to me and rubbed her palms over her large belly.

"I hope you have done nothing foolish," I smiled.

Vadhut giggled. "I have not had the harem wine since I knew I was with child. I remembered what you said."

I looked at her with threefold astonishment: that she would recall my misgivings about the wine, that she would succeed in abstaining from it, and that she would have kept it a secret from me for so many months. I had spoken of my suspicions only once to my friends, long ago. We had been in the harem several months when I began to suspect that the haoma-laced wine prevented the concubines from giving birth to healthy children. The wine was unique to the harem, I reasoned, and the children of concubines fared much worse than Vashti's.

"You were brave to refuse," I said to my friend after a moment. "I am surprised you were permitted."

"They do not know," Vadhut confessed with pride. "No one watches the way they did in the beginning. I pretend to drink and they do not care."

"You kept the secret even from me," I observed with some sadness, though I had, by necessity, kept far more secrets from her.

Vadhut threw her arms around me and kissed my cheek a hundred times. "I wanted to surprise you, and I have. It was hard at first; I wanted the wine so much. But now I never miss it. I hope the baby will be a pretty girl and that I can keep her while she is little."

When I heard her childish plans, a silent cry of woe rose in my throat. I knew Hegai would not change his policies for Vadhut. In the end she would relinquish the baby to a nurse while she underwent beauty treatments to restore her for the king. A terrible scene played out before me: my friend weeping for the baby they had snatched from her arms, the harem attendants forcing the haoma wine into her mouth to calm her.

I looked at Vadhut's rosy smile and round face, and I wanted to tear my golden hair for having inspired false hopes. She would have been better off in the haoma-induced oblivion. Now, if the child died, her grief would be far worse. If the child was born healthy, she would have to give it up. Either way, she would mourn her loss for months.

I searched for words to ease the sorrow that I knew would soon be hers. But I could not stain her innocent smile and simple affection, her dancing curls and her dimpled cheek, with the dark truth. "May you have an easy labor and a healthy child," I wished her, choking on my words.

Her furrowed brow revealed apprehension. "It will be within the month."

"You shall be fine," I insisted, "as your mother was with you."

Vadhut bit her full lower lip. "I want Freni to pray for me. Her God is so powerful that she was able to go home. Perhaps he will keep me safe."

I did not know what to say. When Freni was released from the harem, I had severed all contact with her, hoping the year of her suffering would fade like a bad dream. I wanted no more for my friend than the quiet life she was born into. I had not even sent her gifts, for fear they would remind her of a time she would rather forget. But perhaps I had been wrong. Perhaps she missed us too.

"I could send Puah to see how she is," I suggested with uncertainty. And to pray for me too, I said to myself as I doubled over from a wave of nausea.

Puah was reluctant to leave me in my illness. But Vadhut begged with desperation, insisting that Freni's prayers would benefit all of us. And when Puah saw that I did not object, she agreed to make the trip into the town.

Before she left the room, I reached down under the blanket and removed one of the gold bracelets from my arm, a simple band with a pattern of rosettes.

"Please give this to my friend." I held it out to Puah. I could not compose a message in words. But I knew that none was needed.

I was tired now, and the pain would not subside. I did not wish to distress Vadhut with my weakening condition, so I sent her back to the harem, promising to call for her when Puah returned from visiting Freni. Then I lay down to rest and wait.

But Puah was not gone long enough to journey to the town, or even across the acropolis before she rushed back into the room. She panted for breath and her expression was grave.

"I have seen something you will hear of from others if not from me. Marduka sits barefoot in the town square, dressed in sackcloth. He cannot enter the king's gate in such garb and so he has abandoned his post and his position. They say he refused to bow down to Haman. And somehow it has become known that he is a Jew: I heard him called so."

A spasm of pain passed through my lower abdomen. I could not imagine what had compelled Mordechai to such defiance. He had always been a loyal servant: nothing, not even the God of his father, stood in the way of his devotion to the king's interests. Now he risked his hard-won position, even his life, with disobedience, for no reason I could comprehend.

A riot of possibilities unfolded before me through my pain, each more senseless than the last. He could not force himself to bow down to a master appointed by the one who had taken me, the woman who should have borne his own sons. He had seen Freni in the market square or on the road, and the very sight of her sweet face had inspired him to reclaim all that Marduka the Babylonian had forsaken. He was gathering his strength even now to come forward and demand that the king release me, his rightful wife, to his care. We would return to Babylon and Mordechai would take his place as a scribe to Ezra the scholar and our sons would grow to manhood worshiping the One God in Jerusalem.

Such were my childish imaginings brought on by fear, sorrow, and illness. Such were the hopes I once held and forced myself to bury deep in my heart, before the king made me his.

"Have a servant bring him a clean robe and new shoes," I ordered. "Please hurry to him!"

We settled on to the floor cushions to wait for a report. But too soon the messenger returned with the items. Marduka the Jew stood in the marketplace shouting at the crowd and rubbing ashes into his hair. He would not accept the clothing.

I was frantic for my cousin's safety. If I persisted in my efforts to rescue Marduka from whatever madness possessed him, the truth of our kinship was sure to come out. But I had no choice now.

I turned to Puah, my heart resigned to break the promise I had made so long ago.

"Send for Hathach. Tell him he must rescue Marduka for my sake. Tell him—Marduka is my cousin."

Puah sent Hathach as I instructed. When he returned, he did not offer his usual greetings and I saw fear and agitation on his face. As he stepped over the threshold, his eyes took in the chamber to make sure that Puah and I were alone. He walked to the balcony doorway and released the heavy woolen curtain from its tie to muffle the sound of our voices. We huddled together on my mattress; a single oil lamp on the floor beneath us cast shadows over the high stone walls.

"I have spoken with Marduka," he began. "I found him in the market square."

My face flushed as I imagined my beloved cousin. Once I had looked upon his goodness each day. Now I could not see him except through the eyes of others.

"I told Marduka that I had come at the bidding of Queen Esther," Hathach continued. His wide eyes met mine for a moment, as if to acknowledge that my secret would remain unspoken, even between us, if that was my wish. "I told him that the queen had heard of his refusal to prostrate himself to the king's advisor, and that she was alarmed by this and his public display of mourning. 'Haman has seen your disobedience,' I said. 'You know his power is great and he does not hesitate to use the rope. It is not too late to save yourself.'

"Marduka shook his head. 'Tell the queen that my loyalty is to the king alone.'

"I pled with him. 'She seeks to save you from the gallows.'

"'Tell her this,' he said. 'Her concern should be as mine is, to His Majesty, the king.'

"'Haman is a cruel man to be sure,' I argued, 'but surely you have bowed to many a passing diplomat and advisor.'

"'Never to one with an alien god on his chest,' Marduka replied to me."

I recalled Haman's silver breastplate, embossed with the image of Ahura Mazda. "He would not bow down to an idol!"

"He would not bow to the image of Ahura Mazda on the advisor's chest," Hathach concurred. "When the men at the gate asked Marduka why he would not prostrate himself, he revealed that he was a Jew."

The well of my tears rose and my heart soared like a captive dove released to freedom, high above the crushing confines of the palace, into God's heaven. I had learned to accept Mordechai's rejection of our people's ways. I had come to cherish his kindness and gentleness above the rules of righteousness that my father followed. But I had always told myself that Mordechai would never fall before an idol, the gravest sin of all. And now, I knew that it was true. Mordechai had not abandoned his people. He would rather risk death than defy the One God.

"He did not intend to reveal his secret," the eunuch added. "It came to his tongue as if through his God."

"He is a righteous man," I announced.

"A righteous man hanging from the gallows will do his people no good." Puah's words reminded me that I had little reason to rejoice.

"Marduka expressed neither doubt nor regret as I would have expected from a cautious man. He showed no intention of changing his mind. I tried to employ reason and then I…"

The eunuch broke off and shifted his eyes away from me, as if afraid of my displeasure.

"Keep nothing from me," I insisted.

"I told him that the queen was expecting a child, that she would give birth in grief if her cousin lost all that he had worked so hard to achieve."

Shame rushed through me like the wind across a barren valley. I could not bear for Mordechai to know of the passions to which I had succumbed. "It is God's child," I whispered to myself.

"You are the queen," Puah reminded me. "You have your duties as your cousin has his."

I lowered my eyes to the flickering lamp.

"My arguments did not move him because it was too late." The eunuch's voice dropped. "He showed me the scroll with the king's seal. The Jews are to be slaughtered and their property taken, on a date eleven months hence."

I fell back against the cushions. Now I understood all that I had heard and witnessed the night before: Zeresh's account of Haman throwing the pur to arrive at an auspicious date, Haman's request to exterminate a disobedient people, the signet ring. Mordechai had defied Haman and Hamanhad cast his wrath upon our people. I shook with terror and fury.

"This edict is the work of Haman. I heard him offer the king ten thousand silver talents for the slaughter." I could say no more.

"At least my lady is safe," Puah muttered. Tears ran down the long crevasses in her face. "None but us know ..."

"I cannot let my cousin perish!" I cried out in pain. "Or Freni!" A thousand needles stabbed at me. The shadow of death passed over my heart.

"What is it?" Puah asked in alarm.

"I am not well." And when I rose from beneath the blankets, blood streamed down my legs in a red river.

Twenty-seven

Death ripped though my womb like a hot knife and took my child.

How often had my mother endured this same agony? I lay in my chamber as the child's lifeblood flowed away from me and tried to remember my mother's soothing voice, her sweet face.

"Why do I have no brothers or sisters?" I asked one night as she sat by my mattress, singing me to sleep. A chill had come into the winter air. Her sad smile covered me with more warmth than the blankets she pulled up over my shoulders.

"Please may I have a sister?" I begged.

"Hush..." she murmured. "You are the most cherished child in Babylon. Your father and I have no need for another."

"Ninsun says it hurts to have a baby."

She bent low and kissed my forehead. "After I held you in my arms, I remembered no more than a pinprick."

"I would like a sister or a brother," I persisted.

My mother's eyes filled with tears. "Let us pray that Lilith stays away this time," she whispered, "And in spring you shall have your wish."

But by spring she was dead and I was alone.

Now my own child was gone.

I begged God, in my anguish, not to take from me everything I ever loved. I begged that He leave me Vadhut, Anatana, and Hathach. I begged that He save Puah, Freni and Mordechai from the king's decree. But a bitter spirit settled in my heart. I knew that whatever God gave me with one hand, He took away with the other. However many times I had found my way out of the valley overshadowed by death, the imprint of my footsteps remained behind.

Puah helped me wash and changed my bedding, hiding the sheets until she could burn them. Then she covered me with wool blankets, for a chill had come over me. She called a servant and ordered some warm milk and honey from the kitchens. "The queen is unwell," she explained. "No one but Hathach should be admitted."

I soon felt better in body, the sharp pains subsiding into a dull throb. When I was settled on my mattress again, Puah sat by my side and began to cry.

"You must not be sad for me," I insisted. "It is your safety we must now worry about."

"The child would have been all I had hoped for you," she lamented. "I would have passed from this world content, to know that you had sealed your favor with the king and…"

I interrupted with harsh scorn. "He is a weak and capricious man." Puah had long been my rock, strong and practical. She was never one to see only a flower where there also was a thorn. Now I could not bear for her to imagine a tale that was not true because she would have wished it so.

"A son from would not protect my position," I told her. "Vashti has two sons of royal blood. Surely their supporters would not permit my son to gain precedence without a fight. And I have no special claim to the title of queen. I might soon be banished as Queen Vashti was, for no good reason."

"She was a wicked woman banished for disobedience!" Puah objected.

"She was wicked, but she displeased the king's wine-soaked heart as any woman might," I insisted. I wondered if in fact I would ever have the courage to deny a request from the king. "I shall live in mortal fear of his wayward wrath until the hour he chooses to exercise it."

"God will reward your suffering as He has mine," Puah offered, to soothe my damaged spirits.

"We have only each other to rely upon." The words came from my throat in a stranger's rough voice. I did not even care that I was dishonoring the memory of my father's pious ways, that his ears would have burned in shame to hear such blasphemy coming from the tongue of his own daughter. In my dark sorrow I doubted everything, even what I had just said.

"Lie down now," Puah urged with tenderness, as if I were as young and senseless as Anatana.

I obeyed her and she began to stroke my cheek as my mother used to.

"You have always been my comfort and my rock," I murmured. My eyelids grew heavy with sleep.

"I once wronged you." Her voice trembled. "Many years ago…"

My eyes flew open and I reached for her hand to assure her that I would not be angry.

"When you first came to the harem, before the king selected you as his queen…every day Mordechai walked about in front of the harem gate to learn how you were faring and what was happening to you. He offered the guards payment for news of you. The guards sometimes approached me on his behalf. I told them you were in good health and had many friends. But I did not want your hopes to stray from the harem, to fix on anything but the king. And so I kept silent."

The tears streamed from my heart like blood flowing from an open wound. I squeezed Puah's fingers. "I am glad to know of it now," I whispered. I closed my eyes and turned my head away from her.

I floated into a restless sleep and every ghastly sight I had ever seen came together in my dreams. Aia's scaly head became my father's smashed skull. It seeped across our courtyard to my mother's terrified face, and as I sat by her deathbed the soldiers who took me from Mordechai stood over my hunched figure. The laughter of the woman who stole my mother's shawl rang in my ears. I woke weeping in my chamber, relieved that the past was gone from all but my dreams. But until I remembered that the child I was carrying had been taken from me and Mordechai was in danger. I closed my eyes again, once more seeking refuge in sleep.

Two giant dragons rose from the darkness of the land and the earth trembled in fear. The sun hid its face and the stars grew dim. The lion-headed creatures shrieked and tore at each other's blue scales with claws sharper than knives.

223

And then I saw a small spring gurgle forth from the ground between the two monsters, each holding the other in death's grip. The spring grew larger and became a stream and the stream became a river flowing with the strength of the sea, flooding the earth. Light returned to the land and the turtledove cooed from his perch in a blossoming olive tree.

I awoke on my mattress, my thighs sticky with blood that had seeped through the rags. The fading light in the balcony window told me that it was evening.

I rose on unsteady feet. My knees were like water and I wobbled to a pitcher and basin in a corner of the chamber far from the door. I lifted the pitcher to my lips, then soaked a towel in some water and tried to clean myself. But I was weak and the task defeated me.

Puah found me in a heap on the floor, blood soaked and emptied of tears. "Hathach is eager to tell you the rest of Marduka's message," she whispered, bending over me. "He is waiting to see if you are awake and ready to receive him."

Once again she helped me wash, assuring me that I would soon recover. "I have seen it before. In a few days it will be over."

I smiled at Puah for her kindness and wrapped myself in a shawl while she removed the bedding. "We can not keep this a secret," I observed.

"For another day or two at most." Puah stroked my arm. The king will understand. The king will call for you again and soon you will have another child."

Returning to the mattress, I looked at my chamber with fresh eyes. My people faced annihilation while I sat surrounded by luxury: silk cushions dyed in rich tints of ruby, amethyst, gold, and lapis;

heavy drapery hung from golden rings, the azure and carnelian ceramic wash basin and jug, rosettes carved into the molding and dusted with gold, thick rugs woven with intricate patterns in emerald, wine, and saffron—more brilliant than a garden in bloom—the door inlaid with gilded gazelles. How spoiled I had become! Anything I needed appeared without my asking. If I was sad, Puah and Hathach found ways to lift my spirits. If I was lonely, I could call for company. I gave orders to servants without concern for their burdens and I indulged my sorrows as if I alone suffered.

The light from my dream rose through me. I remembered the monsters and the bird and the spring that grew into a roaring river. I would be that river of strength. I would put aside my sorrows and regrets until I found a way to save those I loved. Another child would not redeem my life if I could not secure theirs.

Hathach entered my chamber with cautious steps, as if he feared that the muffled sound of his sandals against the carpet might disturb me. He offered a deep bow. "Your loss is mine," he said, his voice as gentle as a feather on my face.

"Thank you," I replied. "I am ready to hear more of my cousin's story now."

Hathach nodded.

"When your cousin had word of the decree, he went to a market stall and traded his clothes for sackcloth. He smeared his head with ashes. His cries attracted the attention of many. I came upon him as he was urging Jew and non-Jew alike to pray for salvation."

"There can be no hope," I observed. "A decree sealed with the king's ring is irrevocable. My cousin had better flee than stay. We must help him escape."

"He will not flee," Hathach replied with certainty. "He prays for the rescue of his people."

"He has never been a pious man."

"Perhaps your God will hear him nonetheless," Hathach suggested with more hope than conviction. "Your own love for your cousin seems very great," he added.

I lowered my head to hide my face, embarrassed that the eunuch could read my heart so well.

"Did he send no message to the queen?" Puah asked after a few moments.

Hathach looked at Puah. A signal, I understood, that she should be prepared to comfort and console me.

"He requests that Esther, queen of the Persian Empire, entreat the king on behalf of her people."

As I listened to these words spill from his tongue, a fever rose in my blood. I felt my hands grow cold with certainly that my cousin had gone mad, asking me to risk my life for a hopeless cause. A decree sealed with the king's signet ring could not be revoked. Moreover, as the entire kingdom knew, a supplicant who dared to approach the king on his throne without a summons would be put to death, unless the king showed his favor by extending his golden scepter. Now that I had lost the child, I had even more reason to fear the king's displeasure.

"I…I cannot," I faltered. "I have not been summoned to the king for thirty days. The king does not wish to see me."

And so I refused Mordechai's request, the first he had made of me since I left his household five years before.

Twenty-eight

Hathach returned from speaking with Mordechai to find me pacing in my chamber. His expression was anguished and he hesitated to give his report. But I made plain to him that I would not be shielded from the truth.

He wiped his wide brow with a small cloth and cleared his throat. "When I told Marduka that the queen could not go before the king without risking her life, this was his reply: 'Do not imagine in your heart that you, of all the Jews, will escape because you are in the king's palace. If you keep silent at this time, relief and deliverance will come to the Jews from another place. But you and your father's house will perish...'" his voice trailed off.

If the most skilled Immortal had thrust his sharpest dagger into the pit of my stomach, I could not have been more wounded. My parents had departed this world and Mordechai was the last of his father's house. My child was lost and the king no longer favored me. Mordechai's prediction was close to the truth of what had already come to pass.

"She is not the only one who can go to the king," Puah interceded. "Let Marduka do so himself: his life is already endangered."

"No!" I cried. "I cannot let him perish. He and I are the last of our grandfather's house."

Hathach wiped his brow again and inhaled, filling his chest with air. He opened his mouth to speak. "Marduka's final words to you were these: 'Who knows, Hadassah, if it was not for this purpose that you have come into royalty.'"

"A foolish sentiment," Puah grumbled.

But my cousin's message sent an earthquake through my heart. Puah had once said the same to lift me from the lethargy of sorrow and renew my purpose. Now her scorn served to remind me of what I might have been: a concubine in a stupor of regret, living my days for no greater good than serving the king's pleasure. Puah might yet be a harem servant beaten each night by Nusku. Anatana would never have known the special love of one who cherished her above all others. And Freni's release would have been no more than a dream. Perhaps God's almighty hand would have brought justice to those I loved without my intervention. Mordechai, though he did not live his life by God's commandments, seemed certain that someone would rescue our people. But I could know nothing with surety beyond what my own voice cried out for me to do.

"No one at court is safe," I said to my companions.

Puah raised her eyebrows in surprise. "The decree is against the Jews."

"The decree will come to be against anyone who crosses Haman."

Hathach nodded in agreement. "Marduka is convinced that Haman's ambitions are fixed on the throne." The eunuch lowered his voice. "He suspects that Haman himself stood behind the plot of Bigthan and Teresh to poison the king. Marduka did not tell me all that he overheard that day, for fear of making a false accusation. But they spoke of one who had spurred them on to action, an Elamite who would take the throne and promote them. Now he has no doubt:

Haman promised them rich rewards to kill the king. For this reason as well, he will not bow to the advisor."

I closed my eyes for a moment, recalling the day when I first beheld Haman in the king's chamber. He had been eager to apprehend the eunuchs, to prove his worth by testing the poisoned wine. And he had silenced the traitors by cutting out their tongues before they could speak in their own defense or reveal his role in the plot.

"Haman must realize that my cousin suspects him. We must find a way for him to escape."

For some minutes we sat, absorbed in our own hearts, afraid that an escape would be impossible to execute. A knock at the chamber door broke the silence. Hathach rose to answer and exchanged quiet words with someone. I could read nothing in his expression when he returned, but I assumed the worst: my cousin had been seized and would soon hang from the gallows.

Hathach squatted by my side and whispered, "A woman from the town has asked for an audience with you. She claims to be your friend: Sarah the Jewess."

"Freni!" I exclaimed. I rose to my feet, knowing it could be no other.

"Should you not remain in seclusion?" Hathach asked with concern.

"She should conserve her strength," Puah concurred.

"I must see her," I declared, my voice as tight as a santur string.

Though my legs were still weak, I paced the chamber, picturing my friend as I had last seen her, four years earlier. We had

229

said only the briefest farewell, for I had feared the king would change the release decree. In my excitement, I forgot all that troubled me. I did not ask myself what could have brought Freni back to the palace or pause to imagine her courage in climbing the dreaded stairs by choice, walking under the wings of Ahura Mazda into the valley of the bones. I did not wonder whether I would have risked my freedom even for an hour. Only later did I come to realize how hard it must have been for her.

I did not recognize my friend at first, and took her for a malnourished servant. I remembered her as she was when I last saw her, the flesh on her bones filled out to the plump softness of a well-kept concubine, her long black locks as sleek and glossy as the king's best horse, the delicate features of her face radiant with the rapture of her impending freedom.

But here in my doorway stood a thin, wan creature dressed in a shabby gray robe of rough wool, a threadbare brown headscarf wrapped about her face. She looked up to Hathach, who nodded his permission to enter. She flew to me and flung herself at my feet, begging for mercy on her and her people.

"We have done harm to no one!" she wailed. "My people pay taxes and tribute. They serve in the king's fleet and weave carpets for his palace. His favorite sculptor of stone reliefs is a Jew! Queen Esther, you must save us!"

I sank to my knees and held her while she wept on my shoulder. After a few moments, I pulled away, hoping to see something of my old friend in her face. She was there still, in her big eyes and her high cheekbones. But her skin was wrinkled as one who had been too much in the sun and her hair had lost its luster. Her lips were cracked and I could see, as she offered me a slight smile, that she had lost a tooth. Where once she had smelled of the king's finest perfumes, now she reeked of sour milk and horse manure. I, too, began to cry. For a moment I could not believe that her freedom was worth the price of what she had become.

"Puah is here too," I told her, waving for the old servant, who stood in the shadows on the other side of the room.

Freni looked up and held out her hand to Puah. "How good to see you," she said.

"May God keep you," Puah returned with a tender smile. She showed neither surprise nor disappointment at the condition of our friend.

"Tell us something of yourself," I begged as we settled ourselves on the cushions. "It has been so long since we have seen you."

Freni wiped her tears on her robe. "I have missed you," she admitted. "But God has been good to me. I am blessed with a lord of fine character and gentle ways—he is a wool dyer—and two sons who are the delight of their father's eye." She hesitated for a moment and I expected her to ask if I had any children. But perhaps she read the answer in my eyes, for she said nothing of the matter.

"I wanted to send Puah to you this very day with a gift," I explained. "Vadhut is having a child and wishes you to pray for her."

Puah pulled the bracelet from her sleeve and handed it to Freni.

"It is too fine for me," Freni protested, refusing to take it. "I am a poor man's wife."

"You are my friend," I replied, removing the bracelet from Puah's hand and sliding it onto Freni's thin wrist. "Please say a prayer for Vadhut."

"I shall pray for everyone I love as long as I have breath in my body. But the king has ordered the destruction of my people!"

"They are my people too," I confessed in a low voice, ashamed at having kept this secret from her.

Freni's wide eyes grew even larger.

"I promised my cousin I would tell no one," I explained, my eyes asking her forgiveness. "He is Mordechai the Jew, who sits in the king's gate."

"The very one who mourns and cries for our safety!" Freni exclaimed with admiration.

"My cousin has asked that I go to the king."

"You must!" Freni insisted with a ferocity of a mother protecting her children. She grabbed my hands. "God will listen if you go to the king."

"God cannot hear me," I whispered, holding back my tears. "I abandoned the ways of his people long ago."

"I will fast and pray for you," she insisted. "God will surely hear."

"But the king has not called me in many days," I explained. "I risk my life by going into his presence uninvited."

Freni's hopeful expression turned to grief. "Even now the Jews are being tormented and harassed by those who are eager to exercise the king's decree. People are stealing from our stalls in the market and threatening to sell our children into slavery. Go soon, before we are so abused and humiliated that we long for our deaths!"

I pulled Freni close to me again and the river of my tears mingled with hers.

Freni reached for her necklace, the very one that I had hidden for her on our first day in the harem and that Puah had retuned to her at the hour of her release.

"Please take this in exchange for the bracelet," she insisted, removing the amulet from her neck and sliding it around my own.

I felt the gold amulet slip into place near my heart. Once it had given me courage to face Ishtar. Now it would help me face an even greater danger. I rose to my feet.

"Summon Hathach," I commanded Puah.

"Do nothing rash..." Puah began, urging me to reconsider what I had already decided.

Freni leapt to her feet and ran to the door. She opened it and called for the eunuch who soon appeared.

"Here is my answer to my cousin," I said. "Tell him to assemble all the Jews in Susa and fast for me. Do not eat or drink for three days, night or day, and I will fast too. Then I will go in to the king, though it is against the law. And if I perish, I perish."

Twenty-nine

Mordechai did just as I asked of him. He crossed the Acropolis and descended into the town of Susa where the Jews lived. He gathered them together in the square and told them that the queen planned to seek mercy before the king in three days' time. He urged them to fast on my behalf. Some of the townspeople objected, pointing out that the third day of the fast fell on the feast of the Matzoth. Mordechai replied, "If the people of Israel are destroyed, there will be no Passover to celebrate." And so they followed his instructions.

As Hathach sent my message to Mordechai, I said farewell to Freni, though I would have kept her with me longer. But her lord waited for her at the palace gate and she was eager to return to her sons. We embraced in silence, saying nothing of our hopes to meet again under happier circumstances.

"Remember Vadhut in your prayers." I reminded her as we parted.

"I shall remember you both," she replied, her wide eyes reminding me of the young girl she had once been. But I saw, too, the wisdom of experience in her furrowed brow and hollow cheeks. "You are a righteous woman," she whispered, "a woman of valor. God will reward you." And then she was gone.

Puah helped me onto my mattress and covered me with blankets. When Hathach returned, I sent him to inform the king of my loss. I heard nothing from the king in return, no expression of regret or concern for my well being, no token of sympathy or assurance of his love. I grieved at his silence, though I had expected no better. And I grieved for my own grief. I did not want to regret him. I did not want to weep for someone who had sold my people. I did not want to admit that he had ever been more to me than the one who had taken possession of my body.

I remained in bed for three days, neither eating nor drinking. Puah stayed by my side, joining in the fast, but a raging fever ran through my body and I did not notice her company. In my delirium I saw the dragons again and again, their claws tearing at my skin. They left bleeding welts on my back and my stomach, my arms and my legs. The blood rose into a flowing river that separated them from each other, and I awoke with a terrible thirst. Too parched to speak, I prayed in silence.

I prayed for God to show His mercy on my people and on me. I prayed to bring honor to my father's name through my actions. I prayed for the courage to face the king. I knew I might perish in the effort, and I was afraid. But I told myself that if I did not act, my life would hold no more value than any of the other ornaments that decorated my chamber.

Three days passed and still the king had not asked for me. Puah gave me a cup of water. A single mouthful filled me like an ocean and it seemed that I would burst. Still, I drank it, drop by drop, and some milk as well. Then I rose to prepare for my meeting with the king.

I submitted to the beauty rituals without pleasure. I did not regret that this might be the last time maids would bathe me, strip the hair from my flesh, stain my fingertips with henna, soften my skin with sweet almond oil, and scent it with myrrh. I ringed my eyes with kohl and stained my lips with pomegranate paste, but I did not see my face in the mirror.

I chose a robe of white silk, heavy with gold brocaded flowers and pearls. Gold bands ringed my wrists and a jeweled tiara crowned my head. My hair flowed loose, as the king liked it, over my shoulders all the way down to my lower back. My feet were sheathed in crimson slippers with pointed toes. I hung gold gazelles in my earlobes and a filigreed ring in my nose.

The hours of preparations passed in a haze, as if I were an infant waiting in the shadows of her mother's womb for the moment of my birth. When Hathach appeared, I came back to myself. I stood in the center of my chamber, resplendent in my royal garb and smiled at him. I was calm in my resolve to risk death for the sake of those I loved. I had no plan for what I would say to the king, should he be willing to listen. But I knew that I, a mere woman who had fallen out of favor, could not win against the king's most trusted advisor with weeping.

Hathach gazed upon me and bowed low, in awe. Steadfast in my resolve, I had become the mistress of my own fate. My life was yet unfinished. But whether I spent many more years entombed in this chamber, or met the end of my days in the next few minutes, I would not regret going before the king.

I thanked Hathach and all those who helped me to prepare, assuring them that they had found favor in my eyes and would not go unrewarded. "Now I desire some moments alone," I told them.

No one dared urge me to change my plan, or to ask what I would say to the king if my life were spared. They did what I, their mistress, asked of them, trusting in my decisions. And though the king had crowned me four years before, only now did I feel myself to be a queen.

"A moment," I called out to Hathach as he was about to close the chamber door behind himself. "There is some writing scratched into the wall in the harem, in the small room of the apartment Hegai gave to me."

The eunuch waited for me to continue.

"Vashti," I explained. "I would like to know what it says."

The eunuch bowed and left.

I stood at the balcony door looking out into the garden.

The tulips were still blooming and the jasmine buds were beginning to emerge. The garden and my santur: these were privileges of being queen that I had come to cherish. But I felt no sorrow at bidding them farewell, as I did with the people I might never see again.

I turned my heart to my cousin, remembering my long-held anger that he had let me go without protest. I had been bitter, in my early days with the king, knowing that as Mordechai's wife I would have led a modest and chaste life, safe from the excesses of wine-soaked lust. Bitterness could revisit me, now that I saw my cousin did nothing for me, but would risk his position at court—even his life— for the sake of the people whose ways he had abandoned.

I remembered his confused message, delivered by Hathach. I tried to imagine what he meant, that relief and deliverance would come from somewhere else. Had I become queen for this purpose alone? I could not know God's plan for me, if indeed He had one. I could not know why my cousin's actions had brought the Jews of Persia to this crisis. I could know nothing for sure but the necessity of doing what was right in my own eyes, for those who I held dear in my heart, and to honor the memory of the parents who gave me life.

I spoke the prayer Freni had taught me and then began my own: "Give me courage, King of the gods and the Father of orphans. Make me persuasive before the lion and turn the king's favor from the one who fights against my people. Help me, your servant. Let me be met with mercy by this man whom I will approach against his law, whose wrath I fear. Bring him low before me, for You are the One who humbles the proud. I turn to no one but You, Lord, the One God, God of my Father."

I heard a light knock at the door and called out permission to enter, turning to face Hathach. "You have returned soon," I observed, smiling with gratitude. I moved forward to meet him, but my knees turned to water and I reached out to brace myself against the door jamb of the balcony. The eunuch rushed to offer me his arm.

"I am yet weak," I observed, leaning on him. "You have been a good and loyal servant," I added. I did not know if I would have another chance to thank him.

He answered with a sad smile. I looked at him with expectation.

"The writing on the wall," he whispered. "The words read: 'Death to Xerxes.'"

The depth of Vashti's anger and boldness shocked me. But the legacy of her words only served to heighten my resolve and my purpose. Perhaps I was meant to save not only my people from destruction, but my king as well.

Before the advancement of Haman, the king sat upon his throne most afternoons, receiving dignitaries and reports from all the lands of the realm, and conferring with his advisors. But now he held court only once each week, surrounded by Immortals wielding axes. I had never stepped into this room, where women were not welcome

I leaned against two maids as I walked from the queen's quarters to the king's palace. Puah held the train of my robe until we reached the colonnade. She offered no farewell, in word or gesture. Rather, she turned back to my quarters as one who was sure we would meet again in a few minutes. I took courage in her confidence.

The guards at the portico doorway recognized me and lowered their swords so I might pass. We stepped over the threshold on to a long stretch of crimson carpet that led into the throne room.

I looked to one side and then the other. Advisors, servants, and scribes stood ready to answer the king's call. Their tongues grew still as we passed, and they stared in surprise. Everyone knew the penalty for appearing before the king without a summons. They knew the king did not call for the queen while he sat upon the throne.

I spoke to no one as I walked down the aisle. Haman stepped forward and stared as he never had, his little dark eyes roving over my passive face and body. I lowered my gaze to his hands, one clasped over the other, and saw the king's gold signet ring glimmering on his finger.

Anger consumed my fear: it was unjust that such a man ruled the kingdom. It was unjust that the king did not know the nature of the monster to whom he had forsaken his people. But the king was a proud man. He was more likely to issue my death warrant than admit that he had been a fool to relinquish his authority to Haman the Elamite. Nor would Haman fall without a fight.

I saw the king well before he noticed me. He sat upon an enormous golden throne with a high back, no arms, and feet in the shape of lion paws resting on a silver balls. A canopy of silver netting and gold tassels hung over his head atop a jewel-encrusted gold frame.

The king himself was a dazzling vision of splendor, striking awe in any who came before him. He wore an outer robe of brilliant purple with two gold embroidered lion monsters, one at the throat of another. Beneath this was a purple robe with white fur at the hem. A tall golden crown rested on his turban, and his hair and beard were curled in even rows. Heavy gold cuffs ringed his arms and he held the golden scepter in one hand. If he extended it to me, I would live. If not, his guards stood ready to execute me.

I heard the advisors and servants gather behind me, gasping as I dared step out of the portico on to the purple rug. But I did not look upon king as I advanced. Rather, I saw my own beautiful mother, waiting for me to join her on the shores of the River Euphrates, her gentle face illuminated by the brilliance of God's light. She held out her hand, beckoning to me, and I felt my own face filling with the sweetness of her love.

I rushed to meet her again, the mother who had been taken from me too soon. But my legs were weak. I could not reach her before she vanished.

I stood at the king's feet and saw his powerful hand tightening around the scepter of life and death. The guards began to close in and I heard the Druj Nasu hovering over her mountain, ready to swoop down and seize my bloody corpse.

And then I dared to look up into the king's face. I used my eyes to beg him for my life and my heart to thank God for the gifts I had enjoyed in his world.

Thirty

The king extended the golden scepter in his hand, and I approached and touched the tip. I should have found relief in its cool, smooth surface, in being spared the king's anger and death. But I knew only sorrow: my people were in danger of annihilation, I was still subject to the whim of the king's pleasures, and my mother had been lost to me again.

The king looked upon me as he never had before, without the filter of his cup. His eyes shone like glittering jewels and his face was soft with compassion and love. He gazed into my heart with vision as pure as water from a spring and he saw my distress.

"What troubles you, Queen Esther?" he asked. He stepped down from the throne to embrace me. "What is your request? Even if it be half the kingdom, it will be given you."

The silk of his robe was soft against my cheek and the smell of him filled my nostrils. We could have been the only two people in God's world, a woman safe in her lord's strong arms, and I might have been content.

He stroked my hair and kissed me, his lips sweeter than honey.

I was tempted to state my intention at once, so taken was I by the change in him, by his beauty and his gentle touch, his winsome words and pleasing manner. But I could not forget the signet ring I had just seen on the hand of another. And I knew his cup would not remain unfilled for long. His tenderness could turn to fury in a moment and my pleadings be silenced by Haman's gallows. I needed more time.

"If it please the king," I whispered, resting my hands on his chest, "let the king and Haman come today to the feast that I have prepared for them."

The king's face filled with pleasure. "Hasten Haman to do as Esther has said!" the king ordered his guards.

I bowed low to the king and retreated, knowing that I had little time to prepare. My legs gained strength with my success and I returned to the queen's quarters without leaning upon my maids.

Hathach and Puah were waiting for me just inside the garden door. Their faces filled with relief as I passed over the threshold, but we did not have the luxury of lingering.

"I have invited the king and his advisor to a feast," I explained, my voice trembling with urgency. "They are coming at once."

Puah clicked her tongue with surprise.

"The king has never been to the queen's quarters," Hathach observed.

"Nor has any other with his manhood intact," Puah added.

"I shall reveal the truth here," I explained. "The king does not know Haman has decreed his own queen's death. I must have food and drink for them."

"There is a rare new vintage from Chalybon," Hathach suggested at once.

I looked at the eunuch, hesitating to approve. I had observed the king without his wine and I knew I could find happiness in the arms of that man. Without the wine he might come to see for himself what Haman had wrought. Perhaps his desire to rule would return.

But I knew that the king could not forsake his wine for long. Soon all the sinews and bones of his being would ache for it. He would return to the drink whether I served him or not.

"Several bottles of the new vintage and also the date wine from Babylon," I decided. "And figs and cheese, and sugared almonds," I added. "But you must hurry."

While Hathach was gathering the food and wine, Puah and I readied the dining room. We gathered fine cushions from throughout the queen's quarters and piled them high around a low table. As we spread a shimmering white Egyptian cloth over the table top, incense burners filled the air with the fragrance of sweet cinnamon and clove. Then I went to refresh my own appearance, changing into a Greek gown of sheer white linen with many pleats. Over this I wore a short sleeveless crimson robe with a gold belt at the waist, open in such a manner that only my most secret treasures remained hidden.

When I returned to the dining room, the table was resplendent with fruit and sweets. The wine jugs stood filled and cups ready for the king's enjoyment. The oil lamps were lit and the heavy curtains closed so one would not know whether it was night or day.

"Perhaps the novelty of the location will bring him pleasure and soften his heart," I said.

"May God reward your courage with a good outcome," Puah offered in a low voice. I squeezed her hand in thanks for I knew that she did not call upon God often.

"They are here!" Hathach announced from his post at the door. In a moment I heard a commotion in the passageway.

"By Ahura Mazda that is a narrow stair!" the king's voice rang out.

Hathach opened the door and fell at the king's feet. Puah and all the other the servants followed suit. I bowed as he entered, and began to lower myself to my knees. He held up his hand to stop me, turning to Haman, behind him. "She will spill out of her robe if she goes any lower," he observed with a merry laugh.

I watched the king as I rose, again admiring his beauty and spirit, unmarred by wine. For a moment I regretted all that he might have been and the service I might have rendered him. But then I saw Haman. He stood just behind the king, his eyes darting about the room with suspicion, his hands tense at his sides, his weight on the balls of his feet as if ready to spring into action. The silver breastplate of Ahura Mazda hung from his neck and his turban was as tall as the king's. I could not bow before the idol, for my own sake and Mordechai's. I nodded to him instead.

I waved all the servants away and signaled for Hathach to close the door.

"Please," I said to the king, offering him a place by the table laden with food. "I would be honored to fill your cup myself. And yours my lord," I said to Haman, who had placed himself across from the king.

"He is not your lord!" the king bristled. Then he burst into laughter and rubbed my thigh. "Would you like such a vessel for your use?" he asked Haman, pulling me down next to him. He began to kiss the exposed flesh of my bosom.

"Your Majesty knows I am a man," Haman replied in a guarded tone. But his eyes did not refrain from looking at me.

My heart fell into an abyss of fear. I prayed that the king would not offer me to his advisor.

"I have a new wine from the hills above Nineveh," I offered, to distract the king.

"My Greek doctor has said no more wine," the king laughed, holding out his cup to me. "But he is a fool."

"A fool," Haman echoed, glancing at the fruit and sweet cakes on the table with suspicion, as if he feared they might be poisoned. He looked up, his eyes piercing me with defiance. I returned his challenge with an innocent smile. In my heart I berated myself for underestimating him. He and I both knew that I had not risked my life simply to invite him and the king to a feast.

"I went for a day with nothing but water and beer," the king continued, "from yesterday until now, and it did nothing but cause my head to ache and my legs to shake!"

"Nothing," Haman agreed.

"He said it would invigorate me! But what does a man need for that other than good wine and a beautiful woman?"

"Hear, hear!" Haman concurred.

I filled a cup for the king and another for his advisor. The king drained his at once and I refilled it. Then I sat by the king's side and began to feed him sugared almonds. He accepted them with pleasure, licking my fingers after each offering. Soon he took my hand and rubbed it against his stirring flesh, causing my own desire to rise. But I felt Haman's gaze upon me. I knew it was time to summon the king's jealousy.

I knelt by the table and leaned low across it to offer Haman a piece of honey cake. As I hoped, his eyes lingered on my breasts. The look did not pass the king unnoticed; he grasped my waist and pulled me down upon the cushions, the plate of cakes scattering all around us.

"Let me see what you are hiding," he insisted, pawing at the belt that held the crimson robe shut. When his drunken fingers could not work the buckle, he reached inside my robe from the top and began to fondle me. Soon he was heavy upon my body and I could not breathe. My heart thundered with fear. I did not doubt that he would take me then, in front of Haman. But in a moment his brutal lust subsided and he pulled away. Drinking deep gulps of air, I saw Haman's expression fill with contempt for the king.

"I have other delights to show you," I whispered in the king's ear, stroking his forearm. I refilled his cup once again and went into the next room.

When I returned with the santur in my hands, the king's face brightened. He did not know I had learned to play.

I sat beside him and began to pick at the strings. Soon I improvised a melody that reminded me of a field of fragrant yellow flowers and a soft warm wind caressing my cheek. I closed my eyes and remained there, in the field, chasing a butterfly as it fluttered through the flowers until it flew away into the pale blue sky, beyond my vision.

I had finished my song and looked once more at the king who was now reclining upon the cushions, smiling.

"You have kept this a secret!" he marveled, motioning for me to come to him. I rested the instrument on a cushion behind me and slid into his arms.

"I did not judge myself to have adequate skill to please Your Majesty."

The king ran his fingers through my hair and kissed the top of my head. "Whatever your wish, it will be given you," he insisted. "Whatever your request, up to half the kingdom, it will be done." He looked at me with expectation.

I glanced at Haman who had touched neither wine nor food. I opened my mouth to expose the traitor, but the words did not come. Whatever I said, he would find a way to turn the accusation back upon me. The king's handsome face, filled with affection for me, would change to fury.

I was afraid.

"My wish and my request…" I began, stopping short to stall for time.

And then I knew what I would do.

"If I have won favor in the king's eyes," I said, turning my own eyes full upon him, "and if it pleases the king to grant my wish and fulfill my request, let the king and Haman come to the banquet I will prepare for them tomorrow. Then I will do as the king has said, and reveal my wish and my request."

Thirty-one

Haman went out that day happy and lighthearted. So I heard from Zeresh, who called on me soon after the banquet.

She came into the courtyard garden where I sat, lost in contemplation of my plans for the following day. It was clear that Haman had sent her to find the real purpose of my invitation. After tour last encounters, I no longer pitied her. I had come to wonder if her woeful tales of mistreatment and her sorry appearance were but a ploy to gain my confidence. Perhaps the silver necklace hiding beneath her shabby robe was compensation from her lord for the mask of shabbiness he required of her. But even if all her tales of deprivation were true, my heart would remain hardened to her. She was no better than her lord.

"I wish you good health and happiness," she said. She did not wait for an invitation to sit down.

"Thank you," I replied, offering no good wishes in return.

"I see you are better."

I gazed at the knowing expression on her haggard face. She knew that I had lost the baby and gave herself credit for it.

"I am better." I wondered what reward she had won for the death of my child.

Zeresh looked at me with expectation, but I said no more. Her knowledge of my loss was understood between us, as was my reluctance to discuss it.

"I have come to thank you for the great honor you bestowed upon my lord today," she said after a few moments of silence.

I nodded.

"He renders the king many services," she said, probing for my true opinion of her lord.

"The king has come to depend on him." I considered how I might rid myself of her company without arousing even deeper suspicion of my intentions.

"It is unusual for you to visit me at this hour," I noted. "I hope this means that someone has relieved you of preparing your evening meal."

Zeresh clicked her tongue in disgust. She brought her hands together around her neck, pressing her thumbs into her throat as if to indicate a hanging. "There will be no meal in my lord's house until the Jew at the gate is punished for his disrespect."

Her vile words and gestures made me tremble. "I do not know of what you speak." The words scraped my dry throat like coarse sand on smooth skin.

"The Jew in the gate!" she shrieked. "The one who would not bow! Now he has returned to his post. As my lord left you this afternoon, happy and lighthearted, the Jew would not even look up from his work. My lord said nothing to him but hurried home across the market square. He told me that you had made him guest of honor, and he mentioned the invitation for tomorrow. 'Yet all this is nothing to me,' my lord declared, 'as long as I see Marduka the Jew sitting in the king's gate.'

"'My lord should not suffer this insult day after day!' I told him. And I suggested he build a gallows, fifty cubits high so it rises over our courtyard gate for all in the market square to see. 'In the morning tell the king to have the Jew hanged on it!' I said. 'Then you can go in happiness to the queen's second feast.'"

Zeresh smiled and patted my arm as if to reassure me. "He praised my plan," she boasted. "Even now he is supervising the construction of a gallows from the tallest thorn tree in Susa. In the morning he will go to the king and tell him the Jew must be put to death."

My eyes grew dim and my head spun. I tried to stand, to bring myself back from the abyss of darkness. I clenched my jaws together, swallowing the cries of my tearing heart.

"I am not well." The words came from my mouth echoed as if they were spoken from a great distance. My knees were too unsteady to support my weight, but I walked in the valley of the shadow of death.

I awoke in my chamber with Hathach and Puah at my side. Puah insisted that I drink a brew of warm water, honey, and lemon. I thanked her for the refreshment and took a small mouthful to please her.

"She is still weak from her loss," Puah said to Hathach.

"And the shock of the edict," Hathach added.

"It grows worse," I looked from one questioning face to the other. "Haman intends to bring a death warrant against Marduka tomorrow morning. Even now he is constructing a gallows at this house on the square."

We spoke for many hours, trying to form a plan to save my cousin. Puah believed he would be safest hiding in Egypt; I wished him to flee to Jerusalem. Hathach knew of a guide who traveled the empire buying and selling rare and strange things. At last we agreed that it would be best for my cousin to represent himself as a traveling cloth merchant, and that Puah would gather fabric from the workshop of the royal dressmaker for him.

I was about to send Hathach to rouse the guide and Mordechai when a knock sounded on the chamber door.

"His Majesty is restless," the messenger explained. "He requests your company and the sweet sound of your instrument to lull him to sleep."

"I must dress," I told the messenger, indicating with a nod of my head that Hathach should have the youth wait for me in the passage.

Puah rose to help me change into a robe of fine linen over which I covered myself with the crimson tunic I had worn earlier. "We move forward," I whispered to her. "After I leave, you and Hathach should do what we have discussed. But wait for a message from me, in case I find favor with the king. Perhaps I will yet find the words to save my cousin."

Puah nodded in agreement.

The image of Haman's gallows loomed in my heart, causing me to recall how much pleasure he had taken in the execution of Bigthan and Teresh. Mordechai had saved the king from those traitors, even as they acted under Haman's authority. I needed to find a way to remind the king of Marduka's service, and persuade him to save Marduka in return.

I entered the king's chamber with caution, holding the santur close to my body. More than a month had passed since I was last summoned, but the room looked much the same. The sculpture of my

252

head still sat at his bedside. Perhaps, I told myself, he was more weary with himself than with me. Perhaps, that afternoon at the banquet was not the first time his vigor failed and he had been reluctant to call me for fear that I would discover his loins to have grown weak beyond remedy.

I found him pacing up and down the room, cup in hand, his face pale with nervous exhaustion. But he paused when he noticed me and smiled. "Come, Queen Esther," he beckoned, dismissing his attendants with a flick of his elbow. "I have prayed to Ahura Mazda but He has not quieted my spirit. Play for me that I might drift into slumber."

He drained his cup and tossed it to the floor. Then he let his purple wool outer robe drop to his feet and draped his large and muscular body, clad only a thin silk undertunic, across his mattress. He tapped his hand at his side, indicating that I was to sit next to him.

I crossed my legs under myself, my heart fluttering in confusion. I had never been summoned to the king for companionship and the prospect was more pleasant than I liked to admit. Stretched out before me was not a lustful monarch nor a weak leader, nor a drunken tyrant. Here was a man, like any other, searching for sleep when it would not come to him. He reached over and patted my knee. His hand lingered for a moment and he sighed as if in regret. I might have loved this man, had he revealed himself to me before plundering my innocence.

"I have not enjoyed a woman for some days," he confessed, "and the doctor has told me to refrain from wine. Sleep eludes me. What is left?"

"Your Majesty is exhausted from the cares of state," I suggested. "Perhaps if you heed the doctor's advice you will soon regain your former health and strength."

"But if I cannot sleep…" he objected.

"We all endure sleepless nights," I assured him, bending over the instrument in my lap in order to stroke his wide brow.

"Can this be true?" he asked with surprise. "I have known sleepless nights in battle, but never except by choice."

I smiled down upon his troubled face, restraining my amusement at the life this great warrior had led. His days had been spent with the companions of his choosing who spoke only words he wished to hear. He never made inquiries on matters that did not concern him. How easy it would be to tell him falsehoods about the world of common men and all those things which had never been in his experience!

"Will you play for me?" he asked. Were it not for the long, well-groomed beard, I might have taken him for a small boy.

I plucked the strings with a soft touch, playing an Indian melody that I had learned the week before—a sad song, filled with the longing of a lover whose mistress has been given to another in marriage.

The king's eyelids grew heavy. I changed to a slower song, one that evoked the waves lapping against the shore on the River Euphrates. Then I improvised a tune, much like the one I had played for the king earlier in the day. When I saw his chest rising in the rhythmic breaths of sleep, I rested my weary fingers.

His eyes opened at once and he started up in alarm like one who had seen Druj Nasu hovering over his body.

"My Lord!" I declared, "you are pale."

"I saw a vision…" His voice faltered.

I doubted that a vision could come to one who had been asleep no more than a few moments. The ill effects of too much wine, I assumed.

"A man with a knife!" the king whispered in terror. "He had the eyes of my brother Masistes."

"His Majesty has never spoken of this brother," I replied with caution, for indeed, the subject of his treacherous brother was forbidden in the palace.

"He perished on the road to Bactria, where he was viceroy."

"May his memory be blessed," I said before I could stop myself from offering the automatic response.

"May his memory be cursed!" The king declared, jumping up from the mattress to take up his pacing again. "I sent my army against him when I heard he was plotting a revolt."

"He left you no choice," I assured him.

The king lifted his cup from the floor and held it out to me. I lay the santur down and rose to refill it.

"My own brother would have overthrown my rule."

I said nothing, but looked at him with an attentive gaze to show my eagerness to hear his story. The king waved his hand as if it was nothing but a small matter.

"His wife lost her nose and ears by a knife meant for another," he explained. "Masistes blamed me. I had not ordered the mutilation, but he blamed me. I even offered him any concubine from my harem to replace the damaged wife. But he held on to his anger like a woman.

I recognized the story of the king's niece Artaynta and her mother. The niece, I knew, had since married the king's oldest son

Darius, and they lived in Bactria by the Hindukush mountains. But the king's version stood in contrast to what I had heard from Puah. His own lust had sparked the tragedy, yet now he did not mention his transgressions. Perhaps he did not even remember them.

I watched the king drain his cup as if indifferent to the fate of his sister-in-law and brother. And I knew that it was a monster, not a man, who would hold no regret in his heart for his own brother's death.

The king stopped pacing while I filled his cup yet again. His eyes stared beyond me, as if looking into the past. "I saw Masistes stab me from behind. I turned to him, but his face was different. He resembled...the Elamite."

I held my breath with astonishment.

The king shook his head as if to clear it of confusion. But his brow remained furrowed with trouble. "I must consult a magus about this vision."

"Surely Your Highness has as much wisdom and more." I feared he would send me away before I could speak on my cousin's behalf.

The king smiled down on me as if I were a foolish child. "Perhaps you yourself can interpret the vision for me," he taunted.

Fear gripped me like the hangman's noose. The king might suspect me of deception if I used his invitation to turn the conversation to my purpose. Yet I could not overlook such an opportunity: surely the vision was a gift to me from God.

"Perhaps," I ventured, "your brother regretted his treachery in the end and wished to warn you of another who seeks to overthrow your reign." My voice trailed off, trembling at my own boldness.

The king laughed a bitter laugh. "I do not take Masistes to be more of a friend in death than he was in life. No doubt he sought to have me choose his daughter's husband as my successor, so his own grandson could one day sit upon the throne."

The king finished his cup and threw it down again. His restlessness turned to anger and he took me my shoulders. "I will not see that happen!" he raged through clenched teeth, shaking me as he spoke.

I felt as if my head would separate from my body. I tried to retain my composure, but I could not hold back my tears. The king did not notice. I feared that he was possessed by a demon.

Turning his anger on himself, he released me and began striking his own body, fist against fist, forearm against brow.

"Ahura Mazda, by his will, made my father king of the empire. And by the will of Ahura Mazda, my father made me the greatest after himself. By the will of Ahura Mazda I became king on my father's throne because I was the first son born to him as king. The three before me were not born to royalty as I was." The king muttered this tirade to himself, as if I were not present. "By Ahura Mazda I will not fall for my brother's tricks! The Elamite is sound in his advice that Artaxerxes be taken from his disobedient mother's bosom and returned to court to be named my heir."

I listened to the king, my heart pounding against the wall of my chest as if the king's own fist dwelt within me. Haman had urged him to bring back Vashti's younger son and to promote him over the elder, Darius, whose wife—the king's niece Artaynta—was once the king's concubine. The king could not see the true meaning of his vision, clear to me as water from the River Sha'ur.

257

I struggled against despair in the face of the king's blindness. I feared he would never see the truth of Haman's treachery, no matter what evidence might be presented. I watched him as he continued to beat his fists harder, reliving his brother's betrayal over and over. His face grew as red as my crimson robe.

"Your Highness," I addressed him in a soothing voice as I sought to lay my hands over his, "you shall bring yourself to harm."

The king allowed me to lead him to the mattress. I began to massage his feet and soon his tight muscles relaxed. His face regained its usual tone of soft sandy olive, and no more was left of his anger than the scent of it on his skin, like the smell of damp earth after a short summer storm.

I took up the santur again, playing the melodies that had soothed him earlier. But he was still restless, his arms and legs twitching from time to time as if they were pricked by Aeshma, the fiend of the wounding spear. I wondered if a story might prove a more effective distraction than music, for sometimes the troubles of others caused a man to forget his own.

And then a plan came to me. My fingers went still and I dared to speak.

"When I was a child in Babylon, my nurse used to tell me that the Gods punish a man if he has not rewarded those who do him a service."

The king sat up, frowning. "I have bestowed wealth and women upon all those who have served me well."

"But perhaps one might have been overlooked," I dared to suggest. "One who had done something once, long ago."

"And so forgotten." He spoke with a trace of concern.

I calmed my heart and formed my next words with care.
"Your Majesty could call for the Record Book of the Days."

The king considered this for a moment. "It would be a
diversion," he agreed as he lay back upon his cushions.

Two scribes were roused from their sleep and instructed
them to bring the record book to the king's chamber. They entered
with the scroll, a parchment of such weight that one could not hold it
alone. It held the record of all the events of the court and the
kingdom since the first day of the king's reign. Five years earlier they
had recorded the plot to poison the king on this scroll, just as I had
dictated it to them.

The scribes entered, their clipped beards and the folds of
their tunics indicating them to be of Greek origin. I motioned for the
scroll to be placed on the carpet. As I arranged cushions for them to
sit upon, I bent low to them and whispered, "Find the place where
Marduka saves the king's life and you shall be rewarded."

They nodded without looking up.

I left them on the floor and returned to my place beside the
king.

"It is my wish that you read to me," the king commanded,
raising himself on one elbow to look at the scribes.

"Does Your Majesty wish a certain year?" one scribe asked.

The king shrugged and looked at me.

"Perhaps five years ago, in the seventh year of the king's
reign," I suggested, stroking the king's thigh. "For that was the year
I found favor in His Majesty's eyes. An auspicious time."

The scribes rolled the scroll back until they found the
description of Esther's feast. And then they began to read.

I listened to the account of the day I was named queen and my flesh crawled as if a thousand spiders covered me. I would have given any of God's gifts to me, my health or my youth, my sight or my teeth, to have escaped the life of the palace, to be spared what I had become. I would rather look like Freni and be a slave to a poor man, than sit as plump as a stuffed chicken in luxury as the wife of this king. And then I imagined, for just a moment, that I might meet Mordechai in the dead of night and flee to Jerusalem where we could pass as husband and wife. I would bear him a son who would carry the name of my father and do good in the world.

But I knew I could not let such ideas form in myself. I had come to this day and this place and I could not go back.

Soon the scribe reached the account of the eunuchs' attempt to poison the king. The description of Bigthan and Teresh's treachery roused the king's attention. He leapt from the bed and began pacing close to the scribes.

"Those traitors would have sent me to my death!" he recalled, his voice quivering with excitement. "Were it not for my servant Haman, my elder son would have taken the throne and Masistes' grandson would have followed after him. This is what the vision must have been! By Haman's cunning, the two were stopped. Now I must stop Masistes' heir."

My spirits sank as the king gave Haman credit for Mordechai's deed.

"But your majesty does not recollect the story in its entirety," one of the scribes replied, daring to contradict the king.

"Is that so?" the king bristled.

"It is recorded that the King's treasury official, Marduka, is the one who uncovered the plot. Haman the Elamite provided assistance with the prisoners and the gallows."

"By Ahura Mazda!" the king declared. "What honor or promotion has been conferred upon this Marduka for his deed?"

The scribes bent low over the parchment, both reading on in silence for a moment.

"It appears that nothing has been done for him, Your Majesty," one concluded, his eyes yet on the scroll.

"Who knows the man?" the king asked.

"He is a Jew," I offered, hoping by this to soften the king's heart toward my people.

"He works in the king's gate and is said to be very loyal to the king," the second scribe added.

The king opened his mouth to issue a command. But a noise in the court interrupted him and we heard loud footsteps were tapping on the smooth stone.

"Who is it at this hour?" the king called out. "They will murder me yet," he muttered.

A guard from entered the room and prostrated himself before the king. His golden sword fell with a muffled clatter upon the carpet.

"Haman the Elamite has come," he replied. "He wishes an urgent word with Your Majesty."

Thirty-two

The king said, "Let him in!"

I watched Haman push past the guard, his tall turban rising far above the king's own uncovered head. He did not prostrate himself before the king or acknowledge me, though I held the king's arm. Taking no notice of the scribes or the scroll, he hurried across the room without even seeking permission to approach.

I knew his purpose, yet could not prevent him from voicing it. But before Haman even opened his mouth, the king spoke.

"You are just the man I need!" the king exclaimed this with a cheerfulness of spirit, as if all of the wild restlessness and anger of the past hours had been a trick of my imagination.

"I am honored," Haman replied with a slight bow. He stood so close to me that I could smell his musky perfume.

"Then tell me this," the king asked, "what should be done for a man whom the king desires to honor?"

Had not my cousin's life hung in the balance, I would have laughed at the spectacle that followed. For though the king spoke of Mordechai, I saw that Haman believed the honor was for him. His shoulders drew back in pride and his cheeks expanded as if he held a pomegranate in each. A victorious smile crept across his face, though no battle had been fought. His desire for Mordechai's death gave way to the prospect of increasing his own honor.

"The man whom the king desires to honor…" the Elamite echoed. His voice broke off as he savored all the possible rewards for which he might ask. And as I looked from face to face in the room, I saw no surprise at the advisor's lack of deference. No one else dared speak to the king in such a manner. Yet so elevated in his own esteem was Haman the Elamite that he acted as an equal to the king. Nor did the king seem to take offense. Scorn crept into my heart. A king who allowed his stature to fall so low in the eyes of his court was a weak man and a poor leader.

At last Haman began to speak, his eyes gleaming with ecstasy. "Let the royal robe be brought," he said, "the robe that the king himself wears. And bring, too, a horse upon which the king has ridden, with the royal headpiece upon its head. Let the robe and the horse be entrusted to one of the king's most noble courtiers and let him attire the man whom the king desires to honor. Let the noble courtier lead the horse around the city square. And…" Haman paused, relishing the image. "let the courtier proclaim: 'This is done for the man whom the king desires to honor!'"

The king kissed his advisor on each cheek. "Hurry!" he commanded, "take the robe and the horse as you have described. Do this for Marduka the Jew, who sits in the king's gate. Leave out nothing from what you have said." And then the king dismissed everyone with a wave of his arm. I glanced at Haman. He looked as if he had turned to stone, the expression of pride frozen on his face. What he had imagined as his own coronation, wearing the king's robe and riding the king's horse, would be his enemy's honor. The words that brought such pleasure to his tongue—*the man whom the king desires to honor*—had turned to poison.

King Xerxes took my hand and raised it to his lips. "Come play again," he said, his voice like a raven's feather gliding across the black night. "I have given the man his due and now I shall be able to sleep."

The scribes rolled and lifted the scroll as if their lives depended on leaving the room that instant. Then I smiled at Haman as if he were my friend, though I am sure he could see the laughter in my eyes. His beard quivered and his shoulders sagged, but he remained immobile. Somehow he carried himself off to his task, for after I settled myself on the mattress with the santur, I looked up and he was gone.

I played for the king again and he soon fell into a deep sleep. I held my fingers still and when I saw that he did not wake, I hurried from the room through the colonnade to my garden. I called the eunuch's name the moment my feet stepped over the threshold.

"Hathach!" My voice echoed in the empty courtyard. "Hathach!"

No one answered. I was alone in the world. Panic rose in my throat, and I saw how the yellow irises—as fresh yesterday as Anatana's sunny smile—had faded and withered in the cool shadows of the dawn. Perhaps I had died, I told myself, and this garden courtyard was my eternal prison of loneliness.

I climbed the stairs to my chamber where I found a maid, grown weary of awaiting my return, asleep on the cushions. I did not rouse her; she might be dreaming of a happy place where she was free.

I stood on the garden balcony until sunbeams crept across the floor and kissed my maid's lips. She woke in fear and prostrated herself before me, terrified that I would be angry with her for falling asleep.

"Say nothing more of it!" I smiled. Though I had been queen for five years, I did not enjoy holding authority over others and did not welcome being the object of fear. "Perhaps you know where I can find Puah."

"I was to tell you…" the girl began and broke off, crying with shame for her failure. And before she could collect enough to relay the message, the old servant herself came into the chamber.

"Vadhut has had her baby," she announced, pride and pleasure spreading over her face. "A little girl she has asked to name Esther. It was an easy labor and the child is already nursing."

"May she continue to be well," I wished. And though I held back my tears, I could not ignore the pain in my heart. I was relieved for Vadhut and delighted that the child was healthy; I hoped she could keep the baby and even wondered whether I held enough influence in the court to make that possible. But the loss of my own child grieved me all the more for Vadhut's happy news. The king could no longer give me a child. With or without the extermination of the Jews, my father's line would perish.

Unless I was released from the king and permitted to marry another. In that moment, I knew that my heart would be directed toward this desire forever. I might love or hate the king, I might enjoy the luxuries of my life as queen or shun them, but from day to day and year to year I would mourn my empty womb.

"I must visit my friend soon," I added. "And we should send word to Freni. But not until Hathach has returned with his news."

"Where has he gone?" Puah asked.

"The king has bestowed an honor upon Mordechai," I explained. And despite the threat that still hung over my people, I could not help but smile at the image of Mordechai in the royal saddle, on a horse led by Haman. We settled on the balcony cushions and while we waited for Hathach I told Puah all that had happened the night before.

When the sun was almost at its mid-day peak, Hathach returned. I urged him to tell us all that he had seen and heard of Mordechai's honor.

"At dawn I had word that the king himself had decreed the highest honors for Marduka the treasury official, for the service of saving his life. The whole court was buzzing with talk of this distinction, one that no man had ever been given before: Marduka was to mount the king's best horse wearing the king's purple robe, and then to be escorted through the town by Haman himself. None dared laugh at Haman's humiliation, but never did I see so many faces lowered to restrain a smile!"

Puah grinned, the wrinkles at the corners of her eyes folding even further into deep crevasses.

"Mordechai was already at work," the eunuch continued, "though the first light of the day was just showing. I joined the large group of court servants who went to the gatehouse to witness the conferring of this honor. He was sitting at his place within the inner room, examining account records, when we arrived. I could see from the sorrow and resolve upon his face that he expected punishment rather than reward. But before anyone could speak, the crowd parted for Haman. The wardrobe keeper followed him, carrying a royal robe. The horse master led a magnificent white stallion fitted with a gold and silver headpiece. The harness, saddle, and reins were all encrusted with jewels and gold medallions.

"The Elamite stepped forward to Mordechai. His face was red with fury. He would not look at the treasury official, but kept his

266

gaze focused on the wall beyond. Laughter rose in my throat and I pinched myself to prevent it from escaping. But I was bursting to tell someone that the advisor had spent his night constructing a gallows for the very man now honored by the king. I turned to a companion, the eunuch Harbonah, and whispered in his ear. But Harbonah could not contain himself and released a high-pitched laugh.

"Haman turned to see who had dared to issue such an insulting sound in his presence. Only then did he realize that no one was prostrating before him.

"We held our breaths, waiting to see if Haman would dare order the punishment of the king's servants who had gathered to witness the scene. But the Elamite did no more than throw us a look of loathing before he turned back to Marduka.

"'The king has ordered that you be dressed in his robe and placed on his horse to be taken though the square,' he said clenching his teeth.

"'For what reason am I so honored?'" Marduka replied, rising from his seat. His hands were covered in ink and his beard unkempt. Indeed he looked more like a common scribe than a treasury official.

"'You once saved the king's life!' a voice called out from the crowd.

"I could not see Marduka's response, for Haman quickly covered him with the robe and assisted him in mounting the horse. The crowd followed them out of the gatehouse and down the grand stair, cheering Marduka as Haman called out: 'This is done for the man whom the king desires to honor!'

"Word must have spread to the town below the acropolis, for soon a crowd of Jews came running to witness one of their own in the king's robe. I heard some of them asking each other if this meant that the king's edict yet stood. Others, familiar with the law, observed that such an order could not be changed, but they rejoiced that a Jew had been deemed worthy of this honor.

"'God in His wisdom will save us if we merit saving!' I heard one old man say.

"'The Almighty is waiting to see if we are worthy! I heard another reply. 'We must show Him by rising up to fight for our lives!'

"'Listen to Marduka!' a third called out. 'The words and the deeds of the pious will save us!'

"I pushed my way through the crowd, drawing close enough to the horse and its rider to see Marduka. He was chanting something that seemed familiar to all of the Jews, for one-by-one they joined in until it seemed that even heaven and earth were part of the chorus."

"What did they say?" Puah asked with eagerness.

"It seemed to be a poem," Hathach replied. "But it was in Hebrew, a language I cannot speak. So I turned to a young Jewish woman next to me and asked her to translate. She said it was a poem by David, a great king of the Jews from long ago. 'I will exalt You God for you have drawn me up and not let my foes rejoice over me,' she said. 'Lord, my God, I cried out to you and you healed me.'"

The words entered my ears and flooded my heart until I could no longer remain seated. "Tonight I shall tell the king the truth of his advisor's plots and evil deeds!" I declared, rising from the cushions. "I shall not let my foes rejoice over me!" Then I bent down and kissed Puah, whose jubilant expression had changed to fear. "Do not worry," I assured her. "The One God will hear me."

I sent Puah to check on Vadhut again, to make sure my friend was comfortable and had everything she needed. Then I thanked Hathach for all his efforts. As I instructed him to direct the preparation of the second feast, it came to me that I might gain further advantage over Haman if I met him in the king's part of the palace.

"I wish to entertain the king in his own quarters this time," I said, "for then I will appear to hold influence over the king in his own domain. His Majesty's private gardens are said to be the most beautiful in all the empire. Perhaps we might secure permission from his chamberlain."

"I shall do my utmost," Hathach bowed. "Should your maids be sent in to help you prepare?"

I nodded.

The eunuch left the room and I rose to choose a costume from my wardrobe. Two attendants cared for my clothes and brought me whatever I desired to wear, and I still often sought Hegai's advice in these matters. But today I wished to make my selection alone.

I stood in the wardrobe, which seemed to me as big as the entire house in which I had lived with my parents by the shore of the River Euphrates. Boxes and chests of fine clothing and jewels rose high on the floor. Above them shelves held rows of soft leather shoes and embroidered linen robes. Three chests contained headpieces of gold and veils of sheer lace. Near the door sat a cosmetic table with a special polished stone in which I could see my own image.

I lit the lamp at the table and gazed at myself for a moment, a woman of twenty with good health and a purpose that could not be denied or delayed. I wondered how much of my mother's looks I carried with me, if anyone in Babylon would recognize me as

Hadassah daughter of Avihail son of Shemei. I would never know what it was like to walk in my mother's footsteps, to be regarded by those who knew her as a blessing to her memory.

I chose the plainest, most simple thing amongst all the finery, a soft white linen shift embroidered at the neck with little yellow tulips. My sandals were crafted of saffron-dyed leather and tied around the ankles in the Greek style. I combed my hair and left it loose, a cascade of gold flowing down to my waist. Then I searched the boxes beneath the cosmetic table for a perfume that would give me the scent of a young virgin again, sweet and fresh. I opened two or three vials, but found none to my liking. One bottle had a powerful scent of myrrh and labdanum, both acrid and cloying at the same time. I wondered for what purpose such a scent could have been made, for it smelled like something a demon of the night might wear. At last I settled upon a simple splash of rosewater. The maids arrived as I applied my only cosmetics—kohl around the eyes and a red stain on my lips.

"Zeresh is at the door below begging for Your Majesty," one said, breathless with rushing.

"The guard asked us to tell you," added the other, "For Hathach is not to be found."

"The hairdresser and wardrobe attendants shall be here in but a moment," the first maid added.

"Thank you, but I shall not require them," I replied. "Please bring a garland of fresh white flowers for my hair, and send the visitor to the dining room." I dreaded the prospect of another visit from Zeresh, but I hoped it would be my last.

The maids bowed and took their leave.

I found Zeresh examining one of the silver plates on display in the dining room. She dropped it when she heard my footsteps.

"How could you let the king humiliate my lord in such a way?" she demanded, as if I had awarded Mordechai's honors. "Even now as you take your ease, my lord is suffering humiliation for having led a Jew around the square on the king's own horse!"

"I have no authority over the king's edicts," I pointed out.

"The Jews are rejoicing at the honor bestowed upon their hero!" she hissed, clawing at her own arms as she clutched herself. "They say their people will be saved."

"The order for their death yet stands," I observed.

Zeresh's hands relaxed and the slits of her eyes widened. "You give me a wise reminder," she acknowledged, bowing and fawning as if the falseness of her gestures would escape me.

"Go home and comfort your lord," I suggested my voice as cold as the snow of the Hindukush mountains. I turned away from her and walked toward the door. But I paused and whirled back around to face her. "The Jews are a mighty nation," I said, feeling the strength surge in my own bones and blood. "Your lord will never defeat them."

Thirty-three

Before the king and Haman arrived, one of the king's chamberlains, the eunuch Harbonah, escorted me to the pavilion where the feast was laid. The king's private garden was said to be the most magnificent of the empire. In the early years of his reign, King Darius had built the garden as a retreat from all the cares of state. The voice of the prophet Zoroaster had spoken to him, promising a place of blissful delight on earth if he planted fruit and fragrant flowers, and lay paths of burnished gold. He had carried out this vision and been well-rewarded by the results.

I had heard much of this garden's beauty but had not seen it with my own eyes. I knew from court gossip that Vashti had often walked there uninvited with her attendants. The king was angered by her trespassing, but she had not heeded his demand to stay away. And because I wished to be as unlike Vashti as possible—a clear, calm pool to the raging torrent of her rapids—I had never even hinted to the king that I desired the pleasure of a visit. Nor did the king extend an invitation to me, for after Vashti was banished, the garden became his most cherished private retreat.

But now I stepped over the boundary that I had drawn between Queen Vashti and myself. I could no longer spend my idle days in the queen's quarters, playing my santur and relying upon Hathach to keep me from harm. Even if my people were saved, I knew that I would forever be on my guard against those who would seek to do us harm.

The garden had two entrances. The many workers needed to maintain the rare and profuse plantings used a well-guarded gate near the stables. Harbonah took me to the door that the king and his servants used, behind a curtain in the throne room. As he led the way through the deserted throne room, I stared at the golden throne rising empty before me. I shuddered to recall how the day before I had stepped onto the purple carpet and looked upon the dazzling throne, not knowing if I would live or die.

Harbonah lifted the curtain and we passed through a small door into a dark narrow passage that soon opened into daylight. We stepped onto a path paved with gold-flecked stones. Flowers and fragrant herbs grew in the cracks between these stones and the path was flanked on either side by a white limestone watercourse flowing with clear water that sparkled like diamonds in the sunlight. Beds of low shrubs with glossy leaves and flowers ran beside the watercourses. Beyond this I could see behind them even rows of fruit trees: sour cherry, pomegranate, apple, fig. We continued on the path, which seemed to widen toward the center where many paths converged into a circular plaza. A pink marble fountain rose high here, decorated with white marble animals: ibex, lion, gazelle. Gilded benches offered views of the fountain from every angle and tall date palms rose high above them to give shade.

We did not stop to rest on the benches, but turned onto a path that led away from the fountain toward a gleaming white pavilion. I walked with more speed now, my steps matching the pace of my pounding heart as I rehearsed the words I would use to my lord and king. For though I had already said them to myself a thousand times, I took comfort in reviewing them yet again. I had promised to tell the king my wish and my request on this day. If I could make him see that I lived and died by the fate of my people, perhaps he would turn against the man who planned their annihilation.

We reached the pavilion and Harbonah entered before me. After ensuring that all was in order, he returned to escort me up the low stairs, through the columns into an open room of splendid decoration. I walked across floors of white marble, polished to such a high sheen that it reflected everything in the room. The ceiling was low and ringed with a molding of stone rosettes painted with a wash of lapis lazuli. Hangings of sheer scarlet and saffron dyed linen were suspended around the perimeter of the room from silver rods with golden tassels. A blue and green carpet woven in the style of Tabriz with small medallions of fine flowers and vines lay in the center. On the carpet rested three sofas, each covered with purple fabric as soft as a rose petal, with rolled backs against which to recline and golden legs in the shape of a falcon's talons.

The sofas formed a ring around a low table in the center spread with wine, fruit, and sweets. Servants stood ready behind each sofa with fans, their faces as still as the stone floor. Harbonah seated me where I could see both my guests to best advantage. I lay back to wait.

Haman entered first, escorted by two eunuchs. He wore a dark blue robe and turban which exaggerated the paleness of his skin. His eyes flashed at me even as he bowed, and I knew that Zeresh had told him of our most recent meeting. He sat upon the sofa as if it were his own. He extended his arm across the sofa's rolled back, flexing his fingers so that the king's golden signet ring glimmered against the purple fabric. As I looked away from his hand, he caught my eye. His top lip stiffened and raised in a subtle gesture of superiority and scorn. I felt glass shatter in my skull and fire scorch my bones.

I tried to calm myself by recalling Mordechai as I had first seen him when I came to Susa. His sweet face, his loving voice, his kindness to me: these memories yet dwelt in my heart. The wild tulip I picked for him that first day had been trampled in the mud. But now I intended to deliver a more lasting gift: the defeat of his enemy. I prayed to the One God, asking Him to help me, to make the king strong enough to defy Haman—for the sake of Freni, Puah, Mordechai, and all my people.

The king came fast upon the heels of Haman, eager to see me. I started to rise, but he signaled for me to remain on the sofa. My passions stirred as he bent low over me. He breathed in the scent of the fragrant lilies on my head and then brushed his soft lips over mine.

"I slept like a baby in its mother's arms," he smiled. His face glowed with well-being and I could see that he had not yet indulged in his cup that day. He had donned the attire of a Greek hero: a white, knee-length chiton with many folds, a large section draped over one shoulder, exposing the powerful muscles of the other. He wore a garland of laurels upon his head. And though his hair was pressed close to his head like the Greeks, his beard remained trimmed and curled in the long square style of the Persians. I could not guess what he imagined himself to be, but he seemed to be filled with confidence and energy, as if he had never known the demon of melancholy.

"I have sent for my son Artaxerxes!" he announced, pulling away from me and taking a seat upon the third couch. My heart fell as I watched Haman's ears perk up like a wild animal on the hunt. "He shall come and train to be a warrior and a leader of warriors. And by Ahura Mazda he will take the throne when it is his time."

"His majesty has made a wise decision," Haman observed, the words sliding from his mouth like a serpent slithering through the tall river reeds.

"But let us enjoy today!" the king sang out, clapping his hands and reaching for a bunch of grapes from the table. "Queen Esther has invited us to a feast and promised to reveal her heart's desire to me."

I smiled and nodded at the king as the red juice of the grapes trickled down his lips into his beard, splattering the white chiton like a speckled bird's egg.

"Come," he demanded, wiping his mouth with the back of his hand. "Whatever your wish, it will be given you." He flung his arms out wide to either side as if to indicate that anything I desired could be mine. "Whatever your request," he continued, "up to half the kingdom, it will be done."

I gazed at him with fondness, for I knew his generosity and affection were genuine. I had held a place in his heart far longer than I could have hoped. I knew him to be an impulsive, reckless man, diminished by wine and idleness. He was a warrior who did not fight, a king who did not rule, a brother who turned his lust upon his niece, a father who cared nothing for his children. Yet whenever I looked at him, I replaced the king I saw with the king I imagined, as he might still become. One day, I hoped, the passions of my flesh would be attached to a man I respected and admired.

My head spun and I leaned back against the rolled edge of the sofa. *Whatever your request.* It was time to speak.

I remembered the scarlet wedding belt I wove for Mordechai on that terrible day, so long ago. I remembered the fragrant loaf of bread I had put into the oven. I remembered my black hair and slender body. These were the things I desired. But the king could not return them to me.

The words flowed from me like a river.

"If it pleases the king and I have found favor in his eyes, let my life be given to me as my wish and my people as my request. For we have been sold, my people and I, to be annihilated, killed, and destroyed." I saw the king's merry expression flood with confusion and I hurried to finish. "Had we been sold as slaves, I would have remained silent, for our adversity would not have been worth the bother or the loss to the king's treasury."

I heard my words while I said them, truer than anything I had ever spoken to him. I faced my lord now as I was, Hadassah daughter of Avihail the Jew.

The king's face grew red with rage, spreading to his neck and thrusting him to his feet.

"Who is it?" the king demanded, clenching his fists and drawing himself up to his full height. "Where is the one who dared to do this?"

I glanced at Haman, reclining on his sofa as if nothing I had said could concern him. He was examining his fingernails in great detail, straining to find an imperfection. He brushed a speck off the sleeve of his robe and looked up at me, eyebrows raised, as if to indicate he found the conversation tedious and hoped that I would soon finish.

"He is here, in this very room," I whispered, pointing at the king's advisor, "my adversary and enemy."

The Elamite shrugged. "Women should not meddle in the affairs of state," he said.

"What matter does she speak of?" the king demanded.

Haman remained calm. "An edict authorized by Your Majesty's own seal. Your treasury is ten thousand silver talents richer for it."

I recalled the king's vision of his treacherous brother. "This man is no better than Masistes. Your Majesty has been tricked, deceived, and betrayed."

Haman hissed at me and rose to face the king.

"Need I remind His Majesty that he himself has commanded the wives of the realm to obey the will of their lords?"

The king stood still for a moment, staring at the one man in whom he had placed his trust over the last five years. I could read his face as if it were a book and I a scribe. He did not recollect authorizing the extermination of any people, and he did not yet understand that I was a Jewess. But my accusation and Haman's arrogance had caused him to doubt the advisor's loyalty.

"He has tricked you into signing my death warrant!" I cried. "He has plotted to betray and dishonor you, and this is why he was linked to Masistes in your vision."

The mighty king Xerxes, who ruled from Hindush in the east to Kusha in the west, opened his mouth as if to condemn Haman. But his throat was swollen shut with fury. When no words came to him, he stormed out of the pavilion into the garden.

The king's eunuchs and servants all hurried after him, leaving me alone with Haman. He stared down at me, his face no longer a mask but a seething cauldron of rage. "Do you imagine you can win against the true queen?" he whispered, approaching me with his teeth bared.

I shrank back into the sofa.

"Do you imagine you will ever take her place?"

He bent down over me, pinning his hand against my shoulder and putting his lips to my ear.

"She has killed your child and she will kill you."

My spirit cried out in horror to feel his flesh upon mine. And so I screamed for help as if I were being ravished. The Elamite covered my mouth with his sweaty palm. But the king bounded back into the pavilion, swift and sleek as a panther.

His eyes gathered the sight of Haman upon me and he flew across the floor to my aid. "Would he take the queen with me in the house?" The king thundered. He grabbed Haman by the shoulders and shook him like a hare in the jaws of a lion. Haman's silver breastplate crashed against his chest, as if his very bones rattled in the king's powerful grip.

"You are deceived by a false and immodest woman!" Haman sputtered. "My years of service to you…"

"Years of treachery!" the king raged through clenched teeth. He pushed Haman away with such force that the Elamite fell backwards to the floor. Two of the king's eunuchs came forward to seize the fallen advisor and raised him to his feet. He struggled for a moment until another eunuch came and covered his head with a cloak.

"What shall be done with a creature such as this?" the king asked, his voice filled with the proud disdain of a triumphant warrior. He rose tall and magnificent in the center of the pavilion, a wonder to behold. He knew as well as I that the Elamite had not intended to harm me, and that this was nothing more than a performance to avoid the truth: he had permitted his seal to be used on my death decree. But I did not care. For he stood the master of his realm once more.

"What shall be done with the traitor?" the king cried out again.

I closed my eyes and imagined the gallows in Haman's courtyard, just as Hathach had described it, rising before me. I remembered all those who had suffered at the hands of the Elamite and all whom he would have seen exterminated. I remembered his own pleasure in securing the ropes for the eunuchs whom he had used against the king. And I knew what justice demanded, but my throat burned as if a sword of fire rose from my stomach and I could not bring myself to say it aloud. "The gallows in Haman's courtyard," I whispered to Harbonah who stood next to me. "He made it for Marduka, who saved the king."

Harbonah stepped forward. "There stands in Haman's courtyard a gallows," Harbonah announced. "He built it to hang Marduka, the treasury official who saved the life of the king."

The king heard these words and did not hesitate for a moment. "Hang him on it!" he ordered.

Thirty-four

Haman was sentenced to hang on the gallows that he had put up for Mordechai. And the king insisted that a procession go forth from the palace to witness the execution. He did not allow me to leave his presence, even as he donned his robes of state. And so I sent Hathach to my quarters for a veil and cloak.

The eunuch returned to the king's chamber with the garments, accompanied by Puah. I did not want to subject her to the sight of the execution, but she was eager to witness Haman's end and sought permission to attend me.

We spoke in whispers at the edge of the chamber. I told her how Haman had implicated Vashti in the plan to poison my child and how I feared we must beware of others who might serve as her agents. I reminded them that the Jews were still condemned to die in eleven months' time. "The king does not yet know who my people are," I explained. "He speaks as if the traitor threatened only his rule and my life."

"Where is Queen Esther?" the king called from inside his wardrobe. I kissed Puah's hands, hugged Hathach, and hurried to attend my lord.

He sat in the center of the wardrobe on a sofa, wearing a white undertunic of such fine linen that his manhood was visible to all who dared look. One eunuch curled his hair while another filed his fingernails. A beautiful Greek youth massaged his feet. Such were his preparations to attend an execution.

He gestured me forward with his free hand. And I saw that once again he wore his signet ring. "Queen of my heart!" he sang, "come sit with your king."

Just as his condemnation of Haman had stirred my desire, so had his own heart had turned to lust. I was ashamed for both of us. A traitor stood waiting at the gallows, and death hung over my people. Yet the passions of my flesh seemed to have a life of their own, as if they resided in a foreign country and spoke a language I could not master. Self-indulgence was the privilege of the king's birth and he exercised little authority over himself.

As I approached the sofa, the king dismissed his attendants and sat upright. "Leave us!" he said to the eunuchs as I sat on the edge of the sofa. "But you!" he called out to the youth with big eyes and flowing brown hair. "You stay here," he ordered, indicating a place near the sofa. Then he pulled my robe open and fondled my breasts until the nipples rose hard under his hands. He opened my robe further until all of my treasures were exposed. As he began to caress my inner thighs, I longed to surrender to him. He kissed my hungry lips and waved to the youth. But instead of sending him away, he motioned for him to join us on the sofa.

"Would you like such a vessel for your use?" the king asked. The youth nodded.

The king rubbed his hand over the young man's loincloth.

My desire shriveled like a tulip cut down in the heat. But the king's lust gathered strength from the youth. And so King Xerxes took me there, with one hand remaining on the young man's pleasure as if it were his own.

I rose from the couch as soon as I could. As I hurried to dress, I asked God to take pity on my shame and cause the king to lose the use of his manhood forever rather than permit such a thing to happen again.

I hid my disgrace beneath the veil, so thick with layers of gauzy fabric that none could see me. Puah draped a queen's cloak over my shoulders, scarlet linen with a medallion pattern embroidered in gold. I said nothing of what happened in the wardrobe. I could not look her in the eye and shrank from her touch when she tried to reassure me with a pat on the back. I could not help the revulsion that filled my heart.

We walked to the grand courtyard where the king mounted his finest horse, the very one that Mordechai had ridden earlier in the day. I climbed into a sedan chair made of cedar wood. It held a single seat inside, a wide gilded bench with a plump purple cushion. Four servants lifted the sedan chair's poles onto their shoulders and carried me behind the king toward the gatehouse.

As we entered the gatehouse, I craned my neck out of the window, hoping to catch sight of my cousin. I did not know what had become of him after he received the king's honor. Perhaps he was working late this evening and would emerge from the inner rooms to see the procession. Surely, I told myself, he must be rejoicing at news of the impending execution. A crowd formed around me. I saw the faces of soldiers and officials who worked the gate trying to glimpse the queen. The clamor grew loud and frightening. Members of the king's bodyguard pushed forward to keep a distance cleared between me and the throng. I withdrew from the window.

We soon reached the palace stairs. Five years before, the king's guard forced me to climb them, a terrified maiden held captive. Now they carried me down the same stairs as the queen. I was older in my years and much changed in my appearance. I was schooled in the desires of the flesh and the ways of the court. But I was no less a prisoner than I had been then. I was leaving the palace but I could not leave Queen Esther behind.

The din grew around me as we reached the market square and the people pressed against the circle of guards. They called out in supplication, asking that their wealth be increased, their wives be granted fertility, their sons be healed from illness. Tradition held that an appeal to the queen was more effective than a direct request to the king. People knew that the king's cares of state were always uppermost in his heart. But if the queen spoke on their behalf, they reasoned, the king would be moved to listen. He, in his turn, would appeal to his god, Ahura Mazda. Thus their prayers would have a better chance of being answered.

My father once told me that God listens to a mother's prayers first. As I heard the people, I realized that they were calling out to me as mother of the kingdom. I could be their hope and comfort. And so I resolved that if the slaughter of my people was averted, I would seek the king's permission to receive ten or twenty supplicants each day and help them in whatever way I could.

Comforted by this thought I scanned the crowd again for familiar faces. I knew everyone and no one. My spirits sank for such an opportunity might never come to me again. And then, before a fruit-seller's stand, I saw Mordechai. I brought my hand to my mouth to restrain a cry of joy.

Hathach feared that my cousin had gone mad. I had worried about all that the eunuch and Puah had told me: refusing to bow, abandoning his post to wail in the marketplace, disregard for his own life, visions of a prophet. But Freni had identified him as a hero amongst the Jews. The king had honored him. So much had happened since we parted, I no longer knew him as I once did. He no longer knew me.

I recognized him by his large eyes, heavy lids, and light skin. But he was more changed than I. He was as gaunt as a man too poor to feed himself and stooped like one who held the burdens of the world on his shoulders. His brow was wrinkled and his dark robe was dirty at the hem. But most surprising of all, his beard now flowed, untrimmed, onto his chest. He looked like a Jew: Marduka the Babylonian was no more.

My eyes fixed on Mordechai as the cab passed him. I saw his gaze upon me, though he could not see me through the veil. I wanted to call out to him, to ask him what was in his heart as he looked upon my covered head. And I longed to be an innocent girl of ten again, seeking safety in the arms of my cousin, my betrothed.

I saw the gallows rising high over the wall before we arrived at the traitor's house. Haman stood on the platform, his head still covered, a soldier at each side. None of his family or friends were in the courtyard.

The king remained on his horse, surrounded by his bodyguard, and called for me to join him. Puah and several other attendants ran forward to help me out of the cab and into the king's lap. He tossed the horse's reigns to a guard, and held me close to him with one arm around my waist. The courtyard filled with people coming to witness the execution. I knew that the king would insist that I watch, but as the guards uncovered Haman, I closed my eyes.

The king pulled the veil away from my face. The evening air felt cool and I filled my nostrils with the smell of the world beyond the palace. I tried not to see what was before me: the traitor I had exposed standing at the gallows with a noose around his neck. He stood tall and proud, as if he were a soldier facing his end with honor. But he was pale with fear and his knees trembled.

I told myself that he himself had executed many innocent men. He had sought to kill the king with his own hand, and to hang Mordechai on that very gallows. He would have danced with delight over the slaughtered bodies of my people. I told myself that this was God's justice, not my own. But still I found no relief from the heaviness in my heart. I had never desired to be queen or the instrument of God's justice. I would have been content to live out my days as wife to Marduka the treasury official, the mother of his sons.

"A traitor's property reverts to the king," the king whispered to me as he gave the signal for the hanging to commence. "All of his vast estate will be yours. Such should be your recompense for the threat on your life, my beautiful queen, the only one I can trust."

With this single impulsive gift, King Xerxes made me a wealthy woman, independent of all other beneficence he might bestow or withhold in the future.

Haman did not leave this world with ease. His legs jerked and twitched. His arms flailed. His narrow eyes bulged and his thick tongue shot out of his mouth. It seemed that that he would not die. Burning bile rose from my stomach into my throat, but I held it down with all my will. The king laughed at the sight of the writhing body and tickled my side. Glancing up at the house, I saw black cloth flutter in a window of the second floor. Zeresh must have been hiding there in the shadows, watching her lord's demise. Perhaps she was glad to be free of him.

At last a guard mounted the scaffolding and adjusted the rope. In a moment or two Haman's body hung lifeless. The crowd cheered. I took the veil from the king's hand and covered my head again. And I wept.

Thirty-five

King Xerxes fulfilled his promise to me by announcing his gift of Haman's property in public after the hanging. I remained with the king on his horse for the return to the palace, an uncomfortable ride during which I kept sliding down the side of the saddle. Each time the king hoisted me back up and laughed, as if he enjoyed the game. The people in the market square waved and clapped as we passed and the king whispered that I should return their greetings. "They love their queen," he said to me, "love them back." I tried to wave as if my heart was light and full of gladness. I waved so they would know I was not the wicked Vashti who cared nothing for her lord's subjects. But I could not forget the image of Haman swinging from the gallows.

The gatehouse soon rose above us, beckoning me back to the queen's quarters. I scanned the crowd with frantic desperation. I hoped and I prayed—as if my life were at stake—for another glimpse of Mordechai, or perhaps even Aia or Freni.

But I saw no one I knew amongst the dirt-smudged faces and dusty robes. And I realized that I no longer knew myself. For now, after all my time at court, even the prosperous men and women of Susa looked poor to me. I had grown used to the luxury of the palace, the fine clothes and the furnishings, the gardens and the abundant meals, the immaculate cleanliness. My life was one of luxury and privilege, far above that with which most in this world would be blessed. Yet I had been happier holding my mother's hand on the shores of the Euphrates and helping Aia with the chores. The clothes and jewels, the rich dishes and fine wines, the slaves and servants, the king's attentions: all these trappings had brought me little joy.

As the horse began to climb the wide stairs, it seemed that the king's arm grew tighter around my waist and I suffocated beneath the veil. I did not know how many years would pass before I could again leave the palace. But I knew I would find a way to see Mordechai soon, and I held this resolution in my heart as a salve for my sorrows.

When we reached the palace, the king insisted that we dine in his reception hall. But after three or four ministers came to ask him questions on matters of state and policy, he moved into a smaller dining chamber. But regardless of where we sat, the ministers would persist. For Haman was no longer there to take charge and until the king named a replacement, he himself would have to attend to running the empire.

"If only the traitor had not executed all my worthy advisors," the king complained, draining his third cup of wine and waving the golden vessel in my direction, indicating that I was to pour him another. As he began to eat a morsel of ostrich and pistachio stew, the minister of the royal road was announced. The king threw himself back on the cushions and closed his eyes, groaning.

"Your Majesty," the minister bowed and then prostrated himself.

"Get up," the king snapped, not looking at his minister.

"I have a question of urgent importance from the governor of Media regarding the bridge at the Aspadana river."

"Guards!" the king bellowed.

Four of the king's bodyguard appeared.

"Send this man away," the king demanded. His eyes crinkled in pain and he waved his hands in frustration toward the door.

"But Your Majesty…" the minister implored.

"Let no one come before me unless I request it!" The king shouted.

The guards escorted the minister from the room and closed the doors. I soothed the agitated king by offering him food from my own hands. As I fed him, I chastised myself for imagining that the death of Haman would usher in a new day for the king, that he would rise up and rule as a strong and determined leader. For I saw that he was no different now than he had ever been: he was not a king but a warrior without a war. And as I sweetened the king's lips with honey-soaked almond pastry, I realized that the only way to prevent another Haman from rising to power would be to choose the chief minister myself.

"A king cannot manage all the cares of state alone," I suggested after he had taken his fill of the food and lay back with his cup.

"When my son arrives, I shall be busy with his training," the king confirmed. "Though I have called Gobryas to return to court and assist. There is none braver than he."

"Except for yourself," I added flattering the king.

"Some day you shall see me in battle," he promised, grinning like a boy.

"I heard tell of a Gobryas once," I recalled. "He was a general who helped your father overcome the false Smerdis."

"The very one!" The king slapped his knee with delight as his face filled with the animated pleasure that came only when telling a story of war and battle. "My father loved Gobryas more than all the others and later gave him my sister for a wife. When they were fighting the false Smerdis and came onto the palace where the traitor slept, Otanes—one of the seven who went to reclaim the kingdom—argued that they should wait. But Gobryas and my father plunged into the darkness. They forced their way through the door to the unlit chamber where the enemy was hiding. Soon Gobryas was locked in battle with the usurper. Darius hesitated to help him; he could not see.

"'Strike him!' Gobryas called to his friend.

"'I can not tell which man is which!" Darius returned.

"'Let your sword do the work, even if it strikes both of us," Gobryas insisted. And so my father trusted in Ahura Mazda and struck the blow. Gobryas was unscathed and the false Smerdis dead."

"A brave man!" I exclaimed. I wondered how Puah would feel to see him again. So many years had passed, they would no longer know each other. But perhaps a renewed friendship would bring her joy.

"He will soon be here and you may meet the man for yourself."

"I shall be honored," I replied, eager to tell Puah the news. I refilled the king's cup and returned to the subject of his chief minister.

"While you are busy with matters of warfare and training, you will need an advisor you can entrust with matters pertaining to the administration of the kingdom."

"Where is such a man to be found anymore?" the king complained.

"The son of my father's brother is such a man." My voice quivering with excitement and fear. For I did not know how the king would react to my boldness. "My cousin is a wise and steady man. He has served your interests from his earliest days in Babylon. He left his family to follow the court to Susa. Indeed he even once saved your life."

"Who is he and where is he?" the king demanded, sitting up with interest.

"He is Marduka the treasury official who sits in the king's own gate."

"Send for him!" the king commanded.

Mordechai presented himself in a clean robe of fine yellow linen and turban worthy of a courtier. He bowed low to the king, prostrated himself, and then stood again to bow to me. My eyes danced with happiness to see him and my spirit rose with the lightness of joy. But he did not look at me and offered no sign of recognition.

All the tears I had ever wept returned to my eyes. And though I remained silent, I longed to cry out to him: *I am Hadassah, your beloved and your betrothed!*

The king had servants remove all but the wine from the table and motioned for Mordechai to sit on the cushions across from us. I kept my gaze fixed upon him and met his eyes when he stole a glance at me. I imagined how I must appear to him, a plump and pampered woman with hair dyed golden like a goddess and flesh kept soft and smooth for the king's pleasure. He saw before him only that which I did not want to be: the king's concubine, a vessel for a warrior's lust.

The heat of my anger rose like foam in boiling water. And the floodgates of my heart burst with ugly words of fury. *I am the creature you let me become! You did not take me for your wife, a maiden*

*in your house who longed for nothing more in this world than to serve you
and give you fine sons! You let me go that day, an innocent girl of
fourteen!*

I sat in silence, as the storm raged within me and the king
spoke to Mordechai of matters related to the various provinces of the
empire. But as I listened to Mordechai answer the king's inquiries
with knowledge and wisdom, my heart softened. Mordechai was a
cautious man who knew the manners expected of a courtier. No
doubt my cousin did not wish to appear imprudent or bold before the
king's wife. And perhaps, too, he could not look at me lest he be
reminded of his own sorrow that I had gone from his life and we
could never be husband and wife.

The two men talked and soon a smile of satisfaction spread
over the king's face. He signaled that I should pour our guest a cup of
wine and I selected the most beautiful cup on the table, a golden lion-
monster with eagle's wings. I filled this rare vessel with sweet wine
from Shiraz and handed the cup to my cousin. Our fingers touched
and our eyes met. And I imagined he asked a question I could not yet
answer: *Can you forgive me?*

The king and Mordechai continued their discussion but I did
not listen to their words. Rather, I observed the two men. The king
drank cup after cup, while my cousin sipped only the smallest
amounts. The king was expansive in his gestures and seemed to voice
whatever came to him, while my cousin showed himself to be a man
who measured his words. A well-muscled warrior, the king had a face
of such perfect beauty that he seemed more god-like than human,
while my cousin was plain and gentle, gaunt and stooped with worry.
Whereas the king was like an animal in his lust for wine and women,
my cousin partook of little wine and was as pure as a eunuch.

I looked from one to the other and tormented myself with a choice I did not have. I loved them both. And I hated them both. Neither could ever be a friend to me as Puah or Freni. Neither would know my sorrows and my joys as another of my own kind.

At last the king rose from his cushions, staggering toward the door. I called for attendants to escort him to his bedchamber. I dreaded the moment he would ask me to follow, but he was occupied with matters of state and took no notice of me. Rather, he embraced my cousin as if they were brothers. Then he slipped his signet ring from his own finger and placed it on Mordechai's. "I entrust you, Marduka the Babylonian, with all things concerning the kingdom. Be a loyal servant to me and my queen and you shall be well rewarded."

Mordechai bowed as the king left the room.

I stood alone with my cousin. I looked at his sandals and he at mine.

"You have grown into a woman," he observed, as if he was speaking to a long-absent daughter.

"I would rather have remained a child in your household."

"God does not always grant us what we wish."

I was angered by his reply, for it seemed he was too eager to excuse himself from responsibility for all that had happened to me. But he, too, had suffered and I did not want to mar our reunion with my sorrows and regrets.

"Let us sit in the courtyard." I lead the way from the small dining room, through the large reception hall into the paved court. I had stood here four years before, dressed by Hegai as a goddess, waiting for my first night with King Xerxes. And I saw now that nothing had changed but me. The rushlights were lit and the colored walkway stones glimmered in the flickering flames. I chose a bench and dismissed the servants who attended me, telling them to send Puah. For I knew it was not proper to sit alone with my cousin. We had no more than a few minutes to speak of the five years we had lost.

"I hope Aia is well," I began.

"She is old," Mordechai replied. "Your many kindnesses and your help meant more to her than she ever told you. We both…" His voice broke off, cracked from the fullness of his heart.

I turned my eyes with love upon his face, urging him to continue.

"We both wept when you were taken from us," he whispered. My heart cried out to him when I saw how much he had suffered.

Mordechai reached for my hand and brought it to his lips. Then he clasped it tight in both of his own hands, as if he would never let me go again.

We sat in silence for some time, neither of us knowing what to say.

"You speak of God and have grown your beard like a Jew," I observed after a few minutes.

"When you left I began to pray again," he explained. "I took comfort in praying for your well being and happiness. I prayed that you would bring honor to your people," he added, "and so you have."

My eyes filled with tears at these words, the most beautiful anyone had ever spoken to me. I knew I would cherish them in my memory forever. "Your bravery before Haman inspired me," I replied. "I would not have had the courage to refuse to bow."

"He was a traitor to the king from the first," Mordechai said, his soft voice tinged with anger.

"Yet we are not saved from his evil edict." I knew that however much I might wish to prolong our reunion, my foremost concern as queen had to be for our people. "The extermination of the Jews will proceed if we do nothing more."

"Let us wait a month or two," Mordechai advised, still holding my hand in his as if it were more precious than rubies and pearls. "Let me earn the king's favor as his chief advisor. Let me first purge the court of the other traitors."

"I am sure there are others. My eunuch has spies that shall help you discover them."

My cousin nodded but his expression showed no surprise. And so I came to recall what it was to be in the presence of a sober man who kept his own council and did not reveal his heart by the expression of his face or impetuous words.

"Let us wait a month or two," he repeated, his voice strong and confident, "while the Jews take comfort in my new position and…"

The sound of a woman's cough interrupted him and we looked up from each other's eyes to Puah, standing before us. I did not know how long she had been there or what she imagined when she saw us sitting so close together, my cousin's hand clasped over mine. But I smiled at her with the fullness of my heart and she offered her own smile in return.

"This is my cousin Mordechai," I said, sure she would soon come to love him as if her were her own son.

Thirty-six

I appointed Mordechai over Haman's estate. I could not give away that which the king had given to me, but Mordechai would gain respect and influence much faster if he had vast wealth at his disposal.

The month that followed Haman's execution and Mordechai's appointment were filled with many events. Were it not for the death edict that yet hung over us, the days would have passed faster than the king could drink a single cup of wine. I spent more time with the king than I had in all the years before. He liked to have me wait upon him while he dined. I filled his plate and poured his wine while he entertained me with detailed descriptions of every battle he fought and all his victories, real and imagined. Sometimes he asked me to play the santur for him late into the night.

He began to call for me when he bathed, preferring that I, rather than a servant, wash and oil him. Once or twice he asked that I remove my robe so he might admire my treasures while my hands massaged his well-muscled flesh with almond oil. But he did not take me for his pleasure. After the incident in the wardrobe he had lost his vigor again. He would not believe what his doctor told him: that the only cure was to relinquish his cup. And so he staggered drunk each night to his mattress where he slept alone.

After some weeks, the king took up desperate efforts to regain what he had lost. He watched his guests while they enjoyed the dancing girls. I heard whispering among the youthful attendants that he sometimes asked them to lie with each other in his presence. He tried a hundred different medicines and herbs from the furthest corners of his empire. He replaced his Greek doctor with one from Egypt. But nothing helped. And so I remained the king's servant and nursemaid, thanking God each night for protecting me from such humiliations as the king's dark desires might have inflicted upon me.

Anatana began to visit me again and so our bond was renewed. I was careful not to overwhelm the child with my affections. I had a small santur crafted for her and taught her how to play. She excelled and I soon had to find a better instructor from among the court musicians. We often played together.

One day the girl came to me with a tale of having seen the women in the king's carpet workshop. She wondered if she, too, might learn to weave. Hathach found hand looms for us both and though it had been five years since I had strung a warp, I once again took up the work that Aia had taught me when I was not much more than Anatana's age. My first creation was a azure linen belt for my cousin. He wore it each day, showing me by deed what he could not say in word: that though we were forbidden to each other, his love for me was steadfast.

Anatana spent all her time in the queen's quarters, and such was my position at court that no one could object. Soon I set aside a chamber for her near my own and she came to live with me, returning to visit her young friends in the children's apartments from time to time, as once she had visited me. And though she was only eight years old, I began to plan for her future. When she was old enough to marry I intended to give her part of my estate and choose a lord who would treat her like a princess.

I was careful to say nothing to the king of my renewed affections for the girl or my concern for her well-being. But I continued to hope that he might come to open his heart to her, his own daughter.

After the king granted me the traitor's fortune, I sent Freni a belated wedding gift of five hundred silver talents. I had promised myself not to inflict upon her anything that would bring back memories of all that she would rather forget. But I could not bear to imagine her and her sons living in poverty.

The day after I sent the gift, a warm summer morning, Anatana and I sat with our looms in a shaded corner of the courtyard garden. She was weaving a hanging for my chamber wall while I worked on a ribbon for her hair. The heavy gate opened and I looked up to see the king's eunuch Harbonah.

"I have come with a message from the gatehouse," he explained. "Your cousin sent me to tell you that a visitor has requested to wait upon you that she might express her gratitude for a gift."

"It is Freni," I smiled. My heart danced with excitement.

Harbonah returned with our visitors and I leapt from the bench to embrace my friend. After I pulled away from her I saw the two boys and noticed that she was expecting a third child.

"This is Yeheshkiel," she told me with pride, patting the head of the smaller boy, a charming three year old with his mother's dark hair, delicate bones, and big eyes set far apart on his face. "And this is Reuven," she said, bending low to Anatana who had come to meet the boys.

"Do you like almond honeycomb?" Anatana asked them. Reuven looked up at his mother for permission, and she gave it with a nod.

"Come with me," Anatana ordered, and ran off to find Puah who would give them the treat. The two little boys followed her bouncing curls and flowing pink robe. She took up the role of mother by holding out a hand for each, and they disappeared through the door to the servants' apartments.

"They are good boys," I observed, leading Freni to a bench. "And I see there shall soon be another."

"Perhaps a girl this time," she smiled. "She shall keep me good company as Anatana does you."

"She is as dear to me as if she were my own," I confessed, holding back tears of regret. I knew I might never have a child now, but even as the likelihood grew dim, so did my longing gain strength.

Freni seemed to understand my unspoken sorrow and squeezed my hand in sympathy. "I shall pray for your womb to be filled," she whispered.

"God does not always give us everything we want," I echoed Mordechai's words. "I am blessed to see you and Vadhut well. Vadhut's child is nursing at her mother's breast and no one dares to take the baby away, for they know the concubine is a special friend to me."

"I am happy for her," Freni replied, though her subdued tone reflected a sadness that I imagined she held in her heart for Vadhut's position, and perhaps even my own. She had been the only one of our group to escape the harem and resume the life into which she had been born. She had been the only one to return to the bosom of a loving family.

"I have many blessings," I insisted, as if to convince myself as much as my friend that I should waste no time in regrets. "I am blessed to see my cousin promoted to the highest office in the court."

Freni nodded with vigor. "That is a blessing to us all," she added.

"And I have much yet to do," I continued.

Freni sighed, "You are right: we are not safe yet. We live in fear of our enemies, though we trust in Mordechai the Jew."

"We shall be safe!" I insisted. I watched with fascination as my friend ran her hands across her belly, a gesture I had observed in other pregnant women, who seemed to take a private delight in feeling the evidence of a growing child. She blushed when she saw me watching her.

"This one is a child of love," she confessed, in a low voice.

"Surely you dote upon the other two as much as any mother," I objected, not understanding her.

"They are the light of my eyes," she agreed, "but..." She broke off, her face almost as red as the henna on my fingertips. "I had always admired my lord for his good character," she explained," her smile as wide as Anatana's when Puah gave her sweets. "But now..." she broke off, looking down at her feet as if ashamed.

I understood her meaning and her modest reluctance. "You give each other pleasure as husbands and wives do."

Freni caught my eyes and laughed. Then she shrugged and nodded. I was tempted to advise that she work harder to keep her appearance from fading, to eat well and use oil for her skin and perfume her body with scents such as men enjoy. But I held my tongue. She was no longer in the harem and her lord was not King Xerxes. My father had loved my mother in her plain clothes and lean flesh. She did not devote hours to her appearance and he did not require it. So it would be with Freni and her lord. So it would never be with King Xerxes and me.

We talked for a long time, until the children came back, their fingers sticky and stomachs filled. Anatana began showing them the flowers in the garden, but we knew it was time to part.

"You must come again soon," I insisted. "Come before you have the baby."

"I have not yet thanked you for the gift," she noted, turning shy. "We shall use it for the education of our boys," she replied. "Because of your generosity they shall be scholars rather than wool dyers. It is a blessing we could not have imagined!"

I gazed at Freni's thin face, her earnest eyes and sweet smile, and found that I envied her simple life and fierce attachment to her sons. "I hope I may keep your amulet a little longer," I said, pulling the chain from inside my white linen robe, to show her that I wore it still. "At least until we have found a way to revoke the edict of annihilation."

She held her hand out to me. "It is yours to keep forever," she insisted.

A month later, Hegai left this world in his sleep. His great bulk had grown even greater over the years and he could no longer walk even a few steps, but had to be carried everywhere. One night he lay down to sleep after a large meal and in the morning his attendants could not rouse him. Hathach came to tell me.

I greeted the news with confusion in my heart. Though I had seen less of Hegai in recent years, I knew that I owed him much for all he had taught me. I remembered that he had chosen not to send me to the soldiers, and used all his skills to help me win the king's favor. Yet I also remembered the humiliations I had endured at his hand, the ways in which he had molded my flesh and awakened my desire, his own shameful pleasures, and the use of the haoma wine. I had held no power to change these injustices while the eunuch yet ruled in the harem. Now that he was gone I could hope to do something to help the women of the harem.

I persuaded Mordechai to recommend Hathach as Hegai's replacement. The eunuch had been in the king's service for many years and was a keen observer of the king's tastes and desires. And though I wondered how much Mordechai knew of the king's problem—that it had been many weeks since he called for a girl from the harem—I did not ask. I was content in my own renewed innocence.

Hathach was sorry to leave my service. But he could not refuse the advancement of his position. He trained Harbonah as his replacement, a eunuch he trusted. And even after Hathach assumed the position of head of the harem, not a day went by that he and I did not meet to discuss the affairs of the court. He implemented all the improvements I suggested: the concubines no longer lived in the prison of drugged indifference. He ceased giving the women haoma, and soothed their restlessness with increased entertainments, including music, poetry readings, and other employments such as drawing, needlework, and weaving. The women wore robes that hid their treasures with more dignity, and the children remained in the harem during the day.

Soon after this I sent inquiry to Thriti, who lived in a small house on the edge of the town below the acropolis. I knew she lived without a maid and I asked if she would wish to have Hutana's service. Thriti appeared in person to thank me for my kindness and I saw that a great change had come over the former concubine, in her humbled position. We embraced and Hutana was released to her, their reunion more joyous than I anticipated. And when the king complained at the absence of a dancing girl who was a favorite among his drinking companions, I did not hesitate to tell him a falsehood. I said that she was banished from the harem because her treasure was diseased and rotted and could no longer be shared with his guests. He did not question the truth of what I said.

Mordechai and I saw each other often, but not more than a moment or two at any one time, and often in company. We talked little, and never of ourselves. He worked at a furious pace to put the affairs of the state in order, replacing the ministers who had been in Haman's pay and ruling by justice rather than fear. He began to call himself Mordechai the Jew, even as he gained the honor and respect of all who came to know or hear of him. The king soon found him indispensable, and trusted him above all others. Yet when Mordechai and I agreed that the Jews could let the edict stand no longer, he argued that I would be more effective in pleading our people's cause.

Once again, I prepared to go before the king as he sat in state on the golden throne. But my plans were interrupted by the arrival of the king's son.

Thirty-seven

I had revealed to the king how Mordechai the Jew was related to me, but the subject was of no interest to him and he never questioned me about my people or my descent. The blood ties of family seemed to hold little meaning for him. And so I was surprised to observe his attachment to the young son he had never known.

Artaxerxes had been a newborn when his mother was banished. I knew from court gossip that the king's advisors had recommended the child remain in Susa to be raised at court as befitted his royal position. But though furious with his disobedient wife, the king had taken pity on her plea to keep the child for a few years. Only the king seemed to believe that her maternal feelings were genuine.

Everyone assumed that Darius, the elder son and namesake of the king's father, would be crowned heir to the throne. And so they did not give much consideration to the younger boy. But in his heart the king knew he would rather see the empire fall than bequeath it to his older son, whom he scorned. Darius was weak in body and even worse, the son was married to the daughter of the king's treacherous brother. Were he to take the throne, the grandson of Masistes would one day come to hold it himself. This was a prospect the king could not endure.

The king did not like to talk about the future. Having lost the child he had given me, I was always reluctant to raise the subject of his sons by Vashti. So I could only guess why he prolonged his younger son's stay in Chaldea so many years after he had determined

Darius would not be his successor. Perhaps he had preferred to deny his own mortality. Perhaps, despite all the pressure from the court for him to crown an heir, he could not be bothered. Or perhaps he had been hoping that I, his new favorite, would give him a son.

I dreaded the child's arrival, for he was Vashti's son and surely hated me and the king. Though the child was only eight years old, I expected he would bring dissention and discord into our lives.

"I wish the king had not summoned his son back to court," I admitted to Hathach before the child's arrival.

"It is better that he come now," Hathach observed. "A lust-filled youth is much harder to train and shape than a child of eight. The king will have time to erase the mother's influence."

"But Artaxerxes is her child," I objected. "She can never be erased from him!"

"Perhaps the boy's presence will inspire his loins to renewed vigor," Hathach suggested, trying to lighten my spirit, for he had no good answer to my concerns.

"He would have to give up his cup for that," I retorted with scorn. Though I was glad of the respite from the king's attentions, his weakness for wine diminished him in my eyes a little more each day.

"Every man longs for many sons to carry his name into eternity," the eunuch observed. "Xerxes is no different, though the wine takes its toll."

I bit my lip and said no more. But I could not help wondering if what the eunuch said about every man held true for my cousin Mordechai.

The boy arrived, escorted by the old general Gobryas who was assigned to be his tutor in the art of war. The king sent for me in his chamber to meet them, though the formal ceremony to crown Artaxerxes as heir would not take place until the following day. I entered the chamber through the colonnade but I saw no one except for the guard posted at the door. I heard voices across the long chamber, from the anteroom where ministers and servants waited upon the king even after he retired, should he call for some assistance or advice. And so I crept close to that door, which was ajar and unguarded.

"Tell me what you saw of the child's leave-taking," the king demanded. And so I guessed he was speaking with Gobryas and that the child was not with them.

"The young prince bowed to his mother like a man," the general replied, his voice cracking with age.

"And what of the mother?" The eagerness in his voice wounded me no less than if he had thrust a spear into my heart. For I could no longer hide from myself what I had perhaps always known, that Xerxes had never forgotten the wife who had been born into royalty and whom had been chosen for him long before I ever took my first breath.

I chastised myself for once wishing that I could take her place in his heart and forgetting that I no longer wished to.

"Vashti is as ever." The general was reluctant to speak about the banished queen, though he showed deference and respect in his tone.

"Her beauty must have faded by now," the king observed without conviction, "being well into her third decade. Does her tongue grow even sharper?"

"I saw little of her," Gobryas answered, "and heard less." He paused for a moment, as if searching for a way to shift the subject away from Vashti. "I have heard much of the new queen's beauty and goodness."

"She is a jewel," the king concurred.

But my spirits rose only to fall again.

"Alas," he continued, "she is barren."

I knew he would never admit the truth of the matter to anyone, lest he become an object of ridicule. But I shuddered as he blamed me, wondering if this is what he told himself as well.

"A pity," the old general answered after a moment. "But it is better that the kingdom be spared the fighting. Your Majesty's succession was never in doubt. Still, that was a terrible time for your father, having to choose the son of one wife over those of another," he recalled.

"Indeed," the king sighed, as if he remembered, though I am not sure he did.

I was too upset by all that I had overheard to remain or to make my presence known, but fled back to the queen's quarters to weep alone. I told Harbonah to inform the king that I was ill and begged to be excused until the following day.

I met the boy the next morning, as he embarked on a tour of the palace grounds before his crowning ceremony. I sat in the music room with my santur, attempting to quiet my heart. Anatana listened with great patience as I played a tune of fear and melancholy. And as my fingers moved across the strings I began to hope that perhaps the child might long for a new mother, being separated from the old one. The king would be pleased, I was sure, if I could provide maternal attention and comfort to his heir. If the child could love me, his mother's harsh words might shrivel into dust.

Thus were my foolish hopes as I played. The curtains were open and my song drifted across the courtyard into the palace so that the vaguest strain could be heard in the colonnade, through which the young prince was passing.

His escorts had not intended to show him the queen's quarters or the harem, for though he was only eight, it was still improper for him to have access to his father's women. But the young prince possessed the persistence and quiet determination of one much older in years. Unlike the shallow wailing of a spoiled child, his requests were not to be dismissed. Upon hearing the santur notes carried on the air, he demanded a tour of all that lay behind the tall guarded gate. When his escort explained that no men were permitted inside, Artaxerxes pointed out that he was not yet a man and sent for the eunuch Aspamitres, who had been assigned to attend him in his chamber. The keeper of my door came to inform me of the boy's arrival only moments before his feet were upon the music room threshold.

He was tall for his age, though still shorter than my height, and dressed in a soldier's uniform. A small dagger with a jeweled hilt was tucked into his belt and I did not doubt that it was real. He stood too erect for a child, with an alert and penetrating stare, as if all his senses were aroused, like a lion on the hunt. His face was as pale as the skin of an infant and his almond eyes, in contrast, were dark, as was the mass of thick black waves flowing from his head. I detected his father in the hair, the wide brow, and long, arching nose. Yet his white skin recalled the marble statue of Vashti that had sat upon the king's bed table, long ago. The child looked as if he had no more blood in his veins than that piece of stone. I remembered her cruel mouth, too, the thin lips puckered into a disdainful pout, and I saw this feature in her son.

Anatana and I rose to bow and welcome him. He returned the bow with perfect form, but said nothing. Rather he stared into my eyes like a magus before a fire altar, as if he could see into my future. I grew uneasy with his piercing gaze and looked away.

"Will you play for me?" he asked.

I sat down and took up my instrument again, choosing a cheerful tune such as I imagined a child might enjoy.

He held up his hand to stop me. "That is not what you played before," he observed.

Unsettled that one of his years would prefer to hear a mournful song, I hesitated. But he continued to stare at me with expectation and so I began the song that he had heard over the courtyard wall. He stood transfixed and did not move until I had finished.

"Thank you," he said without warmth. He turned his attention to Anatana who had remained standing near while I played. She was a lovely sight that morning, with her thick curls gathered in a pink ribbon and her lithe form in a flowing yellow robe embroidered with pink lotus blossoms. I could see, in looking from one to the other, that she was a contrast to the prince in all her inclinations: she was cheerful and effusive where he was solemn and self-contained.

The prince walked up to her and she smiled at him in her loving way. He did not return the smile but raised his hand to touch her curls, as if uncertain they were real. "Are you my sister?" he asked after a moment. "I was told the queen had no children."

Anatana looked up at me for guidance.

"She is a daughter of the harem," I confirmed, speaking to the child as if he were a man, for his manner demanded it. I knew that he would have no need of a mother. Perhaps he never had.

The crowned heir began to call for Anatana every evening after his day's training was complete and before he dined. At first this concerned me, because the boy was secretive and cold in manner. But she complained of no ill treatment and amused him with her santur and her smiles. He spoke little, she assured me, though he sometimes touched her curls. I praised her for telling me all that happened when they met in his chamber, and I warned her to be watchful. But she laughed at me as if I were a foolish old woman. That laugh caused me pain, as did her growing eagerness to visit him.

She soon began returning from these visits with gifts: bracelets and boxes, a small carving of a lion, and new hair ribbons. He gave her gold hoops for her ears that she wore every time she went to see him. Her enthusiasm for these trinkets reminded me too much of the way in which the concubines displayed the prizes that they received from the king after he had spent his passion upon them. And so I began to attribute motives to the prince beyond his years, wondering if perhaps he meant to steal Anatana's heart from me to do me harm.

One evening, I formed a plan to overhear the children in the prince's chamber. His tutor was resting and he had sent his attendants away to be alone with Anatana. The chamber door was ajar and by standing in the shadows of the corner behind the door, I was able to see through a crack.

They lay together on the mattress. I saw Anatana, covering the prince's impassive face with kisses. I trembled with fury at the sight, and covered my mouth to keep myself from crying out.

The prince sat up and looked around. I held my breath but he did not rouse himself to investigate. "Get me some wine," he ordered Anatana. And it pained me to see how she complied as if she were his servant, hurrying to pour a cup for him from a little pitcher on his bed-table.

"You are pretty," he said to her as she handed him the cup. "But not as pretty as my mother. She is the real queen."

"Queen Esther is the real queen," Anatana insisted. I smiled to myself, not for her words but rather for her courage.

"She is neither your real mother nor the queen," the boy insisted. "I am your brother and one day I will be your king. The real queen will come back to court and if you are kind to me and obedient, I will let you be one of my concubines."

I fled from my hiding place and found Puah. After I related all that I had seen and feared, we agreed that there was little I could do to prevent the child from working in his mother's interests. And in his presence at court I now saw my own demise. Vashti's son would grow into a man, gathering strength in body and power at court. He had already gained his father's wine-sodden favor: the king spoke of nothing else but how his son excelled in his training and would one day be as fine a warrior as he had been. "Artaxerxes will lead us in victory against the Greeks," the king said to me at least once each day, plotting his revenge through his son. And so in my heart I knew that while I and my cousin might be safe for the moment, the boy's arrival rendered our security uncertain. We would have to maintain our vigilance and as the king grew older, prepare for his passing, when we would no longer be welcome at court. This would be some years hence, for the king was yet in good health.

Puah and I spent many hours in my chamber discussing the child and what might be done to protect Anatana. I could not bear the prospect of sending her away while she was yet so young. And so I formed a plan to lessen the prince's influence. I hoped to enlist Gobryas in this endeavor, for he was the boy's tutor and a gentle man. Puah agreed with the wisdom of my scheme, though we both knew that we would not be able to effect a complete separation of the brother from his sister.

"Please seek out the general and say I wish to speak to him," I asked. Puah had hid from her old friend in the weeks since his arrival, refusing to heed my suggestions that she make herself known.

"I shall send Harbonah," she replied.

"I have asked you to be my messenger." I laughed as she turned red with embarrassment.

"Very well," she whispered.

"You may change your robe first," I added, hoping that she would make an effort to improve her appearance before their meeting.

"I am not a young girl any more," she snapped as she left my chamber.

When she returned with the general, she wore a white linen robe with a lapis blue cloak I had given her long ago. Her hair was braided in a neat coil at the top of her head and fixed in place with one of my own gold hairpins. She said nothing as she ushered in the old warrior. I could see he had not recognized her.

"I hope this day finds you well," I said to Gobryas as he bowed his grizzled head. He was old, almost ancient, but he was yet broad in the shoulders and proud in his posture. I had liked him from our first meeting, and found that I enjoyed his tales of battle far more than the king's. The two of them together were almost a pleasure for their delight in each other's company.

"I am indeed well," he replied, "and rejoice to see that the queen is as fresh as ever."

"I wish to speak to you about one of the king's daughters." I motioned for him to sit on the cushions near me. I held my hand up to Puah who hovered in the doorway. "But first," I continued, "I wish to know if you remember the days of your youth when you went to Egypt under King Cambyses."

"How can I forget the golden past?" he laughed, "when Darius and I fought side-by-side as brothers."

"Yet you have forgotten another friend of those days," I scolded him, with merriment in my eyes. And then I pointed to Puah.

Gobryas turned to look at the servant, many years his junior, yet an old woman nonetheless.

"What fine lady is this?" he asked me. "She will forgive the memory of a withered man."

"She is the child you befriended in your days at Memphis," I told him, watching the color rise on Puah's cheek. "She is the child with whom you played twenty squares. You were forced to abandon her when you were called to overthrow the false Smerdis."

The old warrior looked at me with an expression of puzzlement for a moment before his eyes filled with the light of recognition. Whether this happened by way of his heart or by design, I shall never know for Gobryas was always kind to women. He rose from his cushion to bow before Puah. "What a lovely lady you have become," he said. "Will you not join us and tell me of all that has befallen you these last thirty years?"

And thus was their friendship renewed, much to Puah's joy.

Later, I sent Puah for some refreshment and brought my conversation with the old general back to the subject of Anatana. I was careful to say nothing of my fears about the young prince, for I knew that no good could come from revealing myself, even to one as noble as Gobryas. He was the king's friend and the boy's tutor, and so I could not gain him as an ally by asking him to choose my interests over theirs.

"There is a young girl of the harem who is like my own child to me," I began.

"Indeed," he acknowledged, "the crown prince is very fond of his half-sister."

"I am glad he speaks well of her," I observed.

Gobryas laughed. "He speaks little of anything, that one! He holds his own council. But he learns the soldier's arts with great determination and applies himself to his other studies as well."

"You are fortunate to have such an able student," I smiled, "and one so manly for his years. Yet he has made known to you his affection for Anatana somehow."

"He has asked my advice on gifts such as ladies enjoy," Gobryas confessed as if amused, "and I see how often he calls for her company."

I turned my eyes full upon the general's kind face, pleading in my gaze for his compassion and assistance. "I am afraid he raises her expectations," I explained. "Even were she of full royal birth, it has not been the recent custom in the Persian court for those of shared parentage to marry. And I would hope for more in her future than ending her days as concubine in her brother's harem."

"They are but children playing," Gobryas sought to assure me.

"And so I fear for her all the more," I replied. "The attachments of childhood are fierce and unyielding."

Gobryas nodded.

"She is not too young to be betrothed," I continued. "One can see she will grow into a lovely young woman. Her disposition is sweet and pleasing. And I shall provide a substantial bride-price for her marriage."

"It is a good plan," Gobryas agreed as if considering something more in his heart. And in a moment I saw that his reason was treading upon the very path that I had hoped to lead him. For the king would not object to Anatana's marriage if it were presented by the general as his own wish. "She would be a fine wife for either of my two grandsons," he proposed. "They are young men of eighteen and twenty. One is a bowman in the king's army and the other a seaman."

"I would choose for her whichever is the gentler, and hold the marriage ceremony when she reaches the age of fourteen. But we might seal the arrangement now, if you gain the king's approval." I smiled with hope and gratitude for his help.

Gobryas rose and bowed. "I shall see to it at once," he promised.

He did so with ease, gaining the king's approval to form an alliance between Anatana and his grandson, the bowman. I was able to impress upon Anatana the importance of keeping herself chaste for her betrothed and to capture her imagination with dreams of a future with him.

Artaxerxes was too clever to show his displeasure at my countermove, though I am sure it gave him further reason to despise me. I continued to hope that he would lose interest in Anatana, and insisted that one of my maids accompany the girl on her visits to him. He soon stopped giving her gifts, but I could not extinguish the friendship between brother and sister. Still, I was grateful that he did not seek to punish Anatana for her continuing attachment to me or her enthusiasm about her coming marriage. And if he shared with her any secrets that affected my well-being or that of my cousin, I was sure she would reveal them to me. Nor was there much she could say to him about me that he could not discover by some other means.

And so the second and third months after Haman's execution passed and Mordechai reminded me that I could no longer delay my plea to the king on behalf of the Jews.

Thirty-eight

And again I spoke before the king, falling at his feet and weeping. Again I dressed in the clothing of royalty. I wore a robe of purple silk, which sparkled with silver embroidered lotus blossoms and rubies. My wrists were adorned with gold bracelets and my neck with lapis beads. My hair was braided with pearls and I wore the queen's jeweled tiara on my head. I hung gold circles strung with jewels in my earlobes and a silver ring in my nose. My feet were sheathed in soft leather sandals with golden filigreed ornaments.

Mordechai stood by the king in the throne room and offered a rare smile as I entered. Like the king, he took pleasure in my appearance. For as much as he tried to hide his heart from me, he was a man.

I did not fear the king as he sat in state on the golden throne. I was his favorite, his companion, and the cousin of his chief minister. Yet it was no simple matter to make my request. I did not want to anger the king by causing him to recall his trust in Haman or that he himself had given permission for the massacre to take place. And so I had to exercise great caution in what I said. I planned to win him over as a wife might, with tears, and sorrow, and skillful beguilement. I would remind him of his love for me and soften him with the pleadings of my heart.

The king looked down upon me with admiration and extended his golden scepter. I arose and stood before him.

"If I have won your favor," I began, looking into his dark, yearning eyes. "If I have won favor before you and the matter is right in your judgment," I continued, "let it be written to retract the plot that the wicked Haman conceived, his edict to destroy all the Jews in the king's empire. Because I cannot bear the evil that would befall my people. I cannot bear the destruction of my kindred."

I stole a glance at Mordechai when I finished. I saw neither satisfaction nor disappointment in his expression.

"I have given Haman's property to you," the king replied with mild irritation in his voice. The traitor himself has been hung on the gallows because he would lift a hand against you."

I bowed to the king with gratitude, though in my heart I scorned his weakness. For he would never admit his own role in Haman's edict against the Jews. He would even falsify the circumstances of Haman's condemnation to make himself appear more heroic.

The king nodded, pleased by my humility.

"You may write about the Jews as is good in your eyes," he continued, addressing himself to Mordechai and me together. "You may write in the king's name, and seal it with the king's ring. But an edict written in the king's name and sealed with the king's ring may not be revoked."

My knees trembled and grew weak. For if an edict written in the king's name and sealed with his ring could not be revoked, then my people were doomed. I glanced at Mordechai in alarm. He cocked his head, lowered his drooping eyelids even further, and made a gesture of reassurance with his hand. This was no less than he had expected. He knew the law of the land.

I bowed to the king again, praised his wisdom, and thanked him for his generosity. Then I returned to my quarters to wait for word from Mordechai.

He came late in the afternoon while I sat playing a song on the santur for Anatana in the reception room. He was dressed in magnificent robes of blue and white linen with a cloak of purple wool and a gold-embroidered turban. The king had made a gift of these for my cousin's service to the kingdom.

"I have come to tell you of our progress," he announced in his soft voice. And despite the royal garb, I could see that he was still as thin as a poor man and humble in his manner.

"I am sorry for the intrusion," he apologized to Anatana. "Might I borrow a moment of the queen's time from you?"

Anatana laughed and jumped up from her cushion. "I am going to ask Puah if she will take me to watch the weavers," she said.

"I shall see you at the evening meal," I smiled. As the little girl left, I dismissed the servants and summoned Harbonah to join us so we would not be alone.

Mordechai declined my offer of some refreshment and would not sit near me. Rather he stood at a respectful distance, maintaining a formality between us, as if we were no more to each other than the king's advisor and the king's wife.

"I have dictated the letters," he began. "One to the Jewish community and one to the governor of each province, written in its own script and to every people in their own language. The letters were written in the king's name and I sealed them myself with the king's seal. They have been dispatched with the king's riders on the king's swiftest horses and will travel the royal road across the empire even faster than those who delivered the traitor's message."

"Please tell me what they said," I asked, eager to admire my cousin's initiative.

"That the king has granted this permission to the Jews of every city: on the day of the planned massacre, the Jews may organize and defend themselves against any people or province that attacks them. They may kill and destroy any armed force and its women and children, taking their property for plunder."

I raised my hands to my mouth and gasped at the death sentence for women and children.

"It is no worse than our enemies would have done to us," Mordechai pointed out. "If they do not fear the power of the Jews, they will not hesitate to carry out Haman's plot."

I sighed and nodded. "Let us hope that the people take heed and do not risk their lives by attacking the Jews," I replied.

"The letters will be announced as law and posted in public places so the Jews may be ready for the fight. I will myself go now to proclaim the decree in Susa; I wear the royal robes of honor for this reason alone," he added, embarrassed to be seen in such fine clothing.

"The robes reveal the truth of your character," I dared to reply.

The city of Susa and the town below the acropolis rejoiced at Mordechai's announcement. He was hailed in the square and the Jews proclaimed a feast and a holiday in his honor. And when he made known that he had the king's guard under his command, and that he would use them in defense of the Jews, a fear of his people spread over the land. In many places people even began to call themselves

Jews, thereby hoping to be free from any association with those who wished the Jews harm.

Nine months passed. On the evening before the dreaded day I summoned Freni and her children—the two boys and the infant girl—so they would all be safe in my quarters. But we could not sleep that night. And as the dawn rose, we sat in my chamber with Puah, the three of us awaiting the news, which Harbonah and Hathach both promised to bring throughout the day.

One of the two eunuchs came each hour to report all that he had seen and heard. We were much relieved to learn that few of the townspeople dared fight against the Jews in Susa and that those who raised their swords were soon killed. Freni's lord, who had remained in the town to protect their property, had seen no fighting.

"The ten sons of Haman and their friends have been slaughtered," Hathach reported in the evening, breathless from running. "They have been killed through with the swords of the Jews and the king's body guard to help. Mordechai ordered the headless bodies of Haman's sons to be hanged from a gallows as a warning to all who would harm the Jews. Fifty men in all have been killed on this day." And that was the truth of the battle in Susa, though the number later came to be exaggerated ten-fold in the retelling.

"What of the all the women and children?" Freni asked, her face filled with fear. She still clung to her baby as if we were yet in danger.

"The Jews have neither touched the women nor children. Nor have they taken the spoil," Hathach announced with approval. "For it was whispered amongst them that Mordechai the Jew, the king's chief advisor, did not wish it."

I was sorry my parents were not there to witness Mordechai's triumph. I knew that they would have been proud to have him for a son. I closed my eyes and tried to imagine a picture of my mother and father. I longed to see them again, but their faces were a distant memory. I saw only my beloved companions before me, Puah and Freni. I took comfort in knowing that when they looked upon me they also saw those whose name I carried forward. For though Avihail son of Shemei and his wife had perished by the waters of Babylon, our people were saved and would live on. Our deliverance was theirs.

It happened that the victory of the Jews came to pass throughout the empire as I anticipated. Word came of how many men the Jews had slain and how many more were afraid to challenge them. The king marveled at my cousin's success and the power of our people. He ordered that an account of the events and Mordechai's greatness be recorded in the record book of the days. He continued to rely on Mordechai in all that he did.

And so it came to pass that Mordechai the Jew, chief advisor to King Xerxes, was honored above all in the realm, second only to the king. And he who had once hidden his kindred and his descent now became a favorite among the multitude of his brethren, serving as their spokesman and seeking to do good for the welfare of his father's seed.

Epilogue

Ten years passed. Mordechai remained the chief advisor to the king and I the childless queen. Xerxes loved his wine no less and concerned himself with his son's training at the expense of his own. And so as Artaxerxes grew in strength and reached his full maturity, his father came to be an old man of fifty-two, with nothing but his memories to remind him that he had once been a great warrior.

Artaxerxes changed little in character as he became a man, except to grow even more taciturn. A fine swordsman and better at the bow than most of the king's soldiers, he did not develop his father's fondness for women, wine, or carousing with companions. Rather, he had a brooding, solitary nature. He sought no human company other than that of his eunuch Aspamitres and, from time to time, Anatana, who seemed to provide the little diversion from his studies that he permitted himself. The king came to be in awe of his son's self-discipline. He did not see that the boy was watching and waiting.

I knew from Anatana that the prince was in contact with his mother by way of messenger. I suspected Zeresh of playing some part in the communications between Vashti and her son, but when I had spies follow her, she disappeared. Artaxerxes was not forthcoming about the contents of his correspondence with Vashti. Indeed, Anatana reported that he said little about anything, asking her to play the santur or speak of things that interested her, such as the carpet she was weaving or her growing bridal chest. She often described to me how the prince's tense face relaxed as he lay back on the cushions and listened to her prattle. She was glad of her usefulness and did not fear him. Her future husband was his tutor's grandson, she reminded me, a bowman of great skill. Artaxerxes, unlike the king, would never shame a brother-in-arms by violating his betrothed.

My own name never passed the prince's lips in Anatana's presence, nor did she speak to him of me. I avoided the king's heir as much as I could, though the king often called us to join him at the evening meal. We were polite to each other then, and the king seemed oblivious to the lack of warmth between us or his son's watchful silence. He continued to see only what pleased him. He spoke incessantly of how the court would celebrate his son's eighteenth birthday by sending him out with a rebuilt navy to defeat the Greeks and bring glory to the empire. Nor in all the king's drunken ranting did he notice his son's lip twitch with disdain or my own face lower in shame for his degradation.

The years passed and Anatana grew into a sweet and beautiful young woman. When she was fourteen she was married. I gave the couple Haman's estate in Susa and some land in Media; from this they would have enough income to keep them for the rest of their lives. I was sad to lose my adopted daughter, and the queen's chamber seemed empty without her. But I knew I could not keep her forever, and Anatana was happy with the choice. She made our separation easier by promising that she would never let more than two or three days pass without a visit. But as all mothers know, it is never the same once your child has bound her life to another. Still, her husband was kind and did not object when she returned to see me and, upon occasion, her brother.

King Xerxes tried, for several years, to match Mordechai with a wife. Mordechai declined the king's many offers with steadfast courtesy. Once, during a feast for the New Year, the king leaned over to my cousin and whispered something in his ear. Mordechai bowed as if offering thanks and then shook his head. The king exploded in laughter. "I believe my chief advisor is a eunuch!" he cried out to the assembled guests. "I have offered all manner of diversions to him: my niece, two or three other daughters of the royal family, and a young princess from Kusha. When these did not tempt him, I suggested my beautiful Athenian youths."

The company laughed.

"But he would have none of it! And so he must be a eunuch."

I cringed with embarrassment at the king's drunken words, for his sake and Mordechai's. The king himself had been no more than a eunuch for many years, and this was no secret throughout the court.

If Mordechai was offended by the king's announcement, he did not reveal his true feelings. Rather, he sought to make light of the subject and so save his dignity and the king's. He raised his cup to toast the king. "I thank His Majesty with all my heart for his kindness," he declared in a voice loud enough for the company to hear, "but I would rather serve him and his queen than serve a wife." At this the king laughed and promised to raise the subject no more.

Gobryas met the end of his days five winters after his arrival at court. He was buried with great ceremony outside Susa in a tomb made for him on a high cliff. Puah mourned the loss of her friend for many months, until grief settled into sorrow. But she often spoke of him and of her gratitude for the renewal of their friendship.

And so I reached the age of thirty. I no longer had the beauty of youth, though I retained my health and served my king and his people well. I tried to do good for all those who sought my help and to be kind to every servant. My estate prospered and grew under Mordechai's supervision, and I was comforted by this, knowing that my days at court were limited by the king's own. I imagined that the end of my lord's days and Mordechai's would come together and that I would live out my remaining years in Anatana's household as a second mother to her children.

Peace and purpose filled my quiet days but fear haunted me at night. I drifted into sleep, holding my hand over my heart, where so many beloved friends dwelt with me. Yet I soon found myself in a lonely and barren valley. The smell of death hung in the air—a familiar and overpowering scent of myrrh and labdanum, at once sweet and bitter. A black vulture circled in the dark sky above, its wings casting shadows over me despite the lack of sunlight. I scrambled up a mountain wall to escape that terrible place. The rocky ground tore at the flesh of my hands and feet. I wept tears of joy when I reached the top and looked down upon the Euphrates, the river of my birth. But then I saw that the waters were turned to blood. My mother rose from the depths, her face as white as that of Allatu, supreme goddess of the underworld. My father's brains spilled from his skull into the red river and my mother's corpse floated by. Looking up, I saw a knife drawn over me, and as my face was slashed into disfigurement, I awoke.

The perfume of death still hung in my nostrils as I touched my cheeks to assure myself that it had been no more than a bad dream. What it portended, I could not tell. But any comfort and safety I found as queen was shattered each time I returned from this terrible place.

One morning I awoke from these visions, my night robe drenched with sweat. It was the spring of the twenty-first year of the king's reign, just before the prince's eighteenth birthday.

Puah rushed into my chamber as I was rising.

"The king has been murdered in his bedchamber! We must leave at once, before Artaxerxes takes his father's place."

My head spun and my vision grew dim. My heart tore and a river of blood ran from my eyes.

"One of your informants among the king's chamber boys found him and rushed to tell me before he raised the general alarm. I have sent word to Hathach and Mordechai. We must leave now."

She ran for my wardrobe and I followed, donning two robes, a plain cloak, and my sturdiest sandals. And only then did I learn that Puah had already prepared two large woven trunks, packed with essentials of clothing and bedding.

"You knew in advance and you did not tell me!" I looked at her with disbelief.

"We did not want you to know. You would have perished yourself trying to save the king." She looked up at me without remorse. "It was sure to happen one day."

Hathach came without delay, dressed in a black wool cloak and boots, as if for travel.

"We must go now," he urged. "Mordechai believes that the head of the guard and the eunuch Aspamitres are in the pay of Artaxerxes and did the deed. Your life is in grave danger."

"You cannot give up your position at court for me!" I objected, tears of fear and sadness gathering in my eyes. "I cannot promise you safety or wealth."

"I am to go with you by your cousin's order and my own desire," he replied. "We are to take you to Opis, a city on the River Tigris northwest of Susa. From there we are to find a guide who will take us through the Zagros mountains to your estate in Ecbatana."

I looked from one to the other, my heart a confusion of gratitude, shock, and fear. For if I were in danger for my alliance with the king, so much more so was my cousin. "Mordechai must come with us!"

"He will meet us later," Hathach assured me, his soft brown eyes full of understanding for my distress. "His life is in more danger than your own: once you are gone from the court you will hold no influence and Artaxerxes will not trouble himself. But your cousin is a man with powerful allies and the young king may seek his head. He knew it would not be safe for you to travel together. Anatana will hide him for a day or two. Then he will take the eastern route to Chorasmia and work his way west again."

"Anatana," I cried, another wave of sorrow washing over me for the prospect of parting from her.

Hathach took my hand. "She is safe in her brother's court," he reminded me.

"We must go!" Puah urged, opening the courtyard door.

"My santur," I whispered, my legs unable to move. In my years as queen it was the only possession that I had ever cherished. I could not imagine life without it.

"We shall find you another," Puah promised.

"Wait!" Hathach instructed, turning back. And in a moment he had retrieved the instrument.

We pulled the hoods of our cloaks up over our heads and proceeded with caution through the deserted banquet hall toward the door to the throne room. Hathach led the way.

"I am sure we shall be seen," I whispered.

"Artaxerxes is reviewing the troops in the grand court," he explained in a whisper so low I could just hear him. "The servants are gathered in the kitchens, awaiting instruction for the burial. We will be met at the other end of the garden."

We entered the passage to the throne room, our feet silent on the carpet. The door ahead of us was ajar. Hathach peered in as I came up close behind him. A shadow fell over my heart, as if I expected to see the ghost of the king upon the throne.

Someone sat beneath the silver canopy, a woman wearing rich robes of purple. She was past her third decade but her brow was smooth and wide. Her shining black hair was braided with pearls and twisted in an elaborate sculpture. Her skin was as pale as death. She turned toward us, and I saw the silver star of Ishtar around her neck.

Hathach thrust himself into the room, closing the door behind him all but a crack. I watched him fall at Vashti's feet.

"Your Majesty," he said. He did not dare raise his eyes to the face upon which my own eyes were transfixed. Her perfect beauty seemed to have no more warmth than the marble statue that had once stood beside the king's mattress.

"He is dead and I am restored to my rightful place!" Her harsh voice echoed in the cavernous room. She leaned forward and clawed the eunuch's face with sharp henna-stained fingernails. Bloody welts appeared on his cheeks, but he did not cry out in pain.

"Is she pretty?" Vashti demanded. She lifted her foot to Hathach's chin, forcing him to raise his eyes to meet hers. Her smile was both terrible and bewitching, like Lilith and Lamashtu.

"None can compare to you, Your Majesty," Hathach murmured.

"I shall carve his name upon her face before she dies." Vashti smiled, stroking the eunuch's cheek. She wiped the blood from her palm on to his white tunic and rose from the throne. "Be sure that my apartments are readied for me," she ordered as she swept toward the king's chamber. "Everything of hers must be burned."

The door to the king's chamber slammed and we hurried through the throne room to the garden. My feet trod upon the burnished paths and I clutched my santur, keeping my eyes on Hathach and Puah just ahead of me. We reached the servants' door and Hathach stopped us, raising a finger to his lips. He opened the door a crack and then wider. There, with three donkeys, was Harbonah.

The eunuchs secured our luggage and we mounted the donkeys. We followed Harbonah through an alley to a dark passage that ended at a thick wood door sealed with a heavy beam and an iron bolt. I dismounted to help the two eunuchs. When at last we removed the beam and lifted the latch, sunlight flooded into the passage. We made our way across a dusty court, past the fire temple and a deserted army barracks, on to the rough west slope of the acropolis. Here we bade farewell to Harbonah.

I drank great gulps of air as we began to descend the steep, rocky hill. No one had ever cut a path through this isolated stretch of land and the donkeys moved with slow and cautious steps. I found no assurance in their steady progress for I knew that Vashti would soon send soldiers for us. And though we saw no one I glanced behind with every step. The few minutes of our decent seemed to stretch on like hours.

When we reached the road, I turned back. The palace towered behind us. My heart filled with joy until it burst and I began to laugh and shout with an abandon I had never known. "We are free!" I called out to Puah and Hathach as if I were a child of ten. "We are free!"

I said it again and again until the words were carried away on a river of tears that flowed into the waters of Babylon. I recalled Vashti and the star around her neck. I heard the triumph in her sharp voice as she announced that she was once more queen. But I knew that I was the true victor.

The journey was long and arduous. We did not take the more direct route on the royal road for fear of the king's soldiers. Rather, we went west, across the fertile valley to the River Tigris, following its waters upstream several days to the city of Opis. A bountiful spring harvest there had been the cause of much happiness and the people we met were often merry. We had no trouble securing lodgings or enough to eat, though it was rough food such as I had not known for many years. Yet everything was a wonder and a delight to me in my newfound freedom. I enjoyed watching the antelope frolic on the open plain and the delijah falcons soaring above us, and I rejoiced in being woken by the sound of frogs and bee-eaters in the morning. I did not regret sharing a room with my companions at the squalid inns, the loss of a heated bath—indeed any bath at all—or combing my own hair. I looked forward to the day when the golden tresses that King Xerxes had preferred gave way to the natural black and my skin lost its pampered softness.

Puah purchased plain clothing for us on our first evening away from the palace and we spent four more days on the road to Opis without incident. But when we reached the city, a group of soldiers stopped us.

"Who are you?" one of the men demanded. I saw that we must appear a strange trio, apparently wealthy enough, despite our plain travel clothes, to have a eunuch for a servant. Perhaps they wished to extract a bribe.

"I am Hadassah daughter of Avihail," I replied, my voice steady and firm. "This is my mother and our servant. We travel to meet my brother in the land of the Chorasmians." Thus did I deceive them, choosing a place that was far beyond Ecbatana, to the west and north, but which would explain our need to travel through the Zagros mountains should the soldiers watch us the next day when we left.

The soldier who questioned me was kind and warned us to take care in the high mountain passes where snow was yet on the ground. We thanked the men and they did not trouble us again.

Hathach secured a guide for us, a toothless old man who was from Ecbatana and returned often to visit his family. The guide would not let us begin until we had made the purchase of several wool rugs and scarves from his wife. I had never been so glad to have extra warmth. For the mountains are the highest in the land and colder than anything I could have imagined.

The guide advised Hathach of a clean inn where we could spend the night and secure a good meal. I enjoyed walking along the river's edge to find the place.

The inn was indeed comfortable. After a hearty evening meal of bread and lamb stew I was shown to my own chamber and left to rest. But images of the king closed in upon me in the bed and I could not sleep. After some time I rose and began to pace the room. I recalled the king's ardor for me in the early years of our marriage and how I had returned his passion. I recalled the time of distance between us, when I failed to give him a child and lavished too much affection on Anatana. I recalled his cruelty and his kindness. And I recalled the comfort he had found in my company during his final years. At times I wept, for the girl I was and the man he might have been. But as I stood by the window and watched the dawn rise, I was not sorry to have spent the past hours with my memories. I owed the king at least one night of mourning.

Early the next day we set off to the east, beginning our climb along the cliffs on the gorge carved by the River Gyndes. I grew weary after a day or two but took my strength from the others, who found the sharp air invigorating. I saw snow for the first time and marveled at the way it sparkled in the sun, but I did not wish to linger in such a cold place. At night I slept wrapped in a blanket with Puah to stay warm and we whispered to each other about the memories of our past and our hopes for the future.

One day we arrived at a crossroads known as Behistun. The road from south to north appeared to be more traveled than the road we were on, which continued east. The guide drew our attention to a sheer rock face not too far in the distance, where we saw a carving

taller and wider than any made by the artisans at Susa. Many panels
of what seemed to be script surrounded a scene in which three figures
stood at proud attention before nine others who were bent over like
captives with their hands secured behind their backs. We wondered
how such a relief might have been made and asked the guide its
purpose. He pointed out one man who stood much taller than the
others and told us that this was King Darius. The smaller men lined
up in front of him were traitors who had tried to usurp the throne.
Two soldiers attended the king. The one holding the king's bow, he
told us, was a brave and loyal general by the name of Gobryas.

I turned to Puah and smiled. "It might commemorate the
overthrow of the false Smerdis," I suggested.

Puah's eyes filled with tears.

"Perhaps we shall be able to come back and visit it from time
to time," I suggested.

"I believe we are not far from Ecbatana now," Hathach
agreed.

We stood for a few minutes, staring up at the mighty carving.
And though the fine details were not visible to us, I could make out
the figure of the winged disk hovering above them all.

My bones have risen, I told the king's god. And then I
dismounted from my donkey that I might walk the rest of the way to
my new home.

The next morning we descended the red rock mountains into
a lush valley filled with palm, acacia, and pink oleander. I could see a
village below and a great fortress that rose high on the next slope.
The summer residence of the Achaemenid kings had not been used
since the time of Cambyses. We would be safe here.

Nestled in the foothills of the valley, surrounded by poplar and tamarisk trees, the estate was a small house of five rooms with a modest garden and a separate kitchen building. There was a vineyard and a large pen for sheep, which spent their days grazing on the slopes under the watch of the caretaker's son.

I stood in the little garden while Hathach attended the donkeys and Puah paid our guide. An eagle soared high above me, and the air was filled with the scent of a new day. I thanked God for bringing me to the most beautiful place in the world.

And so here I wait on my estate in Ecbatana, looking down on the village road and the mountains beyond. Each morning I wake filled with hope that this is the day I will be reunited with my beloved cousin. Each night I pray that he will find me worthy of his love.

Acknowledgments

I owe much to two very talented and hardworking women who were willing to take a risk on me: Esther Sung, my agent, and Chris Min, my editor. I have learned more from them than I ever thought possible, and I thank them profusely for their ongoing commitment to my work.

Several friends have stood by me these past years in times of despair and joy. Thanks to Kathleen BelBruno, Marjorie Rose, Sarah Aronson, Nathan Margolis, Marianne Hraibi, and especially to Rabbi Edward Boraz for their unfailing confidence in me. Thanks also to Dr. Gary Schwartz and his Sunday morning Torah study group, where I often found inspiration. I hope Leah Kohn will forgive her mother for the past year: serving as president of our synagogue while writing this novel required a fair amount of sacrifice and understanding on her part.

My deepest gratitude is to Meir Kohn, whose faith in me and support has remained steadfast through many years of hard work. I dedicate this book to him.

Author's Note

I am indebted to the work of many fine scholars. Yoram Hazony's marvelous book *The Dawn: Political Teachings of the Book of Esther* first inspired me to think of Esther as a character with real depth. David Green's masterful translation of Herodotus was a constant resource. While direct quotes from the biblical text are my own translations, I consulted translations and commentary by Adele Berlin, Michael V. Fox, Carey Moore, and Meir Zlotowitz. The fine work of Edwin M. Yamauchi *Persia and the Bible* was indispensable as was A.T. Olmstead's classic *History of the Persian Empire*. For details on art, architecture, religion, and geography, I turned to the works of John Boardman, James Emmons, Stewart Gilbert, Peter Green, Lawrence Mills, Margaret Cool Root, and Houman Sarshar. I learned much about the role of women in ancient Persia from Maria Brosius. For material on Babylon, I turned to a number of sources, including Gwendolyn Leick and Charles Seignobos.